Infinite Worth

Tim Reardon

Infinite Worth

Copyright © 2020 by Tim Reardon

All rights reserved. No part of this book may be reproduced or transmitted in any form or by any means without written permission of the author and publisher. This is a work of fiction. Any resemblance to actual persons, living or dead, is purely coincidental.

ISBN: 9781734685572

Library of Congress Control Number: 2020950137

Author Photo by Claire Reardon

Cover Design by All Things that Matter Press

Cover photo by Kathleen Reardon

Published in 2020 by All Things that Matter Press

Acknowledgements

Thanks to early readers, Bob Dalton and Jim Dekker--English writing icons. Thanks to Dan Harlan for his honest, nuanced, and generous notes. And special thanks to my sixteen years of Catholic school English teachers, some not necessarily loved, but all respected.

For Gina, Kate, Claire, and Lizzy

First Trimester

"May we always care for our children, not counting the cost, so that they may never believe themselves to be mistakes, but always know their infinite worth.

— Pope Francis

Grace

I never see the lady clearly, but I know she's beautiful. I can feel that she's beautiful. Everything is so bright that nothing here has defined edges. The lines on her face blend together so that it's difficult to make out exact shapes or colors. I feel like I'm squinting, but I'm not. I'm not straining at all. I feel peaceful, relaxed. I'm glad to be with her.

"Why I am I here?" she asks, but the question doesn't make sense, and I'm not even sure where here *is.*

"I'm wondering why I'm *here," I say, and my voice sounds different, like I'm me but also more than me.*

She never laughs, but she's smiling now. Her movements aren't necessarily slow, but they're smooth, like an underwater ballerina. Graceful. "How do you feel?" she says and seems to be closer to me now.

"Good," I say but that doesn't really tell the whole story because it's more than that. I feel an almost lazy kind of warmth, but I'm simultaneously strong and alert and safe. I know all that doesn't usually go together, but I'm trying to get this right. I want to explain it so you know what it's like when I'm with her.

"Do you feel that you're ready?" she says.

I don't know what she's asking, but I'm always honest with her. There's no reason to lie. And so I say, "Yes." And it's not a lie because no matter what she's talking about, I do feel ready.

~1~

Principal Pat Ryan had to kick a kid out of school today. It wasn't Pat's first expulsion, and it wouldn't be his last, but he never enjoyed it. These were teenagers. They made mistakes. Couldn't help themselves a lot of the time. Their still developing minds were a jumbled mess of Kanye lyrics, Instagram memes, Fortnite assassins, and porn. With all that ephemera jockeying for position, slugging it out for attention, it was a wonder these kids could complete even the most basic of tasks—setting an alarm, putting on shoes, pouring milk in their Cap'n Crunch. But they somehow did it. They made it to school most days and typically stayed out of trouble.

But not today.

Pat had an unwritten rule that he didn't expel anyone unless they'd brought a weapon to school or got caught selling drugs. Fisticuffs down at the reservoir, sexual liaisons behind the theater, vaping in the bathroom? Of course, no one celebrated these activities, but, for Pat, they didn't warrant expulsion. He liked to give second chances. Thought he could save some lost souls.

Today, however, was a new one for Pat. An offensive lineman named Vincent Allen, who was already on probation for stealing from the lunch line, bullied a transgender youth who went by the handle, Foggy, and was on his way to becoming a girl. Pat didn't know whether Foggy was planning on getting surgery or had already begun some kind of transformation, but the kid wore false eyelashes and shirts that looked to Pat more like something a pirate would wear. Although Pat had been a principal in San Francisco for years, he had relatively few incidents involving kids from the LGBTQ community. Either he'd been lucky or blind. Either way, this was foreign territory for him.

Apparently, Vince not only taunted and roughed up Foggy but also videotaped the whole thing and then posted it.

The video shows Foggy walking down the school hallway. After passing several lockers, he looks over his shoulder directly at the camera and yells, "You're a caveman, Vinny. Go back to your cave and play with your rocks."

Then Foggy turns his attention back to navigating the crowded hallway, busy with between-class chaos—high fives, bulky backpacks, untied sneakers the size of small dogs, lacrosse sticks, and frustrated teachers on their way to the faculty lounge. A typical scene. And the fact that St. Xavier is an all-boys school just added to the frenzied, testosteronal pace of it all.

When Pat had first watched the video, submitted to him by a concerned, unconnected parent, who'd seen it on her son's iPhone, Pat rewound the scene several times. He sat in his office with his Dean of Discipline and listened to Vince laughing at Foggy before saying, "Miss, I think you might have dropped this tampon from your purse," after which you can see Vince's hand in front of the camera, now holding up a tampon, brandishing it as if he were waving a conductor's baton.

Foggy does, indeed, have a purse.

Or it's some kind of satchel with the strap tight and diagonal across his narrow chest. In one swift motion, Foggy reaches into the purse, pulls out something and sprays it at Vince while simultaneously screaming—higher pitched than you might imagine, "Go fuck yourself, Vinny."

Vinny doesn't know it at the time, but the spray is some kind of mouthwash—a breath spray. When Pat was a kid, there was something like this called Binaca Blast. But Vince doesn't know anything about Binaca Blast or whatever this is that Foggy is aiming at him, and he must be at least a bit shocked at the volume and pitch of the scream. So Vince panics and thinks it must be pepper spray.

With the camera still focused on Foggy, Vince bum rushes the boy and yells, "I'm gonna mess you up, fairy." Then the camera gets shaky, but you can see Vince smash the tampon into Foggy's face and then punch him several times, all the while holding the phone with his other hand.

The video provided Pat with an intense ache behind his eyes. Later, in his office, when he showed it to Vince, the kid looked like he was going to throw up or maybe cry, but Vince offered no excuse for his behavior. Pat thought there was a chance the young man might have been confused about his own sexuality, and Pat felt a little sorry for him. But not sorry enough to reconsider the expulsion. Vince had to go. Teachable moment. The best thing about high school kids is that they have plenty of time to turn it around. There are very few things that can completely alter the course of their lives.

~2~

On the ride home, Pat went through the normal litany of emotions. He felt good for having supported a marginalized student, one who certainly made Pat a bit uncomfortable as the head of a Catholic, all-boys' school, but also one who had shown courage and resiliency. The kid knew that he'd be taking crap from the Vinces of the world everyday but showed up anyway and didn't seem to back down from anyone.

But Pat also felt bad for having to let the other kid go. This situation didn't fit into his unwritten rule regarding expulsions—weapons or drugs—but he knew in his gut that the school needed this message, and Vince needed this lesson, or he was going to continue to be a bully for the rest of his time in high school and then end up as a bigger bully walking around the world as an adult.

When Pat got home, he wasn't really rattled by the experience. The crying mom. The confused dad. The stupid kid. All sitting in his office trying to figure out what to do next. Is there an appeals process? *No. Not for this.* Where will he go to school? *I can make some calls.* How will he ever get into college? *There're still options.*

Again, he wasn't rattled, but he also didn't have the energy to make dinner tonight as he did on most nights. He and his wife, Emily, generally got home at about the same time, but she was a lousy cook, and Pat liked the time in the kitchen alone with the news playing in the background. So, most nights, he was happy to put together something creative from the refrigerator and the pantry. Although he was never competing against anyone, he imagined himself a contestant on *Chopped,* trying to utilize beets, ground beef, polenta, and baby kale into something about which Emily and the girls wouldn't complain.

The girls were his daughters, Alice and Grace. Alice was a senior and Grace a freshman at St. Mary's, the girls' high school across the street from St. X, and they could both be brutally critical—*Chopped judges*—when Pat tried something too sophisticated for their pallets. He normally eschewed curry sauce and jerk marinade and mango salsa and anything else that might startle their senses. They just weren't ready for that stuff yet and could be savage in their critiques.

But, alas, tonight he had decided that he would order pizza. Emily would go through the motions of contesting the decision because they were trying to avoid carbs, but she loved pizza and would easily submit as long as someone else called Bambino's. Pat assumed she did this so that she would not be considered an accomplice regardless of how many slices she ate.

When he got to the kitchen, everyone was sitting at the table, and it was clear that Emily and Alice had been crying. They weren't now. They were staring red-eyed at Pat, who was scared to even put down his briefcase.

His youngest, Grace, had *not* been crying. In fact, she looked peaceful—almost as if she were sleeping, but her eyes were open. Her face was completely neutral. Although Emily and Alice were clearly agitated, he couldn't stop watching Grace. Her face looked as though it were about to transform into something that would expose an emotion of some sort, but it didn't. It wasn't frozen. She was breathing naturally, and there was almost a hint of a smile at the corners of her lips, but, otherwise, nothing—like she was in a dreamless sleep or a sleep in which the dream was without conflict or pleasure.

"What's going on?" he said and walked toward the table, still holding his briefcase, squeezing the handle as if he were getting ready to throw it if he had to.

Emily opened her mouth to speak, but before she could say anything, tears streaked down her face so suddenly that the effect momentarily paralyzed Pat. Then Emily immediately started to shake her head so that her hair obscured her face.

"You guys ..." he said but let the words hang in the air as he moved his eyes to his two daughters. For a brief moment, his mind moved irrationally to the subject of the pizza that needed to be ordered, but that slipped away as quickly as it had entered. He was about to go to his wife and put his hands on her, pull her close to him and gently force her to tell him what was going on, or reassure her with comforting words like *What the hell is happening?* But before he chose either of these options, Grace spoke.

"They say I'm pregnant," she said, still no emotion. Not like a zombie or a robot or something. Just with the same countenance she might have displayed if she'd said, "Soccer practice got cancelled today," or "I need some money for a field trip."

Pat's reply was predictable. "What?" he said even though he had heard all four words quite clearly.

"They say—" Grace began.

"I heard you," he said. "Who's *they*?"

"The doctor," interrupted Alice, her face pleading with Pat to fix this problem, this bizarre complication to her otherwise effortless existence that her little sister was now threatening to destroy.

By looking at the placid face of his baby girl instead of the two other demonstrative women in the room, he was able to stay cool. "Who's the father?" he asked and finally placed the briefcase on the floor next to the kitchen island.

"I've never even seen her talk to a boy!" said Alice as she pushed back from the table and walked into the adjoining family room where she sat on a couch and stared at Pat, waiting for his next move.

"Okay," he said, still looking at Alice. "But who's the boy who did this?"

Alice shrugged and picked up a *People* magazine as if she were going to start reading it and then dropped it back down on the coffee table.

Pat looked at his wife and said, "So she hasn't told you guys yet?

Before Emily could reply, Grace said, "I don't know who the father is."

Now Pat could feel his stomach tighten, and he was biting down so hard that his teeth hurt. "You mean to tell me that you've ..." he trailed off, looking for the right phrasing, "...that you've *been* with more than one boy?"

"Daddy," she said, this fifteen-year-old kid, who still occasionally called him *Daddy*. "I haven't *been* with anyone. I've never had sex before. It's like Alice said. I barely even talk to boys."

Emily had her head down and was tracing something on the table. It looked like she was doing cursive with the tip of her finger. "Emily," said Pat. "Do you want to give me some help here? I don't really understand what I'm being told."

"The doctors took urine," she said. "But Gracie insists that she never had sex with anyone."

Pat just stared at Emily, who was trying to smile at Grace, but Emily's mouth was quivering and kept changing shape so that her lips were rapidly pivoting from smile to frown to smile to frown—drama masks, Thalia then Melpomene then back to Thalia again, not sure if this was comedy or tragedy or somehow both. "And I think I believe her," Emily said, then got up and stood next to Grace.

"You believe her?" he said and sat down in the chair that his wife had vacated.

She nodded.

"So, you think the doctor made some kind of mistake?"

Grace was shaking her head. "It's not a mistake."

~3~

When Grace had told Emily that in between her periods she'd seen some blood in her underwear, Emily didn't think much of it. When she was Grace's age, she had cervical polyps, which caused some light spotting but were benign. She figured Grace might be going through the same thing.

But when they got to the doctor's office, the appointment went differently than she'd imagined. After a weigh in, the blood pressure squeeze, and some work on the reflexes, Doctor Ross started in with the questions.

"Grace, how are you doing in school?"

"Good," she said and smiled. Dr. Ross was a regular guy, so even though Grace was sitting in her underwear on the padded table, she seemed relaxed.

"St. Mary's?" he said.

"Yeah."

"And your dad's still over at St. X?"

"Yeah," she said. "Principal."

"That's right," said Doctor Ross as he pulled up a stool so that he was sitting across from her now. Emily felt like a third wheel on a first date. There was a chair tucked into the corner, but Ross never offered her the seat, so she stood, one hand touching the paper runner on the examination table. "He's a good man," Ross continued. "I remember when he was the basketball coach over there." He looked over at Emily and raised his eyebrows as if she were supposed to acknowledge this bit a useless trivia.

She did. She smiled and nodded and said, "Yep. Those were the good old days. I remember it well. Watching game film in bed. Steady diet of gymnasium hotdogs and Skittles. Good times."

Ross nodded at Emily but barely smiled before he turned back to Grace and said, "Do you play hoops?"

"No," she said. "That's my sister, Alice."

Ross nodded again and paused before saying, "What do you do?"

Grace shrugged and said, "I like to write?"

"Oh yeah?" he said. "What kind of stuff?"

"Poems, short stories," she said. "I also write for the school paper."

"Nice," he said. "I read murder mysteries myself, but I respect all writers—sharing a little bit of themselves with the world."

Emily could feel her knees starting to ache slightly. She'd been on her feet all day, so she moved backward toward the corner of the small room and eased into the seat behind her to watch Grace continue her very mature conversation with this nice doctor.

"So, what brings you in today?" he said.

"Well," Grace said, then paused and looked over at Emily, who gave her a *go-ahead* nod. "I 've been seeing spots of blood in my underwear, but it's not during my period."

Emily was proud of Grace. After the initial pause, Grace had been clear and confident.

"Okay," said Doctor Ross. "That could be from any number of things."

"My mom said it's probably policks," said Grace, and Doctor Ross looked over at Emily.

Now it was her turn to be uncomfortable. "Well, no" she began. "I didn't say *probably*." She could feel herself flush. "And it's *polyps*. I had cervical polyps when I was her age, and I thought maybe that was hereditary, or …"

"Got it," he said. "Yes. Polyps are a possibility."

For some reason, Emily felt herself getting up out of the chair and moving toward the examination table again, this time putting both hands on the paper runner just beyond Grace's bare feet.

"Have you been experiencing anything else that's out of the ordinary?" he asked.

Her eyes flashed at Emily so quickly that Emily wasn't even sure if it had happened. "Well," said Grace. "My boobs have actually been kinda tender?" She smiled as if she'd just farted at Easter mass. "My breasts, I mean."

"Okay," he said. "Is there pain?"

"If I bump against something, yeah."

"Gotcha," he said, and Emily caught something in his eye. He wasn't just running through a script now. He was trying to diagnose something that was peculiar to him. Emily saw it. She knew the look. She'd seen that same wrinkle at the bridge of the nose when Pat thought he was about to solve something—the directions to a house on a country road, the final word on a crossword puzzle, a great out-of-bounds play. Something small at play between his eyebrows. She'd seen it in Pat, and she was pretty sure she was seeing it now in Doctor Ross.

"Okay," he said. "Is that it? The spotting and the tenderness?"

"Yes," she said quickly, but after he nodded, she said, "Wait!"

"Something else?" he said.

"Well, yeah," she said. "And this isn't anything, really. I just thought of it, and I think I might have had this before when I was little, but maybe it's new. I don't know. But I feel like I have to pee a lot. Like I feel like have to pee right now. But sometimes I'll go to the bathroom and only a little will come out."

"Got it," he said, but he was looking at Emily now.

And Emily wasn't feeling well. She felt like she sometimes did in elevators just as they started to ascend. A momentary sense of nausea that she could easily fight off with a deep breath, but she was having trouble breathing. Something was creeping into her consciousness and throwing off her equilibrium, but it wasn't there yet. Then the doctor spoke again, and the elevator started its ascent.

"Grace," he said. "Are you sexually active."

"I don't even have a boyfriend," she said and executed an awkward stage shrug. "I just started liking boys last year." She smiled and let those last words float up lightly and dissipate into the vent above the paper towel dispenser.

"So that's a no on sexually active?" he asked again, still genial, getting up off the stool now.

"Yes," she said, then paused for a moment before giggling. "I mean *yes*, that's a *no* on sexually active." Then she stopped giggling and shook her head before saying, "No, I'm not sexually active."

Emily was swimming now, woozy in the thick wet air of the examination room. All she had to do was blink the glaze out of her eyes and return to this moment, but she wouldn't let herself. It must have been some kind of defense mechanism—she had put herself into a standing coma and could feel her fingers tingling.

"Can I ask you to lie back for a minute?" said the doctor.

~4~

After the awkward dinner, Alice and Grace went to their shared room.

Grace didn't show much emotion during her dad's inquiry, and Alice couldn't get a read on her. She knew Grace had to be lying, but her little sister wasn't acting like a liar. Grace had a couple of obvious tells. She would either laugh and wouldn't look you in the eye, or she'd start crying and yelling and defending herself like she'd been falsely accused of murder—really dramatic stuff.

Tonight, she did neither. She was either maturing and getting some control over her tells, becoming a better liar, or this situation was so serious that she was just shutting down emotionally. "So, who was it?" asked Alice once she'd shut the door, and they'd both sat down on their respective beds.

Grace looked confused.

"Was it Max?" asked Alice.

A blink of recognition. "It's what I told you guys," she said. She was holding a stuffed lamb now and was almost cradling it in her hands when she said, "Do you think I would make up something like this?"

"Grace," said Alice and then waited a moment before sitting up straight on the edge of her bed, her hands on her knees, bent forward, waiting for the truth.

"I can't believe you think I'd make this up."

"Of course, you're making it up. What you're saying isn't possible."

"I know it's not," she said, placing the stuffed lamb on her end table. "But it is."

"Oh," said Alice, feeling herself dialing her voice into sarcasm mode. "Did an angel appear before you and tell you this was going to happen?"

"No." Grace was up now, walking toward her dresser, but she stopped short and turned her head quickly toward Alice. She had the expression of someone who'd just gotten the last number on a bingo call. "But I've had dreams."

Alice looked at her sister. They'd grown up sharing the same room, but Grace had never once talked about a dream. "Dreams about what?" asked Alice.

"Well, it's funny," she said. "I never really thought of them as dreams, but maybe that's what they are." Then she came over to Alice and sat next to her on her bed, the good one, near the window.

"What do ya'mean?" asked Alice.

"You know how I've always been a deep sleeper?"

"Yeah."

"Remember I slept through the earthquake even though Sully was supposedly barking like crazy?"

"Okay," said Alice, wondering where this was going.

"Well, sometimes I have these thoughts. I guess they're dreams because I'm thinking them when I'm sleeping. But I feel like I'm not fully asleep, and I can do whatever I want? You know? Can you do what you want in *your* dreams?"

Alice had to think about the question. "I'm not sure what that means," she said. "Sometimes I do what I want, and sometimes I can't."

"Then maybe I'm not dreaming," said Grace.

Alice wanted to find out what Grace was dreaming about, but first she wanted to know if Grace was talking about dreams. "I've had dreams where I want to run but I can't," she said. "Like I'm stuck in mud or something. I guess that's a nightmare because something's always chasing me. Have you ever had a dream like that?"

Grace stood up now and looked out the window, where a set of headlights shone through the glass and flashed around her head and shoulders before disappearing around the corner. "No," she almost whispered. "I don't dream like that. In my dreams, I can control everything. I get to decide what comes next. I think I must be awake."

Alice considered this. It didn't really sound like her own dreams. Sometimes good things happened in her dreams, but she didn't feel like she was controlling the events. They were just happening. "Maybe you're just thinking," said Alice. And then she jumped right to it. "What have you been thinking about when you have your eyes closed?"

"I think about a lady," she said and sat back down on her bed across the room and looked back at Alice.

"Someone you know?" she asked.

"I feel like I know her, but it's not like I can say *yeah, it's the lady who worked coat-check at the father-daughter dance* or anything like that."

"That's strangely specific, but whatever. What does the lady do?"

"We just talk."

"Okay," said Alice. "But you said you control everything that happens. Do you decide what the lady says?"

"It's not like that," she said. "I can control how long we talk or what I'm going to say or maybe even where we are, but I think *she* decides what she's going to say."

Alice was interested, but she didn't know where this was going or why she was pursuing it. "Okay, Grace. That's weird," said Alice. "Can you just tell me what the lady says?"

"It's always something different," said Grace. "One time she told me to pour out my love. I don't really know what that means, but I like the way she says it. I like the way it sounds."

"Pour out your love?" said Alice. "Isn't that a song?"

"It doesn't sound like a song when she says it."

"What else does she say?"

"One time she said, 'Don't be afraid.'"

~5~

Pat and Emily were out on the back deck. It was foggy but not cold. It could get cold in the city in the spring, but there was no wind, and the fog wasn't thick. It was just still.

They were both standing with their elbows resting on the wooden railing. They were looking north at St. Ignatius Church, which was lighted up but looked blurry through the evening fog.

They never ordered the pizza, so Pat had cut himself a few slices of salami and ate them quickly in the kitchen before he and Emily went outside. He could still feel the grease on his fingers as they stood in silence, their shoulders just barely touching.

"You probably shouldn't have raised your voice," said Emily without turning her head to face him.

"Really?" he said. "Grace's is acting nuts. What are we supposed to be saying to her?"

"Not sure yet," she said. "But I know we shouldn't be yelling at her."

"I didn't yell at her," he said and retraced the conversation in his mind. *I want you to tell me right now who the father is. You actually owe it to the boy to let him know that this is happening.* "I would say I was forceful, but I don't think anyone could argue that I yelled at her."

"I know you didn't yell at her, but your tone seemed aggressive."

There it was again. *Aggressive.* When Pat was growing up, being aggressive was encouraged. The aggressive kids were the best students. The aggressive kids were good at sports. The aggressive kids won everything. Now the word aggressive was a pejorative—almost synonymous with oppressive. Aggressive and oppressive are not the same thing. "How was it aggressive to ask her who she had sex with?"

"You're calling her a liar," said Emily, pushing herself back from the railing and walking over to the rusted patio furniture. She let the weight of herself fall into the chair. No tears. Maybe she was too confused for a single emotion to control her, to force her to break down. Maybe the odd combination of emotions was keeping her in this emotionally limbotic state. "By asking her who the father is, you're calling her a liar." She had her face in her hands now, and her voice was a bit muffled when she said, "You're not accommodating her reality."

"Emily," he said. "Please don't do that tonight." She was a marriage and family therapist and would occasionally slip into Dr. Philese with Pat when they were discussing a family issue.

"Okay," she said. "How's this? You're making things worse by telling her that you don't believe her."

"Ah," said Pat. "So, you're asking me to pretend like I believe that my daughter is involved in some version of the Immaculate Conception?" Pat didn't like bullshit. He thought it was a waste of time. But he knew this was Emily's realm, not just because she was a therapist but also because she was a woman, because she was a mom.

She was still holding her face in her hands and was now shaking her head, just slightly, as if she maybe wasn't even aware that she was doing it. Then she looked up with the hint of smirk on her face. "That's the wrong nomenclature," she said.

"Huh?"

"Immaculate Conception," she said. "That's when God made it so that Mary was born without original sin. It doesn't have anything to do with—"

"Yeah, yeah," he said. "I know. Everyone mixes those two up. The virgin birth? Is that what I'm talking about? Either way. You're asking me to pretend that I believe that a biological miracle has occurred."

"Pat," she said. "There's no book that tells you what you're supposed to do when your daughter tells you something like this."

"Well, yeah," he said. "But isn't there a book that tells you what to do when your daughter's experiencing denial or delusions or schizophrenia or whatever is happening here?"

"Denial's usually about things like not recognizing that you have a gambling problem or believing your mom's terminal disease will somehow be cured." She was actually slouching in the chair now and looking up at the sky. No stars tonight. Too much fog. "And short-term denial is actually a fairly healthy coping mechanism ...." She let the words trail off. Her head was still tilted toward the sky, but she had her eyes closed. She didn't look like she was sleeping, though. She looked tortured, like she was getting a tooth filled.

"All right. This could be healthy," he said. "Short-term denial is actually okay. That makes some sense." He stopped for a moment, still mad at himself for mixing up the Immaculate Conception and the virgin birth. He was a Catholic school principal for God's sake. "Short-term, though. Just to get through this initial distressing period. That does make sense. She can absorb it better this way. It'll stop her from going into some kind of psychological tailspin. This is actually okay for now."

"For now," she said, eyes still closed. "That's right. But we have to really watch her, and we have to come up with some kind of game plan. You have to figure out how we're going to handle this at St. Mary's."

"I know," he said. He tried to do the math in his head regarding when she'd start showing. Would it be in the summer? Could they keep it a secret? Could she stay at school? "We have some tough times ahead of us. This is going to test us."

Emily's eyes remained closed, but they could no longer hold the tears that were spilling out now, running down her cheeks.

~6~

"What's the strategy?" said Alice, as she began shoveling scrambled eggs out of a huge frying pan and onto a plate. The family rarely ate breakfast together on weekday mornings, but Emily had gotten up early and was cooking, so they'd all wandered up to the kitchen, hypnotized by the alluring perfume of bacon frying in a skillet.

"What do you mean, strategy?" asked Emily, using tongs to place two pieces of bacon on Alice's plate.

Grace was already working on oatmeal, and Pat, drinking his tea, was sitting across from Grace at the kitchen table.

"I mean," said Alice. "Your youngest child is pregnant, and she's just a kid, she goes to a high school with a bunch of other kids, and a lot of them are total bitches—"

"Stop," said Emily. "I don't want you guys swearing around here."

Alice knew her mom was also directing this at her dad, who swore all the time, but Alice was in a strange mood. She wanted to push things a little bit. She wanted to fast-forward nine months to see what kind of wreckage they'd be dealing with. She wanted to know if her senior year was going to be ruined. "What's the strategy, dad?" she said, knowing that he'd probably stayed up all night trying to figure out how the family was going to get through this.

"We have some time," he said. "We don't need to make any decisions today."

"Yeah," said Alice. "I know that, but I'm also guessing that you already decided what we're gonna do, so I'd just assume you tell us now, so I know how screwed up my life will be when she starts to get big."

"Alice," said Emily, dropping the pan on the stove, bits of eggs jumping out onto the quartz countertop. She pointed the spatula at Alice. "This is still new. Grace is still processing all this."

She'd actually spanked Alice with this same utensil when Alice was four or five and accidentally dropped Grace. Alice had been playing some kind of careless mommy-baby game in the hallway outside the kitchen, and Gracie had slipped right through her hands. Her mom was fuming because she'd told Alice not to pick up the baby. The image of her waving that spatula skidded into Alice's mind and then caught traction and was out just as quickly, but the feeling of that moment stayed with her. "Mom," she said, "is Gracie going to have to drop out of school?"

Grace looked up from her oatmeal but didn't say anything.

Pat placed his mug on the table and said, "We're going to be fine."

Alice frowned. "What does that mean?" she said.

"What do you think it means?" he said and took an almost dainty sip of tea, clearly trying to focus on keeping his cool this morning but coming off as a wimp.

"I think it means you don't have a plan, but you're saying everything's fine because you're either trying to convince us or yourself that this'll blow over or something." Alice could hear the cutting of her voice slicing through the greasy, bacon ripened air, and she didn't like the sound of it, but she also wanted her dad to take some control here. Sometimes he needed some prodding.

He had both hands on his mug and was silent for a moment before saying, "As far as the rest of the world knows, except for the doctor, I guess, the Ryan family is no different today than it was yesterday, so we don't need to make any big decisions yet."

Alice was standing in front of the table and looking at her dad, then over at Grace, then back at her dad again. "That's it?" she said. She had that sensation wash over her again, the yearning to see into the future, to just know.

"For now," he said, but he was looking over Alice's shoulder now, presumably at her mom. "Can you just give me a little time to ...?" It felt like the beginning of something more. Like he was going to continue with words of comfort: *... some time to solve this problem ... some time to protect our family ... some time to discover the antidote.* But that was it. He just wanted time.

"Grace is still processing this," said her mom from over by the stove. "It's important for us to let her come to a clear understanding of her situation before we decide how to best move forward."

"She's sitting right here," said Alice. "Shouldn't we ask her what she'd like to do?" Alice didn't really know what she was asking, but it occurred to her that the question in another household might be taken as a reference to abortion. But that's not what she was asking. That option wasn't really on the table. The family had never really talked about the topic, but they were Catholic. There were other solutions.

What Alice really wanted was for Grace to enter into the discourse. She wanted to know what Grace was thinking, but her little sister was still just sitting there, now wiping some oatmeal off her uniform skirt. "Can we at least do the math now, so I know when we will be *forced* to have a real discussion about this?"

Her mom was piling up pans in the sink, making a lot of noise. But she turned off the water and said, "She's three or four weeks pregnant. It's February 26th. School's out in the beginning of June. We could realistically get through the rest of the school year without saying anything."

Alice felt a moment of guilty pleasure in the fact that she could graduate without having to go through the drama of this pregnancy scandal while she was still at St. Mary's. She knew she should be thinking of her sister, but this was a reflex. Self-preservation. She would be the sister of the pregnant girl. She was tough, but she didn't think she'd have the guts to make it through something like this without scars, deep ones.

Grace clanked her spoon into the empty bowl and said, "What about when the summer's over?" She was looking at their dad now. No emotion except in her eyes, slightly narrowed and maybe a little wet. "Then what?"

~7~

On the way to school, Pat kept thinking to himself that he needed to just do his normal thing today. There was absolutely no reason to rush into any decisions. He had things to do at school, and he should just work on getting those things done. Why rush? That's when you make mistakes, right? Grace was still holding on to her virgin narrative, so Pat should be able to allow at least a day of straight up denial and not think about any of this until tomorrow or maybe tonight when he and Emily had a quiet moment to share ideas.

But that wasn't how it went. By lunch, he hadn't done much. He'd signed some advanced purchase orders for computer paper and a down payment on the prom venue. He'd written a short blurb for the weekly newsletter. And he'd stared at the computer screen. 346 unopened emails. Some junk mail. But mostly stuff he had to address. Just not now.

His mind was alternating between two modes: first, a lightening mode in which images and ideas were sparking into his consciousness so quickly that the new thoughts overlapped with the old ones until the superimposed ideas formed a kind of sloppy Max Ernst photomontage that had no meaning at all.

That feverish pace sporadically interchanged with the slow-motion, glacial mode, in which his eyes were glazed over, and he would let himself stare blankly across his office at unimportant items: the light switch, the corner of a picture frame, the dish under the flower pot, until the photos in the collage would drop off one by one, and his mind would become an empty wall. Navajo white. Tabula rasa. And ideas would stroll up, knock once or twice, and then leave without further discourse.

So after a couple of hours of this nonsense, he decided that he'd call Jenny Daly over at St. Mary's and see if she wanted to have lunch. It was his turn to walk across the street and eat in her cafeteria. He would be happy to get out of St. X for a bit and talk to an adult—maybe get his mind functioning again in some semblance of normal cerebral activity.

Jenny was the Dean of Academics at St. Mary's but, for all intents and purposes, was the Head of School. Sister Margaret had kept the place going for decades, but she was mostly a figurehead at this point, and Jenny ran the day-to-day operations. She and Pat had taken Masters classes together at USF and had become fast friends, and Pat really valued their friendship. She was blunt, and Pat sometimes needed that. The two of them had gone toe-to-toe on a few issues over the years. but they'd always ended up in a place of mutual admiration.

***

There were a few men who worked at St. Mary's but it was mostly really talented, passionate women, who had forgone the higher pay in the public schools because they were serious Catholics or serious about single-gender education. Either way, Pat respected them and got along well with all the St. Mary's teachers he knew.

And he didn't mind walking on their campus despite the fact that his two daughters attended the school and might be embarrassed by his presence. In fact, they never were. When they would see him on campus, they'd invariably run up to him to say hi. They were usually happier to see him at school than they ever were when he was home.

Today, when he walked across the cafeteria to the table at which he usually sat with Jenny Daly, he saw Alice sitting with a bunch of seniors, the cool kids. Some were on a table with their legs dangling off, the plaid skirts probably a bit too short. Some were standing, eating off paper plates or scooping healthier, homemade food out of Tupperware containers. Alice was sitting and laughing with two other girls, one of whom was doing a kind of puppet show with two pop tarts that had been chewed to look like animals.

When Alice saw him from across the cafeteria, she smiled and waved but didn't come over to greet him today.

He kept walking and saw Grace sitting near the salad bar with her friend, Jill. The two were talking quietly. Neither was smiling but they were paying close attention to each other, sharing freshman ideas over mac & cheese.

By the time he got close to his spot, he saw Jenny, who was carrying two trays over to the table. She wasn't saying anything, but girls were hustling out of her way. One girl stopped to ask if she needed help, and Jenny shook her off with a quick glance.

When she placed the two trays on the table between them, she said, "Bon appétit."

"Thanks," he said as he looked down at a compostable bowl filled with mac & cheese and on the tray next to it, an apple. "You always seem to take into consideration my sophisticated palate," he said.

"It was this or the chili," she said. "You want me to get you the chili?"

"No," he said. "This is perfect. How you doin'?"

"How am I ever doing?" she said. "I'm worried about enrollment, and the girls keep clogging up the toilets with tampons."

"I could write a country song with those lyrics," he said and laughed a little at the thought of it.

"Yeah, well, if you make any money off it, you could help pay for a plumber," she said, then nodded and shoveled a big spoonful of mac and cheese into her mouth.

"Hey," he said. "Speaking of tampons. What happens at St. Mary's if a girl gets pregnant?"

"What?"

~8~

Alice didn't know how Grace was going to hold it together today.

Dad had parked the car, and as they walked from the St. X lot across the street to St. Mary's, Alice asked Grace if she would be okay today.

Grace kept looking straight ahead when she said, "I'm fine," in a kind of *don't worry* singsong voice, the kind she might use if she had a test that day for which she hadn't studied. Or, if Nordstrom didn't have the dress she wanted in her size.

Alice stopped in the middle of the crosswalk and said, "Are you sure?"

Grace kept walking but looked back at Alice and said, "Yeah."

Alice and Grace were always among the first girls to arrive at school because their dad liked to get to St. X early. Unlike other sisters who split up as soon as they opened the door, these two would usually sit on stools at a tall table together in the student center.

When they got there today, they both unloaded homework from their backpacks, but before they started to work, Alice whispered, "Did you have any dreams last night?"

Grace's face lit up. "I did," she said.

"Was the lady there?"

"Yes."

"What did she say?"

"I'm not sure I'm supposed to tell."

"Did she tell you not to tell anyone?" asked Alice, looking around to see if anyone was close enough to hear their conversation.

"No," said Grace. "She didn't say that."

"Then why don't you tell me what she said?"

Now Grace looked behind her. A few more girls were entering the student center, but they were moving toward the benches on the opposite side. "She didn't tell me that it was a secret, but when she talks to me it feels like a secret."

Alice was playing with the zipper on her backpack now, squeezing it until it hurt her fingers. *Calm down. New strategy.* "Okay, you don't have to tell me." *Open book and pretend to be reading about the three branches of government. Don't look up to see if she's watching. Move eyes back and forth even though everything's a blur.*

"Maybe she wants me to tell you," said Grace.

Alice held strong. She didn't look up yet. *Wait for it. Wait for It ...*

"I think I'm actually *supposed* to talk to you about it," said Grace.

Alice looked up from her book. "Are you sure?"

"Yeah."

"Well ..."

"I did a lot of the talking this time," said Grace.

"Okay. What did you talk about?"

"I told her about Mom and Dad," she said. "How they're sad about all this."

Alice felt bad for Grace. Grace was special. She was kind to everyone. The fact that Mom and Dad were sad because of something she did was new to the whole family. "Why do you think they're sad?" asked Alice.

"It's not that I *think* they're sad," she said. "I *know* they're sad. They liked their life. Their lives. They were happy with everything. And now it's all going to change, and they're probably scared and sad that they'll be different people now."

"Gracie," said Alice. "Everyone's going to be the same person no matter what."

Grace didn't react. She looked like she wasn't listening. And she was looking toward Alice but not *at* her.

"Grace?"

Still another moment of silence before she said, "The lady wants me to be brave, but I'm not really scared. Don't you have to be scared so you can be brave?"

"Brave is the opposite of scared," said Alice.

"I know that," said Grace. "But isn't the bravery part when you're really afraid of something but then you stand up to your fear? You actually do what you're scared to do?"

"I guess that's right."

"Well, the lady told me I need to be brave, but I'm not scared of this, so I don't really think that's being brave."

"You're not scared of what?"

"Having the baby," said Grace, but it was quiet in the student center at this time in the morning, and she made a face like she'd rung the bell at the wrong time during Sunday mass. She looked around to see if anyone had heard. Then she whispered, "I'm not scared to have this baby."

Alice wasn't sure how to respond to this. She guessed that it was good that Grace wasn't scared, but fifteen-year-old girls are supposed to be scared to have a baby. So, Alice was worried about her sister, worried that maybe she was going a little crazy. Alice figured it might be time to make this more real. "Grace," she said. "You need to tell me who the father is. If you're not scared to have this baby, then you shouldn't be scared to tell me who you slept with."

Grace smiled at Alice as if she were looking at a confused fifth grader in *Family Life* class. "Alice," she said, shaking her head a little bit. "Do you still think I'm lying to you?"

"I don't think you're lying," she said. "I think you're confused or in denial or something, but I think you need to snap out of it and tell me how this happened." Alice stopped to see if she could read Grace's expression, but there was nothing to read. It was the same face that was explaining the situation to their dad last night. "It's okay to be scared," said Alice. "Anyone would be, and it doesn't matter that you lied in the beginning. You were probably in shock."

"But I'm not."

"You're not scared? Or you're not lying? Or you're not in shock?"

"All of the above," she said, still with the smile, not a care in the world. "Or none of the above, I guess. Everything I've told you is true, and I'm not in shock, and I'm not scared." Then she paused for a moment and let the grin turn into a full smile. "I have *you* guys. That's what the lady said."

"The dream lady?" asked Alice, though she knew.

"Yes."

"What did she say about us?"

"She said you're my shield."

***

Alice couldn't focus on her morning classes. She kept thinking of her sister and her dreams and the idea of a shield. Alice would be turning eighteen in a couple of months and would be a legal adult, but she didn't think she was ready to be anyone's shield. In fact, even though she had good grades and was having a solid basketball season, a lot of the time she felt as though she was the one who needed to be shielded.

By the time lunch came around, she was letting herself enjoy a moment of levity. Tracy from her AP Lit class had chewed her pop tarts into the shapes of pigs: Napoleon and Old Major from *Animal Farm,* which they were studying this week in class. The dialogue that Tracy was mocking was neither accurate nor funny, but her improvised snorting voices and the fact that pop tart crumbs were rocketing out of her mouth made Alice laugh.

And then she saw her dad walk into the cafeteria. He must be eating with Ms. Daly today. Alice smiled and waved to him, but all she could think about was Grace saying mom and dad were sad now. Did the lady tell Grace that, or did she come up with that on her own? Alice couldn't remember. Either way, her dad did seem like he was slouching a bit. She wondered if she was imagining this.

~9~

Of course, Jenny Daly had considered the question of what the school would do if they had a pregnant girl, but she didn't expect the question to come from Pat. "Is one of your boys pregnant?" she asked and with her fork, pushed around the runny mac and cheese cooling in the bowl in front of her.

"Do you guys have a written policy?" he asked, deadpan. Apparently not in the mood today.

"Yep," she said. "Why does it matter to you?"

"Just curious," he said and raised his eyebrows before jamming a forkful of mac into his mouth.

"Well, that's a weird question to ask out of the blue like that," she said. "Are there any other St. Mary's policies you'd like to discuss today?"

"No," he said, distracted, looking around the cafeteria like there might be something more interesting to look at than Jenny or stalling for some reason. "I was just wondering. Was thinking about what would happen if one of our gay teachers got married. Like what would the archdiocese do in that case?"

"You know there's a clause for all that in the faculty handbook, right?"

"Yeah," he said, pausing again and looking up now, like she'd asked a question he knew but couldn't remember the answer. "But what about your policy on pregnant girls? You said you guys have one."

"What do you want to know about it?"

"Well," he said and tossed his fork into the empty bowl. "Do you guys kick the kid out?"

"You think this is 19th century Ireland?" she said. "We're going to kick these kids out and make them do laundry somewhere?"

Pat looked a little embarrassed. His smile flattened. Just a thin line below his nose. "I guess not," he said. "It's just that I remember hearing about kids not being allowed to graduate or some such thing. I don't know where I hear this stuff."

"That probably happened somewhere else," she said. "And probably not that long ago. Some really conservative places might even still do it. But there's a school of thought on the matter that kicking kids out will actually encourage abortions."

Pat nodded. "Girls don't want to be expelled so they get rid of the baby?"

"Yep," said Jenny. "But there's another school of thought that we're supposed to be preaching abstinence. Chastity. I know it sounds old fashioned, but that's supposed to be the party line at both of our schools."

"I know it," he said. "It's complicated."

"Some people think—" she stopped short. "Hey," she barked. "Pick that stuff up, ladies." She hated that. There were garbage cans everywhere, but these girls would finish lunch and just walk away from the tables like the trash would simply disintegrate upon their departure. "Some educators at these conservative places in the Midwest think that if we allow pregnant girls to stay, that it will encourage pre-marital sex. It will signal to the girls that we're okay with it. What do you think of that?"

"What do *you* think of it?" he said.

"Pat," she said. "It's just us here, and you brought it up. Which one of these philosophies makes sense to you?"

He stood up with his empty bowl and walked it over to the garbage can at the end of the row of tables. He was walking slowly. He dropped it in and scanned the cafeteria. Jenny wondered what he was looking for. Then he shuffled back to his plastic chair. Stalling again. She wasn't even trying to argue. Now she was just curious. He sat down across from her again and looked at her without saying anything.

"Well?" she said.

"Well, what?" he said and started shining his apple with the palms of his hands.

"Pat," she said. "Do you think schools should throw the kids out or let them stay?"

"Both can work," he said, nodding. Then he continued, "Neither can work."

"Yeah," she said. "That about sums it up."

"But I think we're supposed to be doing everything we can to promote life here, right? That's part of our mission at Catholic schools?"

Jenny nodded.

"Then I really think we have to let these kids stay and try to support them." He seemed suddenly tired and maybe a little sad. "I don't think that if you had a pregnant girl walking around in here other girls are going to run out and have sex because they think the school is endorsing it."

"Exactly," she said. "I think once they're pregnant we need to help these girls have the babies. We need to let them know that it was a mistake, but they're forgiven and now things can be all right."

"Have you ever had a pregnant girl at St. Mary's?" he said.

"Heavens, no!" she said. They'd never had a girl get pregnant and carry the baby to full term while remaining a student at the school. "That never happened. Could you imagine the press?"

~10~

Grace was sitting with her friend, Jill. They'd known each other since Happy Times preschool. Back when Grace came up with the nickname Jilly-Bean. It stuck. When she was in a playful mood, she still called her Jilly-Bean.

She wasn't playful today. Her stomach was making ridiculous noises, and she was so tired she could barely keep her eyes open, even though she and Jill were talking about a party.

Freshman didn't go to many parties. It just didn't happen. They sometimes met up with boys and drank at the Marina Greens or the Grove, but actual house parties were a rarity.

"Remember that party at Max's last month?" asked Jill.

"Parts of it," said Grace, trying to be funny but also honest.

"Yeah, well, he's having another one next weekend."

"Oh fun," said Grace, now trying to make her voice sound like there wasn't anything more exciting than another freshman party. And there really wasn't. Except that she didn't feel very well most of the time, and obviously she wouldn't be able to drink now.

"I guess he says that his parents are going to Cabo, so it's just him and his brother in that big house."

"His brother?" Grace had known Max since junior high, and she didn't know he had a brother. "You mean his St. X brothers?"

"No," she said. "His older brother, Tony."

"That's so weird," said Grace. "I've never met him. Never heard of him."

"He's like five years older," she said. "Went to a boarding school back east. I think he's kind of a bad boy."

"Does he look like Max?" said Gracie. She liked the way Max looked. Curly hair. Tan. Always smiling. Perfect teeth.

"Kind of," she said. "But he—wait—you know what he looks like. You met him at the last party."

Grace shrugged. There were a lot of people there, but she drank too much. She didn't throw up like some of the other kids apparently did, but the whole night was a blur. Once people told her about stuff that happened, she could remember those details, but she couldn't sit there and narrate the events of Max's wild bash. She needed to be prompted to recall all the crazy stuff that happened.

"He's taller than Max," said Jill. "And his hair is kind of long and greasy. But his face looks like Max's."

"I must have met him," said Grace, ready to close the topic for now.

"You did meet him," said Jill, laughing and yelling a little bit now.

"Okay," said Grace, a little frustrated that she couldn't remember. "Yes, the tall guy. Dark hair?"

"Yeah," she said, apparently happy that Grace was pretending to remember. "He bought all the beer. You guys were talking in the hallway when you were in line for the bathroom. I was coming down the hall, and you smacked my butt when I walked past you guys."

"Oh yeah," said Grace, giggling some, but still not recalling any of it. Maybe Jill was the one remembering wrong. Grace never met this guy. She would remember someone who looked like Max.

***

When she got up to religion class in 205, she was dragging. They were working on the New Testament. Mrs. Kelly was trying to use the gospels to relate to their everyday lives, but Grace couldn't see how the loaves and fishes story could relate to her current situation. And wasn't that the same story as "Stone Soup"?

These are the things Grace was thinking when she decided to rest her eyes:

The lady is clearer today. The room isn't quite as bright, so I don't have to squint at all. But it's as warm and comfortable as it always is. Since I talked a lot the last time, I feel like I should wait and see what she has to say. I don't want to be rude.

"Your body is changing," she says, quiet, almost like she's singing me a lullaby.

"I know," I say. And then without thinking, I blurt out, "I feel like I have to fart all the time." Before I can even catch my breath, I say, "I'm sorry." And I

should feel embarrassed. I mean, normally I'm embarrassed when I say things without thinking. But not with her. I feel like maybe this is what it's like to be hypnotized.

She doesn't laugh at me. Instead she says, "Protect yourself."

"Okay," I say. And I want to ask, "from what?" but I don't. If she needed me to know, she would tell me. That, I'm sure of.

And then she comes toward me, but she gets fuzzier the closer she gets, like she's ruining the focus. She reaches out to me.

Mrs. Kelly was a cool teacher. She placed her hand on Grace's shoulder but didn't squeeze and she kept talking. Grace started to come out of it just as Mrs. Kelly was saying, "There are twelve baskets of bread and fish left over after everyone has eaten. Does that number mean anything to any of you?"

Even though she still felt half-hypnotized, Grace said, "Twelve apostles," and she was surprised at how full her own voice sounded. They were reading a story in a different class in which a girl's voice was described as sounding like *mountain water in a silver pitcher*, and Grace felt like that's the way her voice sounded now in class, but no one looked at her funny, and Mrs. Kelly just kept going.

"Good, Grace," she said. "What else?"

"Twelve tribes," said another girl in the back.

"Right," said Mrs. Kelly, and she took her hand off Grace's shoulder now and started to walk toward the white board in the front of the class. "Twelve seems to be some kind of mystical number," she said. "Where else do we see it?"

Kids started yelling stuff out now: *Eggs ... Juries...Clocks... Donuts ... Calendars ... Zodiac ...*

Grace had never really thought much about it, but her birthday was December 12.

~11~

At about three o'clock someone had sent out the "Bat Signal" on the group text. It was a simple message: *Anyone?*

There were seven people in the group, and everyone knew what the message meant. On Friday afternoons for decades at around 4:30 p.m., Pat and his buddies would meet for an early drink at the Dubliner on West Portal. The bar had been called a few other names during that time—The Fishbowl, Joxer Daly's, Fahey's— but the set-up had remained the same. Long bar, wise guy bar tenders, lots of regulars, and Friday afternoon beers that sometimes dominoed into longer sessions if there was a game on, any kind of game when they were a younger crew, but a more selective slate now.

As the group had gotten older and started families, they didn't necessarily meet every week, but when someone sent out the message—*Anyone?*—Pat and his cohorts knew the query's unabbreviated dispatch asked, *Is anyone going to the bar today?* Pat rarely sent out the message, but he always felt the tug when he saw it, and today was no different.

It had been almost twenty-four hours since he'd heard the news about Grace, and he and Emily had not created even the semblance of a strategy. But a couple of beers at the Dubliner wasn't going to make the situation any worse, and Pat had skipped the last few weeks.

The bar's tagline was very San Francisco: *Foggy Nights, Foggier Mornings.* But that would not be the case for Pat. Emily would expect him home to make dinner, and he needed a clear head to participate in the discussion with Grace as she would probably be slipping out of her *temporary denial* by the time he got home.

Two beers. Home by six. Really. No screwing around. Then he'd find out who the father was.

***

By four o'clock, St. X was a ghost town. Pat's assistant, Doris, had left him next week's schedule, and he watched her water the plants before the weekend. He had organized the two mountains of papers on his desk into one mountain and four smaller stacks, foothills, that he would climb if he came in over the weekend, which he usually did, or first thing Monday morning if there was something going on after Mass, and Sunday wasn't an option.

"Have a good weekend, Pat," Doris called to him before she put on her jacket and hustled out.

He heard the door shut, just as he was saying, "Same to you."

He was holding his reading glasses, getting ready to leave. With the glasses, he tapped the top of each of the foothills, mentally organizing the order with which he would assail these when he was back in the office. Because it would be impossible to ever get to all of it, he nodded at the stacks, folded up his laptop, slid it into his satchel, and made his way to the parking lot.

***

The Dubliner looked and sounded like it always did. Van Morrison was mumbling a song on the jukebox, and the rabble of city workers, contractors, fireman, and cops were mumbling the same complaints they'd been spewing for years. Today's topic sounded like Warriors-gab, a common topic since the Dubs had started their five-year dominance in the NBA. But the guys at the Dubliner could always find something about which to argue. Today, it was whether or not the Warriors could win without Durant. A stale topic as far as Pat was concerned.

"Time-bomb," someone shouted at him as he walked past the cluster near the door. An old coaching moniker that had stuck even though he'd been out of the game for a few years now and didn't really earn many technical fouls in those last few seasons. The nickname came from his earlier days as a coach.

Pat sat down next to Jack Meehan, who pushed a Coors light in front of Pat and said, "How're things at St. X?" Most of the patrons at the Dubliner had attended St. X or one of the other two Catholic high schools in the city, but Jack was a diehard St. X fan. Not just the teams, but the school in general. He had a good job with Public Works, and he'd sent his kids to St. X. He felt that the other Catholic schools in the city were catering to rich kids and that St. X was the last school supporting working class families.

"We're getting by," Pat said to Jack and smiled as he grabbed his beer.

Jack held up his bottle, "Slainte," he said and took a swallow.

"How's your boy doing?" asked Pat. He knew the kid had gotten into one of the UC's, but he couldn't remember which one.

"UC Davis," said Jack. "Studying viniculture."

Pat raised his eyebrows.

"I know," said Jack. "It's the science of wine or how to grow grapes or some shit. I don't know."

"Yeah," said Pat. "Apparently, it's big business." Then he looked all the way down the crowded bar and didn't see a single wine glass on the counter. "Just not in here."

Jack laughed. "Not in here," he repeated and used his longneck bottle to point down the bar and then at the tall tables that lined the wall behind them. "But I'm supporting the kid. Someone's drinking wine, and someone has to grow the grapes, and someone has to make the stuff, and a lot of people make a living out of it. Why not him?"

"I really do think it's a serious course of study up there and down at Cal Poly as well," Pat said.

"Yep," said Jack. "It just kinda took me by surprise is all. The kid never struck me as someone who'd be interested in wine."

"Maybe he's interested in the business side of the industry," said Pat.

"Could be," said Jack, and then he was silent for a long moment before he said, "It just never made sense to me that these kids—at eighteen years old, mind you— are supposed to be mature enough to pick a career. Think about that."

"Didn't you start working for the city right after high school?"

"I did a year at City College," he said. "But that's the point. I didn't have as many options as these kids. Most of the jobs young people are trying to land didn't even exist when we were kids. Do you know what a *user experience professional* is?" he asked.

Pat shook his head.

"Exactly," he said. "They have too many choices, and their brains aren't equipped at that age to weed through so many options."

"That's true," said Pat.

"It ain't like when our folks were young, and a lot of 'em were getting married and having babies not long after they got out of high school. Shit, my kid's been so sheltered he can barely cross the street on his own."

Pat had three quarters of a beer left. He drank it in one long series of swallows. "I gotta get out of here, Jack," he gasped after a quick suck of air and a stifled belch. "I'll talk to you soon." He popped the beer down on the counter and felt the crisp bubbles stinging the back of his throat. He needed to get home.

~12~

Emily smelled beer on his breath when he walked in, but she wasn't going to make a big deal out of it. She was happy he was home and happy the girls said they would cook dinner. They were doing tacos, which would be a mess, but Emily was thankful for the fleeting normalcy of it all.

"Let's take Sully for a walk," she said to Pat, "while the girls make dinner."

Sully heard the word *walk* and immediately ran to the hall tree to get his leash.

Pat had already sat down on the couch in the family room and flipped on the TV. Whoever had used it last had it turned to MTV, so when the screen came to life, Pat was greeted with an episode of *Catfish,* a show about people involved in online romances. Sometimes these folks assumed fabricated identities and built relationships based on these fictional characters that they'd invented for a myriad of bizarre psychological reasons.

The show invariably followed a basic construction. The host, a guy named Nev, did a kind of half-assed digital investigation to locate one of the parties involved. Then he ultimately tried to bring the two people together. Sometimes it ended up being just two shy, lonely people who needed some nudging to finally meet each other in person. But mostly the show featured a different type, an odd kind of introvert who was afraid of an authentic relationship, but who had the time to build with photos and fake posts and videos, a realistic online persona.

As a therapist, Emily was fascinated by the show. Who were these people? What had happened to them that they would end up participating in these strange charades? And she had to hand it to this guy, Nev. He had a way of getting the subjects to admit to the reasons why they'd committed these acts.

Much of the time, the people who'd assumed the false identities were young adults who came to a point in their lives in which they had lost all self-esteem and felt that their real personalities, their real selves, weren't worthy of attracting genuine partners. However—and these were the ones Emily really enjoyed—there were other more complicated motives like online fakes, seeking revenge on past lovers, members of the LGBTQ community who had various reasons for establishing their relationships online, and people who had dozens of online personalities and dozens of fake relationships. And there were really bored people, who simply had nothing better to do.

All the scenarios were interesting to Emily. She was a blunt person, who'd never been afraid to speak her mind and be herself, so when Nev started to peel back the layers of these peculiar online onions, Emily was fully absorbed in the stories. To her, living a lie was always harder than living the truth—even an ugly one—and the twisted plots involved in the concealment of the truth on this show were worth investing an hour in front of the TV.

But not tonight.

Pat looked tired and didn't even notice the leash that Sully had dropped on his lap.

"Pat," said Emily. "Let's get some fresh air while the girls make dinner.

Without responding, he pushed himself out of the chair and secured Sully's leash. "I'll meet you out front," he said. "I have to change my shoes."

Emily was in her yoga pants and a long-sleeved tee shirt, always ready to sneak in a quick workout when she had some time to spare.

Pat walked out of the house in his work clothes—khakis and an oxford button down—but now he was wearing New Balance cross-trainers instead of his standard loafers or desert boots. It was an awful look, a dad uniform, but Emily was happy that he'd agreed to walk with her.

"Buena Vista or down toward Kezar?" she asked. If they went toward Kezar, the walk back up the hill would be a challenge, but she was a little scared to go to Buena Vista Park at this hour because they might encounter a coyote. For some reason, these wild animals that the city allowed in the parks liked to show themselves right around dusk, and Sully couldn't help himself. He was a very protective border collie, and, if he were off leash, he would chase the coyotes. Emily had done her research. If the coyote wanted to hurt Sully, it would be pretty easy.

"Let's do Kezar," he said without prompting, and Emily wondered if he was considering the coyotes as well. Pat had actually taken a picture of one from about ten feet away. Pat and the Urban 'Yote were having a stare-down, and Pat wanted a picture to prove that these things were taking over the park. So, he snapped it and brought it home to show the girls and tell them to stay away from Buena Vista until further notice.

"No speed-walking," he said to Emily now. "Let's just take it easy."

"Okay," she said. "So have you done any thinking about Grace?"

"I had lunch with Jenny Daly today," he said.

"You didn't tell her, did you?" she asked. She liked Jenny, but she didn't really understand the relationship with Pat. She was a single lady, and Pat seemed to share a lot with Jenny about the family. It seemed weird to Emily.

"No," he said. "But we did talk about the St. Mary's policy on student pregnancies."

"How did you bring that up?"

"I can't even remember," he lied. "But she didn't ask. Wait ... she did. She wanted to know if I had a pregnant kid at St. X."

"Funny," she said and almost tripped over some uneven pavement just as they were about to cross Ashbury Street from Frederick. She looked back at the spot she'd lost her balance but couldn't see anything on the ground. Then she looked at Pat to see if he'd even noticed. Pat and Sully were now about five feet in front of her because Sully was pulling hard to get to the water bowl that Bob, the owner of Ashbury Market, would leave outside the door. Emily felt some stinging in her toe as she limped to the corner where Pat and Sully were. Pat was looking back at her now, squinting, and Sully was lapping up the water and checking to see if Bob was going to come out.

He did.

"How's Sully?" said Bob. Sully turned around and jumped at him, paws landing on the Bob's thighs. Bob scratched behind the dog's ears and then produced a treat from his hip pocket. "There you go, boy," he said and held up the biscuit so that Sully would have to stand on his hind legs, and then Bob dropped the snack into Sully's mouth.

"How are you, Bob?" said Pat, pulling back on the leash so that Sully wouldn't jump up again.

"Good," he said. "I love the dogs, you know?"

"Yep," said Pat. "I guess you haven't seen this one in a while."

"Sully?" he said, reaching into his pocket for a second treat. "I see him with your daughter all the time." This time he tossed the snack up in the air, and Pat let the leash have some slack as Sully jumped up and snatched it out of the air.

Emily was confused. "Which daughter?" she asked.

"Long hair, light brown," he said. "Very lovely. Hope?"

"Grace?" she said.

"Yes," he said. "Not the athlete. The younger one. Grace. Lovely and nice."

Emily didn't know that Grace had been walking the dog much and certainly didn't think that she'd have come down to this part of the neighborhood. Emily knew that she was staying away from Buena Vista Park, but she assumed Grace was just taking the dog down to Corona Heights and throwing the ball in the dog park. "How often do you see her?" asked Emily.

"Not so much the last couple of weeks," he said. "But she was coming around a lot about three weeks or a month ago. I don't remember so good anymore."

"Got it," said Emily, wondering what else Grace was doing without Emily's knowledge. "Good to see you, Bob," she said and started walk toward Cole Street.

Pat followed and said over his shoulder, "I'll talk to you soon, Bob." Sully looked back at Bob and barked once before catching his stride.

"I like that guy," said Pat.

"You don't think he's a little weird?"

"In this town?" he said. "No. He's one of the most normal guys I know."

"I guess," she said but was still curious about Grace hanging around on Ashbury. "I didn't know Grace walked the dog down here."

"Yeah, well," he said and paused, "apparently she's doing a lot of things we don't know about."

"What's the St. Mary's rule?" asked Emily.

"Huh?"

"The St. Mary's rule on pregnant girls."

"Oh," he said. "This is actually some relatively good news." They were walking up Cole Street now, and no one was sitting on the bench outside of Finnegan's Wake, so Pat sat down, and Sully curled up under the bench. "They don't kick the girls out," he said.

Emily was relieved but simultaneously anxious. She was happy that Grace would be allowed to continue to attend the school, but she also knew that if Grace stayed, there would be a public scandal. The ladies on the Mother's Guild would eat this up. "I guess that's good news," she said.

"Should we do the math?" he said.

She knew what he was talking about. "I think Gracie will be able to get through this year without showing. She'll be right at the end of the first trimester. She can wear baggy clothes, I guess, and be fine."

"Okay," he said. "That will buy us some time, but by the end of the summer, she'll be at six months. She'll start the school year looking very pregnant."

Suddenly, Emily felt like she was going to cry. It actually started in her chest and rose up in shivers through her throat and to her eyes, but she was able to stop it, like an aborted sneeze, and spoke with only the hint of trembling in her voice. "Do we even want her going back there?" she asked.

"Well that's something to consider," he said. "There's the possibility we could have her do summer school somewhere else to get ahead. Some school where no one knows her. And we can have her take online classes at home for the fall semester. Then by the time she has the baby in October or early November, she'd be able to have some time with the baby until January when she could return to St. Mary's."

"Is that possible?" she said.

"I don't know," he said. "To be perfectly honest, I'm just considering all this now. I haven't really had a chance to really check on all the details."

"Oh," said Emily. She was actually somewhat soothed by the blueprint that Pat had rolled out, but the continued uncertainty was tightening her stomach. "What do you need to check on?"

"I think I need to see if Jenny Daly will accept summer school and online classes for that first semester."

"What do you think she'll say?"

"I actually think it could work," he said. "I'm worried about after she gets back to school."

"You mean how the other girls will treat her?"

"Emily," he said. "I haven't even thought about that yet. I'm trying to figure out how this family is going to take care of a baby while the mother is a sophomore in high school, and the grandparents both have full-time jobs."

Grandparents she thought and again felt the vibrations of a sob rumbling in her chest somewhere, rising up.

~13~

Alice had told Grace to work on the guacamole, and Grace was doing a good job. All she wanted was for Grace to get the avocado into the bowl, and then Alice would add her special touches. She liked to add lime, garlic, garlic salt, a couple of tablespoons of pico de gallo, and a dollop of sour cream. Came out perfect every time.

Alice was currently working on getting all the fixings into separate bowls so that everyone could build his or her own taco. She knew Mom and Dad would forgo the tortillas and try to make some kind of ridiculous taco salads, and that was fine, but she and Grace were going to melt cheese onto the tortillas and build from there. When Alice went over to the pot to stir some green chilies into the ground beef mixture, she heard Grace behind her.

"Do you think they went on the walk to talk about me," she asked.

"Yep," said Alice.

"Do you think they're mad?"

Alice had to think about this. They weren't acting mad, but they should be mad. Their little girl was pregnant. "They haven't really yelled at you," she said. "I don't think they're so much mad as they are worried," she said and that sounded about right to her.

"I agree," said Grace. "But they shouldn't be."

Alice stuck the wooden spoon in the pot. It had been about twenty-four hours since they'd told their dad about the baby, but it felt longer. Alice had a towel over her shoulder, and she used it to clean her hands before she turned to Grace. "To me, it doesn't make sense that you're *not* worried," she said. "The rest of us are definitely worried. This could actually make it really hard for dad at work."

Grace was finished with the avocados and was dumping the skins and pits into the garbage. She turned her head quickly and said, "Why?"

Alice assumed Grace had considered all this, but maybe she hadn't. "Grace," she said. "Have you ever heard of a pregnant girl at St. Mary's?"

"It's just my first year," she said. "But I haven't seen any."

"Well, I'm almost finished at St. Mary's," said Alice. "And I haven't heard even one story about a pregnant girl at this school."

Grace stuck a tortilla chip into the unfinished bowl of mashed avocados but didn't say anything,

"I gotta put all the stuff in there," said Alice as Grace crunched away at the chip. "St. X is our brother school, and Dad's the principal. Don't you think it might be a little awkward for him if his daughter is across the street with a belly out to here?" Alice held both hands out in front of her and posed as if she were carrying an invisible beach ball.

Grace smiled. "Dad can handle it," she said and reached into the bag for another chip.

Alice pulled the guacamole bowl away so that she could mix in the rest of the ingredients. But before she started squeezing the lime, she said, "Why do you think dad will be able to handle it so easily?" she said and tried to imagine the kind of scrutiny he would suffer and the humiliation he would endure. She couldn't. It was all too much.

Grace had taken a bite out of the chip. She was holding the other half between two fingers and looking out the kitchen window at nothing in particular, but she was still smiling. She said nothing.

"Can you answer me, please?" said Alice.

"Because it's a blessing," said Grace and stared deeply at Alice, who had lime wedges in each hand. Grace looked older when she gazed like this. She looked almost old enough to have a child.

***

When her parents got back home with Sully, the meal was ready to go, and, predictably, both Mom and Dad made salads out of the taco ingredients. Alice didn't question the choices. Her mom looked amazing, and her dad needed to try something to reduce the stubborn gut that he'd been carrying for the last few years. It just didn't seem to Alice that a tortilla could be such a health risk.

"Nice job, girls," said her dad as he sprinkled some chopped onions on top of the mound of ground beef that smothered the shredded iceberg lettuce beneath it.

"Thanks," said Alice. "Did you guys figure anything out while you were with Sully?"

"We did," said Emily. "We think we know how we'd like to proceed."

"Oh," said Alice, surprised that they'd made that much progress on their thirty-minute walk. She knew it would sound selfish, but she couldn't help herself. "Are you going to wait to make any announcements until after graduation?" she asked and immediately felt ashamed. But Grace didn't blink.

Her dad made a face that said, *Really, Alice?* but he said only, "We think everything will be fine if we can make it to summer."

The table was silent for a moment, so he continued: "Grace probably won't be showing much until after your graduation, so we don't feel an immediate need to notify the school at this point."

Grace's face could have been on a church statue. No emotion, but still somehow expressing kindness and empathy in her eyes.

Their mom apparently didn't like the silence that had crept into the room after Dad's matter of fact statement about the next three months, so she decided to fill it with a random question. "Gracie, honey," she began. "When were you walking the dog a lot down in Cole Valley?"

Grace was holding a taco, the juice dripping out onto the heel of her right hand and down onto her wrist and elbow before trickling to the plate below her. She tilted it up to prevent more leaking and took a small bite from the end that had the seepage. The bite was so small that she chewed it quickly and swallowed before saying, "I used to walk the dog down there because Max lives on Parnassus, near the Walgreens. That was just my route, and I would stop by to see him sometimes."

Alice watched her dad's eyes shift quickly to look over at her mom, but neither said anything.

"Why do you ask?" said Grace.

"We saw Bob from Ashbury Market," said Mom. "And he told us he used to see you down there a lot." She paused for a moment before saying, "We didn't know is all."

Alice decided to jump in. "Is Max your boyfriend?" she asked. She knew the kid and liked him but wasn't sure who he hung out with or what he was into. All she really knew about the family was that the dad drove a new Tesla with a butterfly door, and that there was an older brother a little older than Alice, who went away to a boarding school. And the parents went on a lot of trips.

"Alice," said Grace. "I've told you before. Me and Max are just friends."

Alice's mom said, "Have the two of you ever gone on a date?"

Grace smiled. "Do you guys still think that I had sex with someone?"

Dad said, "Well, it sounds like you might have been alone with Max on occasion, and …." It sounded like he was going to say something else, but he just dropped it.

Grace placed her taco back on her plate, wiped the juice off her hands, and said very calmly, "Tell me what I can do to prove to you that I have never had sexual intercourse with anyone."

~14~

Emily was already in bed, and Pat was brushing his teeth. He couldn't stop thinking about Grace's challenge to him to figure out a way for her to prove that she was still a virgin but somehow happened to be carrying a baby.

He stepped out of the bathroom while he was still brushing and said, "*Shoo we gi huh a lie detecka?*

"Go spit," said Emily.

He went back into the bathroom, spit, and washed his face. When he came out, he said, "Does she want us to give her a lie detector?"

Emily didn't nod or shake her head. She thought for a moment and then said, "Can someone be lying and not even know it?"

"Um ..." he said. He knew this. "I don't think so."

"But what if someone really believes what they're saying?"

"Then I don't think it's a lie," he said, and grabbed the remote control. All the bedrooms were downstairs, and the girls would probably hear the discussion unless the TV or radio was on. He turned on the Ten O'clock news on Channel Two. He had a secret crush on the weather lady.

"No," said Emily. "What if the person is saying something untrue but believes it to be true."

"Yeah," he said. "I get it. But I don't think that's a lie." He was sitting on her side of the bed, and his feet were cold despite the fact that he was wearing socks.

She was lying down, but she adjusted her pillow and sat up now. "You don't think it's a lie when someone says something that's not true?"

He smiled. "We're just arguing semantics, hon. All I'm saying is that in order for it to be considered a lie, the person has to intentionally tell a falsehood in order to deceive someone. I think that's a lie." He got up to turn off the light and walk around to his side of the bed. "What Gracie is doing is different. If she's not doing it on purpose and if she's not trying to mislead us, she's—"

"What?" said Emily. "What is that? What's she doing if she believes she's telling the truth?"

"Isn't that more your expertise?" he said. Again, it was just semantics. It didn't really matter what it was called. The two of them agreed that they were saying the same thing. "Does it matter if there's a term for this?" he said.

Emily had her phone out now.

"Do we really need to know a word for this?" he said.

"This is just for me," she said, scrolling. "It's bugging me."

Pat moved the remote control off the bed and onto his end table. "Knock yourself out," he said and climbed into bed.

"This is actually ridiculous," she said. "I don't think there's a word for it. When I put in *unintentional lie* it says that's a contradiction in terms."

"It is."

"Okay," she said. "What if she's not lying *or* telling a falsehood?"

"When you say *telling a falsehood*, you're talking about the idea of the unintentional lie?"

"Apparently that's a contradiction in terms, but yeah, that's what I'm saying."

"Emily," he said but didn't say anything else. Sure, he'd had ridiculous thoughts that there was some kind of miracle going on here, but he wasn't going to entertain those thoughts with anyone else. That's a good way to make yourself go crazy. Gracie would have this baby, and no one would love it more than this family, but he wasn't going to pretend that there was any way for this conception to have occurred except for the old fashion way.

"What?" she said. "Why can't we even discuss the possibility?"

"Emily," he said. "We've got a lot going on here. My career is in jeopardy. I don't think we should spend any time on that kind of hopeful thinking. It will just allow Grace to continue her denial longer than it's a healthy thing to do."

"Of course," she said, now in a sad kind of breathy whisper, the air coming out of her like the last few gasps from a deflating air mattress—nothing left to keep her floating, the buoyancy of the delusion slipping away. "But what about something else," she said.

"What do you mean?"

"What if she got pregnant without knowing it?"

Pat heard what she said, but he wanted to take a moment with it. He could only think of one possibility, and he didn't like it at all. "Do we want to go there, Emily? Because that's a dark place, and I don't think you're ready for that."

She turned on the light on her side of the bed. She was still sitting up. When Pat looked over at her, she had a strange look on her face, like she was scared and mad at the same time. "What are you saying, Pat?"

He assumed that she could figure this out. She was a very smart woman. Was she just trying to force him to say it? "The only other alternative. And you know exactly what I'm saying."

"I don't have any idea what you're saying," she said. "I was thinking maybe some kind of biological anomaly. What are you thinking?"

"Emily," he said, and he heard himself raising his voice, so he reverted to a whisper. "The only way she could have gotten pregnant without knowing it would be if she was drugged and raped." It sounded horrible coming out of his mouth, a foul banshee that he'd released into the room and then immediately regretted it. But he felt the need to elaborate when he heard Emily let out a small cry of helplessness. "Someone could have slipped her a mickey," he said.

"A roofie?"

"Yeah," he said and suddenly felt as if he were about to cry.

Grace

This is the first time that I see the lady outside. I don't know exactly where I am, but it feels like Golden Gate Park on a sunny day. No sun in my eyes. Not hot. More like room temperature only in the middle of a park. I don't think it's the Japanese Tea Garden, but it looks like it. There are narrow streams and tiny bridges and flowers and plants and creeping ivy all over the place. No people, though.

We're sitting on a bench, but it's not like a normal park bench. It's more like if someone told me to get into the most comfortable sitting position and then built a bench under me. I can barely even feel it. I'm in the kind of spot where I could lose a couple of hours just sitting. In fact, I'm hesitant to say anything to the lady because I'm so content just being.

But she speaks first this time. "Don't let them," she says, and as always, her voice is a song. It's soft bells, wind chimes, reaching my ears like they're coming from inside my own head.

I usually don't question her when she gives directions, but these words sound distressed even through the music. "What do they want to do?" I ask but immediately feel regret. I should know the answer. And maybe I do know if I'd only try to think differently.

"They want to make you doubt," she says.

I don't say this to her, but I've spent my life doubting. I question everything, so this might be a tall order for me. "I'll try," I say, and I feel myself smiling like I've seen Alice do when her basketball coach is giving her directions. She's always eager to please. She wants to do what her coach told her so that her team will win.

I feel the same way, but I'm not yet sure who's on my team.

~15~

Emily hadn't slept for a week after Pat told her that Grace could have been raped while unconscious. He'd also talked about bringing Grace to someone who could administer a lie detector. But, as they'd discussed that night, Grace might be telling a falsehood without even knowing it. A lie detector wouldn't pick that up.

Emily also thought about bringing Grace to see a hypnotherapist. Emily actually knew one who worked in the building next to hers. But that didn't seem right, either. So she and Pat were talking about whether or not it might be a good time to see a therapist or a psychiatrist.

"I know you've told me the difference before," Pat said and turned down the car radio. "But can you just refresh my memory?" It was a stoplight, so he was looking at her with apology in his eyes, sorry that he never listens.

"Pat," said Emily. "This is simple. I've told you a hundred times. A psychiatrist has to go to medical school and can prescribe drugs. I cannot."

"Yes, yes," he said. "Of course. I know that. So what do we need?"

"I think we can start with a therapist," she said. "And if the therapist thinks we need more, he or she can refer us."

"This is also going to sound stupid," he said as the light turned green. "But I'm going to ask anyway because these are difficult times, and we're both going to be really patient with each other."

"Go ahead," she said.

The driver of the car ahead of them was riding the brakes, which would normally elicit at least a tightening of his grip on the wheel and a subvocalized directive, but today, nothing. "There's a reason *you* can't be her therapist, right?"

Again, he should know this, but he doesn't listen. "Do you think we would have better results getting to the truth if I continue to ask Gracie the same questions we've been posing for a week, or do you think it's time we put it in someone else's hands?"

He was in the left-hand turn lane near West Portal and taking a U-turn to go the opposite direction on Sloat toward the beach. By the time they turned around, they were looking right into the sunset, and he put on his shades against the glare but didn't answer the question.

"Is it ever a good idea for a parent to be a child's therapist, Pat?"

"I think we've had this argument before," he said. "I think all parents should be therapists for their kids. It's part of the job."

"Well, thanks for reminding me how much you value my work," she said. He'd done this before. He'd sat in front of the TV and said that he could come up with the same answers as Dr. Phil, and he had. People would come on the show and talk about their problems, and, invariably, before Dr. Phil would give his advice, Pat would beat him to it and provide almost the exact same counsel that the learned doctor would postulate.

"I'm not minimizing your work," he said. "I'm just making the point that parents should be advising their own kids. If anyone should be able to help their teenaged girl, it should be a therapist and an educator." He was going about fifty miles per hour now in a thirty-five, and Sloat was a speed trap; it even had those cameras at the traffic lights.

"Slow down," she said. "And we *were* the first ones to advise her, Pat. We always have been, and now we have a child who believes that she is experiencing a virgin pregnancy. Don't you think it's time to bring in someone else?"

They were whizzing past Sigmund Stern Grove on the right and the reservoir on the left. Hardly any traffic at all moving west. Pat was being stubborn. Not answering the question even though the answer was obvious.

There was a slight marine layer, so the glare was minimal, and the shape of the sun was visible as it began its steady dip into the cold Pacific. It didn't plunge into the salty waves the way Alice did on summer days—a dramatic, instantaneous dive into the breakers. And it didn't employ Grace's in-and-out method of dipping her feet, running away, and trying again until she could bear the cold. It was steady. It was going to do its thing without interruption, like it was simply sprawling into a warm bath.

"Do you know someone?" Pat asked.

"I know lots of people who would be good," she said.

"Do you have someone particular in mind?"

As Pat was slowly coming around on this issue, Emily decided to take her time and make him suffer a bit. "Yeah," she said. Then, "Where are we going?"

"I was going to stop by Java Beach and grab a beer or a coffee," he said.

"Which one?" she asked.

"Whichever one would result in the least amount of crap from you," he said.

"Do you really need a beer?" she asked.

"No," he said. "But that doesn't mean I wouldn't like one. Do you want one?"

"Not really."

"Coffee?"

"I guess."

They passed George's Liquor and Pasquale's Pizza and found a spot just around the corner from Java Beach in front of the Irish Cultural Center. Pat knew the owners of the coffee shop and entered to make the orders. Emily sat at one of the outside tables. She was listening to the monkeys chattering from the zoo across the street while the colors blossoming from the sunset had pedestrians stopping to watch. In the few minutes that she was waiting for Pat, several cars pulled over to take in the spectacle.

When Pat came out with the coffees, he didn't even notice the view. He put the two cups down on the table and asked, "So who do you have in mind?"

Emily had many friends in the business—psychiatrists, psychologists, and therapists—but she thought Cindy Parker would probably be the best bet. Cindy had teenaged girls of her own, and she and Emily had always gotten along very well. And Cindy was Catholic. Emily wasn't sure why this felt important to her, but the idea had been orbiting the perimeter of her mind since the possibility of a therapist had been introduced, and now, as the notion broke through the heat of re-entry, she was sure that Cindy was the right choice.

"Cindy Parker," she said.

"I like Cindy Parker," he said. Then he took a deep breath, leaned back in his chair and said, "Jesus, look at that sunset."

~16~

Jill had known Grace since they were little, and they both had become good friends with Max over the last couple of years. So, it wasn't a surprise when Jill got the group text from Grace asking that the three of them meet up for something important.

Grace was usually pretty direct, but this text had a sense of mystery to it: *Can you guys meet me this afternoon. I have something kind of big to tell you.* That's what it said. Nothing else. But that was enough for both Jill and Max to reply almost immediately and ask when and where.

West Portal Park. 5pm.

The park was actually a playground for little kids. It was perched above the streetcar tunnel that opened up onto West Portal Avenue with all its stores and restaurants and bars. And even though the park was really for little kids, Jill's group still liked to meet there. It had benches around the swings and slides, and it was funny to watch the little kids if they were there in the daytime. If it was nighttime, it was a great place to sneak some beers before walking down the hill to get a pizza at Mozzarella Di Bufala or see a movie at the Empire.

There was also a big patch of grass away from the play structure, and if it was a nice day, they would sprawl out on lawn and talk there. This afternoon was warm, so they set up camp in a loose triangle right in the middle of the grass area.

"What's the big thing?" said Max, while Grace was still spreading out her hoodie on the grass so that she wouldn't get her jeans wet when she sat down.

Jill almost chimed in with *Yeah, what is it*? But Grace's face changed right away to something that Jill had never seen before. She looked like someone who'd been crying so long that she didn't have any more tears. She looked tired and older. So, Jill didn't say anything. She waited for Grace.

Grace had her head down now and was playing with the cuff of her sweatshirt sleeve, which was on the ground beneath her. "You guys have to promise not to tell anyone," she said, and it surprised Jill that Grace's voice was clear, a mature person making a serious request.

Max said, "Grace, what is it?"

Jill just nodded, a little scared now that this was not going to be fun gossip. It was more important than that. Grace might be in trouble. Were her parents sick? Did something happen to Alice? Was the family moving away? Divorce?

"This really has to be between just us," she said. "I'm serious. My parents would kill me if they knew I was meeting you guys down here."

"Grace," said Jill. "Are you trying to scare me? Because this is getting scary. Are you okay?"

"Perfectly healthy," she said. "I've been to the doctor a couple of times the last few weeks.

Max was losing patience. "So, what is it?" he said.

"You're not going to believe me, and I'm not ready for you guys to react badly to this, so please be nice to me."

Jill could hear a few kids playing in the park, and the L Taraval streetcar was making its honking sound as it turned up Ulloa Street toward the library. Max was silent.

"I'm pregnant," said Grace, and she almost smiled, not with her teeth or anything, but a kind of a smile like the saints on the stained-glass windows at church.

Jill heard herself say "Oh my God," and she put her hands up to her mouth as if to stop whatever would come out next. Grace was so beautiful sitting there. Jill wanted to say something comforting, but she couldn't think of anything except to ask who the father was, and she didn't want to do that. She wanted to let Grace tell this however she wanted.

When Jill looked at Max, he was just staring at Grace, his eyebrows maybe turned down slightly. He finally said, "I assume you're joking."

For some reason, Jill knew it wasn't a joke. And she actually thought that Max knew as well, but he just didn't know what to say. So, he'd offered this lame line.

Grace didn't like it. "You really think I would joke about something like this?" she said, her hands out in front of her now and shaking a little bit like she was about to catch a football. "What would be funny about that?"

Max stared. "I didn't mean that kind of a joke," he said. "I meant like you're playing with us. You called us here for something else and now you're messing with us before you tell us why we're really here." He was shaking his head a little bit at the end as if to say *I don't even know why I'm trying to explain this now. I believe you.*

"Do you understand now that I'm not joking?" she said.

His eyes were cast downward. He was looking at his shoes like he'd never seen a pair of Jordans before. He nodded but never looked up.

"Jill?" she said

"I don't know what to say," said Jill. "But you know we're here for you. We'll help you any way we can." Jill was still being careful, not sure what kind of mind Grace had at this point. "How many weeks?" she asked after a moment.

Before Grace could answer, Max said, "Are you going to keep it?"

Grace took a moment to pick at some grass near her feet before she answered. "They think about five or six weeks," she said, the orange glow of the sunset forming a fuzzy outline around the roofs of the houses across the street.

"Who's the father," said Max.

"That's the thing," Grace said.

~17~

Pat parked on Ocean Avenue between 19th Avenue and Junipero Serra Boulevard. He knew people called it Lakeside Village, but, like many San Francisco neighborhoods, he thought the name was a misnomer—like *pregnant virgin*. Lake Merced was at least a mile or two southwest of the three-block commercial district where Cindy Parker's office sat between an optometrist and a tuxedo rental place. Areas called *lakeside* should at least have a view of a lake.

Emily and Grace jumped out of the car quickly. They didn't want to be seen walking into a therapist's office. Pat knew this was all going to come out at some point, but he wasn't ready yet either, so he hustled to put some money in the meter and followed them in.

By the time he walked through the door, Cindy was out near the front desk hugging Emily. Cindy saw Pat over Emily's shoulder and came over to shake his hand. "Hi, Patrick," she said and gave him one of those shakes where she put her left hand on top. Without thinking, Pat did the same and immediately felt ridiculous.

"Good to see you, Cindy," he said. "Do we all come in, or …"

"We'll start together," she said. "And then Grace and I will have some time to chat on our own."

Cindy led them into a small office. No books on shelves or degrees on the walls or a big desk. Just a couch and a love seat, an office chair with a small table next to it, and a Ficus growing out of a clay pot in the corner of the room. There was also a small window, with a few succulents in small containers on the sill. And a portrait hanging on the wall behind Cindy's chair.

Pat looked at it for a long moment, even after Cindy had begun to talk. It was a painting of a man and a woman standing close to one another: almost all greys and charcoals and blacks. Smudged, rudimentary figures. There was no real distinction of separation in their torsos. It was clear that the woman was turned slightly toward the man, but the man was looking straight forward. The only splashes of color in the whole painting were the woman's open lips and the man's right ear.

Both were painted bright red. The woman was standing to the man's left, so the red ear was not on her side.

Why doesn't the man want to hear her? he thought. What's he listening to beyond the frame when she's right there trying to tell him something?

"Pat," said Emily, and Pat looked over at the three of them, all watching him. "Are you with us?"

"I like your painting," he said to Cindy, feeling his face begin to flush as he sat down by himself on the loveseat.

"You like the red?" she said.

"I do," he said. "It tells the story."

"I agree," she said and took a quick peek over her shoulder at the painting. "So, what are we here to talk about?"

Emily said, "Well, we found out some really big news last week, and we just want to talk it through, make sure we're handling everything the right way."

"Okay," said Cindy. "That sounds like a good reason to have a chat. Does someone want to tell me the big news?"

Pat was certain that Cindy knew what had happened, but this was probably her way to get Grace talking, and it worked.

"I'm pregnant," said Grace. "It's pretty big news for our family because I'm only fifteen, and I'm not married."

"Big news, indeed," said Cindy without seeming surprised at all. "And I assume you all have talked about Grace's options?"

"Well, no," Emily began. "We don't—no—we haven't ... no—"

"We're Catholic," said Pat and left it at that.

"I see," said Cindy. "But Grace should understand—"

"I understand," said Grace. "I'm fifteen."

"So you're planning on having the baby," said Cindy and wrote something in her notebook before looking back up to Grace.

"Yes," she said. "I believe that I'm supposed to."

Cindy sat up straight and said, "Because of your religion?"

"Well, yes," she said. "That's part of it." Then she paused and looked over at Emily before continuing. "But I also think there's something special about this baby."

"Yes," said Cindy. "Of course."

Pat was relieved. He thought Cindy might try to introduce other options, and despite all the repercussions the family would face when Grace started to show, he was committed to making sure this baby would be brought into the world the way he was supposed to be.

"All babies are special," said Cindy. "And it's a positive motherly instinct for you to think of your baby in this way."

"No," said Grace. "This is different." Grace reached over and held Emily's hand for this part. "This baby *is* special. More special than other babies."

"Again," said Cindy. "Those are important natural instincts. They will help you be a good mom."

Pat was starting to think that Emily hadn't told Cindy about the virgin pregnancy component involved here. Otherwise, Cindy would certainly have just asked Grace why this child was so special. He looked over at Emily to try to confirm this theory, but Emily was focused on Grace.

Grace moved forward on the couch. She had her elbows on her knees like the sixth man on a basketball team, not in the game but ready. She said in an almost defiant voice, "I've never had sex before." And Cindy smiled at her before Grace said, "That's why this baby is special."

Pat was impressed that Cindy didn't even blink. Maybe Emily *had* told her.

"That would make this baby really special," she said. "But we're all here to support you, Grace. Your mom and dad aren't mad at you. They don't want to punish you. They want to make sure that you're safe and happy and protected from anything uncomfortable that your pregnancy might conjure."

She made a funny face after she said *conjure.* She'd been so careful with her words, and this was a strange choice. This wasn't a séance. But what she said made sense for someone who hadn't been dealing with this situation and maybe thought that Grace was lying to her parents because she thought she'd get in trouble.

However, the family was simply beyond that at this point. Grace was going through something else, something that needed a thoughtful treatment. Cindy was going to have to crack through whatever shell

Grace had formed to protect herself from whatever truth she couldn't reveal.

"I'm at peace with the pregnancy," she said. "My parents are being really supportive."

"Well, that's very brave, Grace," said Cindy. "People react in a variety of ways to unexpected challenges, to moments in their lives when they don't feel safe." She was nodding at Grace now, trying to somehow convince her that she knew how this baby got inside her. "And one of those reactions is to convince oneself that the bad thing that happened didn't really happen. Does that make sense?" she asked.

"Yes," said Grace. "That's denial. But I don't think anything bad happened to me. I believe this is a gift."

"Yes," said Cindy. She looked different now. Maybe a little frustrated. Maybe just curious. But her face didn't have the same relaxed expression it had at the beginning of this discussion. And she seemed less confident. Like she was just going to try some things now because the normal stuff wasn't working. "As I referenced earlier, babies are blessings to their mothers, and you have a healthy instinct in this regard. Can you tell me why you used the word *gift*?"

Grace smiled. "Not really," she said. "It just is."

Cindy smiled back, then looked over at Pat and Emily. "Maybe this is a good time for Grace and me to have a chat on our own."

~18~

When Alice received the call from Jill about Grace's confession, Alice didn't want to immediately tell her parents that people knew. She first wanted to find out what the hell Grace had told them. So, she asked Max and Jill to meet her at the McDonald's on Ocean. It was close to school, and there was a chance that someone might see them, but she knew they were only freshman and didn't have transportation, and even if someone saw them, there was no way anyone could guess what they were talking about.

Alice drove, so she beat them there. She ordered a bunch of fries and was sitting in the corner booth when she saw them arrive together. She wouldn't categorize them as being in the popular group, but they were cool. Max caught her eye, and she waved them both over.

They sat down opposite Alice, and Max said, "Are these for us?" pointing at the three orders of fries sitting on a tray in the middle of the table.

"Yeah," said Alice. "Thanks for coming."

"Do you mind if I grab some ketchup?" he said, half-standing as he waited for a response.

"Sure," said Alice and watched him hustle up to the front counter. When she looked over at Jill—*Jillie Bean* is what Grace called her when they were little—Jill rolled her eyes as if the ketchup request was an embarrassment to the sanctity of this meeting.

"It's okay," said Alice, just as Max was returning to the table with a handful of about twenty ketchup packets.

He sat down next to Jill and squirted the contents of one packet onto a napkin. "Sorry. Go ahead. Fries without ketchup …" he started but abandoned the thought.

"So, what exactly did Grace tell you guys?" asked Alice.

"She told us everything," said Jill and Max nodded.

"What does that mean?" asked Alice.

Max had a mouth full of fries and was fiddling with another ketchup packet when he said, "That she's pregnant and doesn't know the father."

"Okay, hold on," said Alice. "You mean she told you guys she had sex with a guy but doesn't know him?" This would be a step toward solving the mystery, but it didn't sound like something that Grace could have encountered.

"No," said Jill, looking over at Max like he was a mental patient who had sat down at their table without asking. "That's not what she said."

"So, what did she say?" asked Alice.

"She told us that there was *no* father," said Jill. "That she just *became* pregnant."

So, Grace was staying consistent. But that didn't mean these two didn't know something, even if they didn't even realize they knew something. "What do you make of that?" she asked.

Max had dipped two fries into the puddle of ketchup, but he laid them down on the napkin before saying, "I really like Grace." Then he paused and looked over at Jill before turning back to Alice. "I mean, I like-like her. I have for over a year now." He seemed slightly embarrassed, looking out the window for a moment, but also a little hurt and impudent. "In all honesty, I kind of thought she was my girlfriend, so this is kind of messed up for me."

Alice had to ask. "Did you guys ever have sex?"

"We never even made out," he said. "I think we were close to that—making out, I mean—but it just hasn't happened yet."

"Max," said Alice, sighing, playing it up a bit. "This is serious. You bullshitting us isn't going to help Grace."

Max slouched deeper into his seat now. "Are you saying that you think I *did* hook up with Grace?" he said and didn't wait for a reply. "'Because that didn't happen. Believe me. That's not something I'd forget."

Alice looked over at Jill who was nodding now. "What?" said Alice. "You can confirm that Grace and Max never hooked up?"

"Yes," said Jill. "She would have told me, Alice. There's no way."

Alice was aggravated. She guessed that she just wanted it to be Max. Then she'd know. And it would be this normal kid, and it would be two high schoolers who'd made a mistake like teenagers had been making for hundreds of years, and they could get on with their lives in this new, screwed up form, but at least they could get on with things. The way it stood, she had no idea what was going to happen, so the pressure just kind of built up for her in the McDonald's and then exploded like someone had stepped on a ketchup packet and the words came out almost violently, condiment shrapnel spraying across room. "Well, who the hell knocked up my little sister?" she whisper-yelled to the two freshmen sitting across from her. "You're her two best friends. How do you not know what's going on?"

The two of them sat mute. Max ignored the fries and looked like he might cry. "I thought she liked me," he said, and his voice cracked a little bit.

Jill put her arm around him. "She does," said Jill. "None of this makes sense."

"Did Grace tell you anything about how she thinks this happened to her?" said Alice.

Max looked like he was done talking. Probably scared that he would cry in front of two girls if he tried to say anything else. He actually had his arms crossed in front of him now like a little kid who got punished at school for fighting, only it was the other kid who started it.

Jill smiled at Alice in a way that made Alice feel like Jill felt sorry for her before Jill said, "Grace said some pretty weird stuff."

"Like what?" said Alice.

Jill picked up a couple of fries, put them in her mouth, and chewed thoughtfully for a moment. "Alice," she said. "Grace told us that she's been seeing this woman. Like in dreams, or she's appearing to Grace or something? Did she tell you about that?"

"Yeah," said Alice and again pondered whether or not Grace might be losing her mind. "What did she say that made you think these visions weren't just dreams?" asked Alice and didn't like her own use of the word *visions.* That word seemed to elevate whatever it was that Grace was experiencing.

"She said she saw the lady at school once," said Jill.

"At school?" said Alice. "Like in the bathroom or something?"

"No" said Jill. "She saw her in class. But she might have fallen asleep in class, which means that she might only see her when she's dreaming."

"Did she tell you anything that the lady said to her?"

"Comforting things," said Jill. "I think that might be why she's handling this so well."

Alice nodded and looked out the window, where a streetcar, the K Ingleside, was scooting past Beep's Burgers up the street. There were at least fifteen or twenty St. X and St. Mary's kids loitering in their school uniforms at the picnic tables out front. Somebody had to know something. One of these two across from her should know something, but, if they did, they were doing an excellent job of hiding it. Max's near-tears were a nice touch, but she still wasn't sure that he was completely innocent. If Jill thought Max was Grace's "boyfriend," then who else could her sister have hooked up with. It didn't make any sense. Someone knew something. Grace knew something.

Alice wondered if the therapist was getting anywhere with Grace. If she didn't tell these two anything, Alice thought it was unlikely that Grace would open up to a stranger. "Did you guys ever see her with any other guys?" she asked even though she knew it might hurt Max more than he was already hurting. "Did she go to any parties that you know of?"

Jill was still doing the talking. "The only real party that we've all been to was at Max's."

Alice nodded. She was aware that Grace was beautiful and that older guys were always checking her out, but the schools were small, and Alice knew everyone. If some older St. X pig was hitting on her, someone would have reported it to her. "You don't think she went to any parties with older kids, maybe without you guys?"

Jill looked at her like she thought Alice was nuts. "C'mon Alice," said Jill. "You know Grace better than we do. Could you even imagine it?"

The answer was *no*, she couldn't even imagine it. But what else could have happened? Alice wondered. She wished she could talk to the lady in Grace's dreams and ask her what to do. Alice could use something "comforting" about now.

"Will you guys tell me if you hear anything that might explain this?" she asked, and she felt sorry for Max now. He was probably in love with Grace and thought he had a chance because he'd known her before she was beautiful.

Jill said, "Of course."

Max nodded, but he was looking out the window, up toward Beep's Burgers and the rest of the kids, who were probably talking about the talent show or Mr. Loftus's chem exam or the new transfer student from Vermont, stuff kids were supposed to be talking about. Not this.

~19~

When Grace and Cindy walked out of the office, Grace was already looking at her phone. "Can I walk up to West Portal to meet my friends?" she asked, and Pat looked over at Emily for help but got none.

"Is she all done?" he asked Cindy.

"She is," said Cindy and her tone suggested that things didn't go well.

"We'll drive you, honey," said Emily.

Grace and Cindy replied simultaneously. While Grace was saying *I'd rather walk,* Cindy was saying *We need to talk.* The effect was that Pat, a former English teacher, somehow clearly heard both speakers and appreciated the syncopation and rhyme. If they'd done it in harmony, he might have applauded.

Emily didn't hear it the same way and was confused. "Is the session over?" she asked.

Cindy smiled and said, "I'd like to talk to you two for just a few minutes," and she took a step toward her office.

"You're okay walking?" Emily said to Grace.

"Mom," said Grace. "It's only a couple of blocks, and my friends are already there." She looked back down at her phone for a moment and swiped something before continuing, "Apparently, Alice gave them a ride."

"Alice?" said Emily.

"I guess she saw them somewhere after school," said Grace slipping into her jacket. "I won't be late," she said, at the door now. "I'll call you guys or Alice for a ride home. See ya." Out the door.

Pat kept looking at the door even after it was shut. He couldn't figure out when they'd lost her when she'd created this other life. He always thought Alice might be the one to get in trouble. Grace didn't have a hunger for adventure. She was happy with a book. God, she did jigsaw puzzles just this past summer. When did she leave the safety of that little girl existence? What were she and her friends doing tonight?

Neither woman had said anything for a few moments, so he turned back to them. They were both looking at him. "Why don't we step into the office," said Cindy. "This will only take a few minutes."

Once they'd all found a seat, Cindy began, "This is a tough one."

Pat didn't like the sound of it.

Emily needed to speak. "Is this a total outlier? I've never dealt with anything like this?"

"Me neither," said Cindy. She stood up and walked over to a cabinet from which she removed two room temperature bottled waters and placed them on the table in front of Pat and Emily. "I thought I'd run a few tricks by her to see if I could get her to admit that she'd been intimate with someone, but she was either on to me, or she really believes that she has never had intercourse."

Cindy got up and went back to the cabinet. She pulled out another water for herself, opened the top, and drank about a third of it in a series of gulps before catching her breath and putting the cap back on the bottle. "If I'm truly honest with you," she said. "I'd say she might be delusional."

Up until a couple of weeks ago, Grace was as clear-minded a teenager as Pat had ever encountered in all his years in education, so hearing the word *delusional* put him immediately in defense mode. "That kid's one of the sanest people I know," said Pat. "And I know a lot of people."

"I'm not saying she's having some kind of psychotic episode," said Cindy. "But something is going on here. She didn't appear to be lying to me. It's my opinion that she really believes this is an immaculate conception."

Pat was tempted to tell her that she didn't understand the term *immaculate conception*, but he held back. She was a smart woman, and she was trying to help.

The room was quiet now. Pat opened his bottle and took a small sip before putting it back on the table. Emily picked hers up but then put it back down before she said, "What if this *is* a virgin pregnancy?"

It was quiet again. Pat felt himself nodding in agreement even though he knew this couldn't be the case.

"You want to hear my theory?" said Cindy.

"That's why we're here," said Pat and then realized that he sounded a bit curt. "Yes, of course. We trust your judgment."

Cindy smiled at Pat. "Guys," she said. "This is just my theory after one forty-five-minute session. It might be total bullshit." Emily's hand was on the armrest of the couch, and Cindy reached over and put her hand on top of Emily's. "This is complicated, but I'd like to take a shot, and Emily, you can use your expertise to troubleshoot my explanation."

"I watch Dr. Phil," said Pat.

"He watches Dr. Phil," said Emily.

"Well, great," said Cindy. "The two of you can use your combined expertise to analyze my theory and hopefully among the three experts here, we can come to something like a consensus."

Pat was back to liking her again. "That sounds good," he said.

"Good," said Cindy. "Here's what I think." She held out a finger now as she grabbed for her water with the other hand. She took one more sip and said, "Am I to assume that Grace has led a pretty charmed life up to this point?" Pat and Emily were both nodding. "Good grades, lots of friends, she's absolutely lovely. Things probably come really easy to her."

"That's all true," said Emily.

"Okay," said Cindy. "Now imagine all that suddenly being taken away from her."

"But it's not," said Pat almost immediately. "She's still smart, and kind, and beautiful."

"Of course," said Cindy. "But she found out some shocking and scandalous information about herself. She's only fifteen. She doesn't have enough experience to know that she'll get through this fine. That she'll survive because she's smart and kind and beautiful, and she has you two and Alice. Part of her brain shut down to protect herself from what really happened to her because she felt as though the only life she knew—a great life—would be over."

This made some sense to Pat, but he asked, "So this can happen to a smart person, who has never shut down like this before?"

"That's precisely who it would happen to," said Cindy. "Have you ever read *The Price of Privilege* by Madeline Levine?"

"We have," they said together. Then Emily said, "We've actually seen her speak."

"But we're hardly privileged," said Pat. "That book was about really rich kids from Marin. We're not really that."

"Stay with me for a minute," she said. "A lot of those kids in the study have psychological problems because their parents never allowed them to fail. Are you with me?"

Pat had read the book and was angry with the parents portrayed. They were helicopter parents. Steamroller parents. Because they put their kids in only situations in which the kids could succeed, when the kids eventually had to make it on their own and predictably failed, the kids had no strategies to deal with the failure. And they ended up cutting themselves and starving themselves and dropping out of school and killing themselves. He knew *he* wasn't one of those parents. It wasn't the way he was brought up, and he knew that he hadn't treated Alice or Grace that way. Emily was one of eight kids. She certainly hadn't been raised that way and was totally fine with the kids losing from time to time. It was natural.

"We're not like those parents, Cindy," he said. "We're just not. So, we might as well move on to another theory." He felt himself shaking slightly, so he reached for his water bottle. Before he drank, he said, "I'm not one of those guys who thinks he's the perfect dad. I'm not. I screw things up every day. But I'm not one of *those* parents, either. Without sounding too defensive here, I hate those parents."

Cindy sighed, and Pat immediately felt like a fool. "Can you let me finish?" she said.

"Yes," he said and went to take a sip of the water only to find that it was empty.

"Do you want another one?" she asked.

Pat shook his head.

"I'm not saying you guys are like those wealthy parents," she said. "But I want you to think about this. Couldn't Grace have ended up in the same psychological state as those privileged kids simply because she grew up really happy, just on her own, without either of you clearing a path for her success?"

Emily said, "So are you saying that Grace is paying the price of privilege even though it has nothing to do with wealth or power, of which we have very little?"

"I think so," she said. "Like the Marin kids, Grace has gotten almost everything she wants, not because you have set that life up for her, just because she has natural talents that have led to her relatively unchallenged existence. It has been nice for her."

"Then suddenly," said Emily. "It's not so nice, and she has no tools to fix it, so ..." and then she paused for so long that Pat nearly intervened before Emily turned her hand palm up and moved it horizontally in front of her like a game show spokesmodel showcasing a new car. "We have this."

"Wait a minute," said Pat. "Those kids in the study had eating disorders and depression and other stuff, but you're saying Grace is *delusional*. That doesn't seem to fit the theory."

Cindy seemed to be enjoying the discourse. Maybe that's how therapists think. "No," she said. "Grace is different. As you said, she didn't grow up with the same kind of privilege as those other kids, some of whom feel guilt when they get older. But she's suffering from the same kind of disillusionment, so her mental state is being challenged, but her symptoms are manifesting themselves in a different way."

"That makes sense," said Emily, and Pat decided to let the real experts hash this out. "But I still feel like denial would be a closer diagnosis to what she's experiencing."

"In the beginning," said Cindy. "Yes. Of course. She didn't want to face this difficult reality. But here we are two weeks later." She used a quieter, more soothing voice to temper this last enlightening assessment, but it didn't help. Pat felt sad for his daughter. This sounded like it was beyond anything he could do to help.

"No, I hear you," said Emily. "The denial has extended longer than a safe duration. And it's really just semantics, but delusional still feels like the wrong word."

"Well, yes," said Cindy. "Until you consider the lady."

"What lady?" said Pat.

Grace

This is the first time that I'm walking with the lady. All the other times, we were sitting or standing in one place. It's nice to be walking. I can barely feel my feet touching the ground. It's a nice way to travel. The traffic sounds are muffled, so I hear only the wind rustling the trees and her voice, which seems like it's somehow part of the wind.

"Your strength is growing," she says, and I can feel her soft breath in my hair.

"Doesn't seem like it," I say and think about how I was tempted to make up a lie and tell the therapist what she wanted to hear.

"The struggles are exercises, building muscles inside you against doubt."

Sometimes she talks like that. She says things that, at one level, I don't really understand. But at some other level, some deeper place, they mean something. As if the words are somehow free and wandering someplace inside of my mind, but they find each other and band together. Then she pulls them out of me in the strangest ways and gives them back. Not in my syntax. Not my diction. Not really my opinions, but maybe my beliefs. If that makes any sense.

The thought of muscles has me flexing my bicep as I walk and looking at my arm to see if there's any definition. Not much. But a horn honks, and I look up to see Alice driving the opposite way. She's laughing and shrugging at me and mouthing something through the closed window. I can't make it out, but I realize that she must have seen me looking at my muscle and thought it was funny. I guess it is funny.

Alice already has muscles.

"She's going to help you when you think you're alone," the lady says, and, again, I feel like I already know that. But it's scary to think of myself as being alone. I've never really been.

~20~

Pat and Emily were standing on the sidewalk outside of Cindy's building. They maybe had a better idea of what was going on in Grace's brain, but they weren't any closer to figuring out how to help her.

They rarely showed any affection in public, but Pat had his arm around her waist and was pulling her close against the wind. He pointed across the street to Villa D'Este. "You want to go for one?" he asked.

"There?" she said.

"Why not?"

"I thought I wasn't allowed."

Pat and a few buddies had been meeting at the old restaurant for years. It had a little six-stool bar near the entrance and a beautiful dining room with huge chandeliers and extravagant crown molding. It hadn't been updated in a long time, but that was part of its charm.

Pat's group would sometimes meet there on random Wednesday afternoons, and they liked the place because they absolutely knew that they wouldn't see anyone they knew. Aside from the anonymity, there was also a fantastic bartender named Ramon, whose family had owned the place for decades.

Everyone loved Ramon.

When Pat first went to Villa D'Este years ago after getting a call from a couple of guys who were going to meet there to organize a Texas Hold 'Em tournament, Pat asked for a bourbon and ginger ale. Ramon said *just a moment,* left the restaurant, went across the street to Walgreens, and came back with a two-liter bottle of Canada Dry. He mixed the drink and then asked the other guys what they wanted. He was that kind of guy.

Emily didn't think she was allowed in because one of the lads had brought a girlfriend once and ruined everyone's afternoon. Pat came home complaining about it.

"It'll just be us," said Pat and guided her across the street with him.

When they opened the door, Ramon was standing behind the bar and brightened up immediately. He had never met Emily before and said, "Pat, I've missed you, but I can't allow you to have one of your students in the bar area."

Ramon was already making Pat a bourbon and ginger. It wasn't Pat's favorite drink, but he always had it here. "It's okay," said Pat. "She has a fake I.D."

"Okay," he said. "Just this once. What'll it be, miss?"

"I'm Emily," she said. "It's nice to meet you." Ramon held out his hand, and they shook. "I've heard a lot about you, Ramon."

"I can't tell you anything I've heard about you," he said. "This is like a confessional in here."

"Understood," she said. "Do you have the same deal with all the other wives?"

"You're the first one to come in," he said. "And might I say, it's refreshing. I have no idea how this man ended up with you. Did he drug you?"

"No," said Emily. "He visited me in prison."

"Ah," he said. "Smart man, the principal."

"How about a glass of chardonnay?" she said and took off her coat.

"Right away," he said and walked to the other side of the bar to pour.

"This guy's great," she said.

"The best," said Pat.

Ramon placed the glass in front of Emily without a word and wandered back to the other side of the bar. It was one of his great talents. He could disappear like a ghost until you needed another drink. Then he'd be there just before you ordered.

"Did the session with Cindy go as planned?" Pat asked.

"I didn't have a plan," she said and took a sip of her wine. She grimaced slightly and shot a glance over to see if Ramon was watching. He wasn't. There was a college basketball game on the little TV in the corner, and he seemed immersed in it.

"I know," said Pat. "But did anything surprise you?"

"I thought Cindy might have a breakthrough and get Gracie to talk about the night, or day, whatever, that Grace got ... that the baby was conceived." She had the stem of the wine glass between her middle finger and her index finger, but she wasn't swirling the way people do. She was just looking down, seeming lost in the moment. "I want that part of this to be over."

"Me too," he said and used the small straw to mix the bourbon and ginger. Then he placed the straw on the cocktail napkin and took a long drink. "I was surprised that she got into all that stuff about *The Price of Privilege*, but I was glad she made the distinction between us and the steamroller parents. We've never been like that."

"We haven't," said Emily. "Don't worry. She wasn't accusing us of that."

"I know," he said. "I'm glad she separated us from them. We've made it a point to avoid that kind of stuff."

"Yeah," she said. "Don't worry about it. Aren't you curious about this recurring dream she's having, though?"

"I guess," he said and was glad she called it a recurring dream rather than a *vision*, which is the word that Cindy used. "It's probably just another way of coping with the stress. Her brain is trying to fight against a reality that she doesn't like."

"Agree," she said. "Your Dr. Phil studies are coming in handy."

"Cindy said she tried some tricks to get Grace to admit to having sex with someone," he said. "I kind of agree with that tactic. I feel like if we could get her to realize what happened, then she could start to come to terms with it. And stop with the delusional stuff."

Emily took another sip of her wine and didn't wince this time. "Do you have a way to get her to realize whatever the truth is?"

Pat had been thinking about an old documentary that he'd watched a hundred years ago. It was about a tribe of people, an island tribe, and the elders of the village would actually conduct a physical test on the girls before they got married to see whether or not the girls were virgins. If you asked him for specifics, he couldn't remember anything, but he did remember an old man doing the examinations on young girls, and then he would proclaim virgin or non-virgin when he was done. It seemed primitive, but if he could do it in a bamboo hut, why couldn't Grace's doctor figure all this out in his office?

"Do you think we should bring her back to Dr. Ross and have him do a virginity examination?" he said. "That way, she might snap out of this idea that the baby is some kind of divine gift."

"First of all," she said. "Are you a complete moron?"

"What?" he said, holding his drink in front of him, feeling the condensation on the palm of his hand but waiting to take a sip until she told him why he was a moron.

"One, she has not once referenced God in this, so I'm not sure where you're getting this *divine gift* idea. "

"Fair enough," still waiting to find out why he was a moron.

"Two," she said. "This exam you're talking about doesn't exist."

"It does," he said, ready to prove his vast knowledge on the subject. "I saw it in a documentary."

"Those exams are totally unreliable," she said.

"Have you ever heard of the hymen," he asked.

"Pat," she said. "You're being a fool. If anything, that kind of test could be even more traumatic than what she's already gone through, and it won't tell us anything definitive anyway."

"What exactly did she go through?" asked Pat.

"I know you're going to think I'm nuts," she said. "And I've asked this before. But we both know Gracie. Is there any way that there's something transcendent happening here?"

"A miracle?"

"Yes," she said. "Or some kind of biological glitch?"

~21~

St. Mary's and St. Xavier were having their annual dual rally. As a freshman, Grace didn't really know what to expect, but she liked the fact that they could sit wherever they wanted and were allowed to mix with the boys. She was sitting in the stands between Jill and Max, and they were mostly surrounded by freshmen from both schools.

The Activities Directors for the two schools were taking turns with the microphone. They were telling the crowd what was going on, but the sound system wasn't very good, and most people weren't really listening, except the student councils for both schools. Those kids were standing around the perimeter of the gym floor, and they looked sad that no one was paying attention.

Every couple of minutes, someone would come up to Max and ask him if the party was on for Saturday, and Max would give the same answer in a slightly different way.

Tarique, the six foot four inch center from the frosh basketball team, leaned over about five people to get in close, and he whispered, "What up for Saturday, homeboy?"

Max nodded, trying to look cool, and said, "We good to go, TQ."

"That's what I'm talkin' 'bout," said Tarique and slapped hands with Max. "You two gonna be there?" he said and looked at Jill and Grace.

They both nodded and smiled.

"Good shit," he said and used people's shoulders to push his way back out of crowd and into the aisle.

Grace was still unsure if she'd go. It was fun last time, but she knew she couldn't drink, and she didn't want people asking her why.

Mikey Firpo was one of the kids Tarique climbed over to ask about the party. He was sitting next to Max. "What's happening on Saturday?" he asked.

"I'm having a party, Mikey," said Max. "But I can't have the whole freshman class there."

"Wait," said Mikey. "*I* can come though, right?"

"Yeah," said Max. "But you can't tell everyone. This one has to be smaller than the first one, or my parents are gonna kill me."

"I'm not gonna tell anyone," said Mikey. Then, to Grace and Jill, "Are you guys going?"

Grace and Jill smiled and nodded.

"Sweet," said Mikey and then directed his attention back to the gym floor where a St. Mary's senior and a St. X senior were doing some kind of obstacle course competition.

Both were holding baseball bats to the floor. They had their heads pressed to the knobs and were spinning around as if they were using their foreheads to drill the bats into the hardwood. Grace had seen this before. The idea was to try to get the participants dizzy before they moved onto the next obstacle. In this case, it was a slalom course of orange cones.

When the boy finished his ten spins, he stood still for a moment and shook himself before he started through the cones. The girl finished just afterward, but she didn't pause. She started right at the cones and made it through the first two but then started to drift off course. Instead of stopping to get her balance, she just kept moving. Her arms were pumping like a normal runner, but her legs were taking her on a bizarre diagonal toward the scorer's table where a bunch of teachers were sitting, including Grace's dad and Ms. Daly.

Now the girl was tilted and totally off balance. Gravity was controlling her, and she had a full head of steam behind her. There was no way she could stop, so Principal Ryan ran out from behind the table and tried to catch her, but the two of them went tumbling into the table before they ended up on the floor.

There were several pie tins with whipped cream resting on the table, but now Mr. Ryan and the senior girl were sitting on the floor with whipped cream all over them. The girl had her arm around Grace's dad's shoulder like they were old pals, and he was licking whipped cream off his tie.

The place was going crazy.

The senior boy was finishing off the obstacle course by throwing nerf balls into a laundry basket. The senior girl stood up and pumped her fist into the air. It seemed like everyone was cheering for her even though the boy had won.

"Oh my God," said Jill. "Look at your dad."

Ms. Daly was helping him up, and he was laughing, but his shirt and tie were a mess. And when he stood up, he had whipped cream on his butt, too. Ms. Daly went to wipe it off with a paper towel, but then she stopped herself and handed him the towel so that he could do it himself. Everyone was still laughing, but the Activities Director from St. X didn't think it was funny. "It looks like the pie throw is cancelled," he said and looked at some kids who were supposed to get to throw pies at some teachers. The kids looked pissed off.

"This is embarrassing," said Grace.

"He saved her from running into the table," said Max.

"Did he?" said Grace, and she started to feel a little dizzy. She took a deep breath to try to fight it off, but it hit her fast, and she started leaning into Max for support.

"You okay?" he said, but her head was swimming.

Grace

The lady is actually in the stands with me, and she says, "Let them help you." And that's it. She's gone as fast as she came.

"Whoa," said Grace. "I just got really dizzy." Her ear was up against Max's shoulder, and she lifted her head just as Jill was saying something inaudible. "What?" Grace asked.

Jill said, "Your sister's up next."

"Wait," said Max. "Are you okay? Do you need to see the school nurse or something? Do we even have a school nurse?"

"I'm okay," she said. "That was weird. How long was I out?"

"Just a couple of seconds, I think," said Max.

"Out where?" said Jill and then shouted, "C'mon, Alice."

Alice was at one end of the court shooting three-pointers, and Dante Westbrook was on the other end doing the same thing. The scoreboard showed Alice up by three shots, and the clock only showed twenty seconds, but Dante made his last four, and Alice went cold at the end, so St. X won another competition. Alice and Dante ran to half court and hugged, and everyone in the gym let out a collective ,"Aww," before the Activities Director from St. Mary's was back on the microphone shouting directions for the next contest, which looked like it involved the choirs from both schools.

"Are you sure you're okay?" asked Max. "I mean, I don't think that's supposed to happen."

Grace really did feel much better. "I'm fine now," she said. "I skipped breakfast this morning. I guess that was stupid."

"You gotta take care of yourself, Grace."

"I know," she said. "Do you think I should skip the party on Saturday?"

"You don't have to drink," he said. "Just go and have fun. Watch everyone else act like idiots."

"I just don't want everyone asking me why I'm not drinking."

"Just put water in a red cup, and if anyone asks, you can say it's vodka," he said. "But no one's gonna ask."

"I guess that could work," she said just as the St. Mary's choir started doing an acapella version of the Lady Gaga song that was in that movie, *Shallow*. It sounded pretty good.

"When do you think you're going to start telling people?" asked Max.

"About the baby?" she said.

"Yeah."

She took a moment. She knew her parents' plan to just get to the summer, like somehow that will make everything all right. During the pause in the conversation, she heard the choir:

Crash through the surface
Where they can't hurt us
We're far from the shallow now

"I'm supposed to wait until the summer," she said. "That's when I'll probably start to get fat."

"Oh," he said, like this was the first time he thought about the fact that there was going to be an actual kid growing inside her and that her belly was going to get huge.

"But I'm not sure I'll wait that long," she said. "I don't like having the secret. I feel like I'm lying every minute of every day."

~22~

Grace was rarely home alone, but this afternoon she was, and she continued with the research she'd been doing for weeks. She was reading a message board regarding the question of virgin pregnancies. Most of it involved questions about whether or not sperm could swim through someone's underpants or tread water in a hot tub long enough for an unsuspecting girl to wade in close enough to get pregnant. She was also texting Jill at the same time and relaying some of this information, which Jill thought was hilarious.

There was even a very involved tale about a civil war soldier who was shot in the crotch. The way the story went, the bullet passed through the scrotum and into the abdomen of a virgin, impregnating her. Jill texted *That's enough for me! I'm outy.* But Grace kept reading.

Many people wrote in to debunk the story, and that thread turned into a lengthy discussion about where sperm is stored. It seemed there was some confusion as to whether it was the testes, the epididymis, or the prostate. But none of that mattered to Grace because she believed that there was no sperm involved in her pregnancy. She was hoping to find something that could explain her situation. And although she found some articles that had data regarding a certain percentage of women who claimed virgin pregnancies, no one on this thread seemed to take the notion very seriously.

Grace usually just *read* the posts on these sites but never posted anything of her own. However, today she was frustrated with the discourse. It was almost all scientific, but Grace knew that what happened to her could not be explained through science.

Without thinking much about it, she posted the following: *Is there a way to get pregnant without any sperm at all?*

After she hit submit, she sat at the computer for a few minutes to see if anything would happen. Then she started rereading the previous posts and realized that the last person to write anything on this message board did it back in 2017. She had been thinking that she was in some kind of live chat room on which people had been posting all day, but it turned out that no one had posted anything in two years.

She clicked to another site that had the word Christianity in the title. It featured a long sermon by a female minister who believed that there was a lot of evidence in the Bible, particularly the gospel of Luke, that Mary was *not* a virgin. This minister's theory was that Mary was a young girl, who was raped by Roman soldiers as some kind of military tactic, one that is still used today in some countries.

Grace didn't like what she was reading, and she actually thought her dad would be upset if he saw the material, but it was an interesting theory to Grace. To her, it was just another story. If she took out the fact that it went against her deep beliefs and that the baby in the story was the Son of God, it was still a really dramatic story about a teenage girl from long time ago, who had a baby that went on to be really famous.

Of course, the theory seemed crazy to Grace. It was so different from what she understood from eight years of Catholic education. But she liked the woman in this strange version, which portrayed Mary as a heroine, who had to do what she had to do to protect herself and her baby. In this story, she was in danger of being stoned because she'd become pregnant out of wedlock. This Mary was a fugitive, a revolutionary, a radical.

Grace was old enough to recognize that the reverend who wrote the piece was a feminist who referred several times to the fact that all sacred stories have been written by men. That men have decided which stories have made it into the sacred canon of scriptures and that men have been the ones to analyze and preach the meanings of the stories from pulpits for thousands of years.

Grace didn't see how this new version made Mary any better than the original stories. She didn't see this alternate Mary as being any stronger or more feminist. Grace liked both Marys.

The article was long, and she was dozing off a bit as she read, until she heard the front door slam. She woke up, looked at the computer screen, and clicked back to the message board that she'd been on before. She didn't want her dad to see what she'd been reading. It felt to her like it was against the rules to even *read* things that talked about Mary this way. Maybe it *was* against the rules.

When she looked at the bottom of the message board, there was a new post. Right under where Grace had said, *Is there a way to get pregnant without any sperm at all?* there was a short response from someone named Sophia: *Let's talk offline.* Then it provided an email address before it said, *I'm going to delete this post in thirty minutes.*

Grace heard her dad say, "Hi Grace," and she heard his hard shoes on the floor in the kitchen.

"Hi dad," she said as she scrambled to find a pen. She knew it could be getting close to the thirty minutes.

She copied down the address and then stared at the message on the screen. She had been to enough school assemblies during which someone would tell them not to enter into an online dialogue with anyone she didn't know. There were predators out there, and they would say anything to get you to give them personal information. Grace knew all that. She'd seen shows on TV about these creeps.

But she also knew that she was going to contact *Sophia.*

~23~

Pat looked at his watch and saw that he had time to take Sully on a quick walk before dinner. On a whim, he called down to Grace's room. "Do you want to come with me to walk Sully," he said with no expectation that she would agree.

"Where you taking him?" she said.

"Buena Vista."

"Sure," she said.

Pat used to take Grace with him to Buena Vista when she was in elementary school. To a little kid, the park must have felt to her like a forest. Obviously, it wasn't huge like Golden Gate Park, but it had its own sense of vastness. It was all hills and mature trees and paved paths and unpaved paths. A dog-walkers heaven. Grace had written an essay about the park for a fifth-grade project. When she was doing the research, she found an article which explained that the park had once been a cemetery. People in the city probably still called it a graveyard back then. And apparently when they moved the cemetery down to Colma, they kept a lot of the headstones in Buena Vista to create the retaining walls and drainage troughs. The landscapers and builders were careful to turn the headstones upside down, but, on occasion, Pat and Grace had found letters on some of the stones lining the paved paths in the park. Just fragments of names and epitaphs—etched slivers of past lives.

Pat heard Grace grabbing the leash. Sully must have heard, too, because he came sliding across the hardwood floor past Pat and down the stairs with a tennis ball in his mouth.

Pat put on a fleece and met Grace in front of the house. As they started to walk east toward the park, he realized that this was the first time he was alone with her since her original doctor's appointment. Either Alice or Emily was always there. He wondered if Grace had been avoiding him.

They didn't say much before they got to the park. As was their custom, Pat had used his phone to tune into the daily mix from Spotify. Somehow this service had figured out his affinity for the 70s, and although Grace wouldn't admit it to Alice, she really liked the songs as well.

They had listened to a Jackson Brown song and were halfway through Three Dog Night's *Mama Told Me Not to Come* when they got to the long ramp on Buena Vista West. After they let Sully off leash and walked past the coyote warning signs near the entrance, Sully decided to climb a mountain of woodchips and stare down at the two of them.

"What's all that for?" asked Grace.

"They're probably going to distribute it to different parts of the park that need cover," he said, guessing. He'd rarely seen the park maintenance workers or gardeners, but the place always looked good.

Sully ran ahead of them now, waiting for Pat to throw the ball. Sully was a strange dog in that he didn't like to play a traditional game of fetch. To the contrary, he preferred to give Pat the ball, run ahead, and then try to catch the ball when it was thrown in his direction. If they were on a slope, after he'd caught the ball, he liked to simply drop it and let it roll back to the thrower as the dog crouched and watched gravity take the ball down the hill. In a sense, it was more a game of catch than it was fetch.

"That was quite a show today," she said and smiled up at her dad.

"The whipped cream?" he asked.

"Yeah," she said and looked back up the hill at Sully, waiting for the ball.

"I'm surprised that girl didn't get really hurt."

"Well, you saved her," she said and looked back at him.

"We both ended up on the gym floor with whipped cream all over us. It didn't feel like I saved anyone," he said, wondering if his pants were ruined.

"It coulda been worse." she said.

"You can say that about nearly anything," he said and wasn't sure why he said it. He was pretty sure it was a line from a movie that he'd seen long ago and hadn't thought of since, but the idea made sense. Everything was relative. As sick as he'd felt the past few weeks about Grace's situation, he also knew that there were people with worse problems and that it would be okay, especially if Grace could get past this initial emotional response, the confusion and denial. The *visions*.

"Yeah," she said. "You're right. What's a situation you can think of where you wouldn't be able to say *It coulda been worse*?"

"Being married to your mother?" he said.

"Ha-ha," she said. "I'm gonna tell her you said that."

"I'm joking," he said. "How about being a Dodgers fan?"

"That makes more sense," she said. "Throw it. Sully's losing his mind up there."

Sully was still down in a Border collie crouch, flat on his stomach, paws out in front of him, ready to pounce as soon as the ball was thrown in his direction. Pat threw it up the hill just past Sully, and Sully chased it down, catching it on the second bounce and then dropping it and watching it roll back down the hill toward Pat and Grace as they continued to walk up toward the little patch of grass at the top of the hill. That area featured an unobstructed view of the Golden Gate Bridge and the Marin headlands.

When they got to the top, Bob Segar was finishing off *Still the Same* and the Marshall Tucker Band was starting *Can't You See.*

"So," said Pat as they looked out toward the steeple of St. Ignatius Church in the half-light of the late afternoon, "have you had any visits from the lady lately?"

"You don't have to talk about it so weird, Dad."

"I'm just asking a question," he said.

"I guess I have," she said.

"Why do you say it that way?"

"Because it's not really a *visit*, y'know? That's a weird way to talk about her." Grace walked away toward the path where Sully was waiting for them. When she got there, she grabbed him behind the ears and scratched.

"Grace," said Pat, following her to the path. "I'm just trying to figure out what's going on, what kinds of things she's saying to you."

"She says good things. Doesn't that make you happy?"

"Yes," he said and threw the ball down the path. He watched Sully scramble after it and said, "That actually makes me really happy. That's good. What kind of stuff?"

Sully came back and sat on Pat's foot. The dog looked bored with the conversation.

"She basically supports me, Dad. She tells me to be strong and to trust you guys."

"I like this lady," he said. "She sounds brilliant."

Before Grace could respond, Sully shot down the path toward a young couple holding hands. One of Sully's most annoying habits was that he always wanted people he didn't know to throw the ball for him. When he got close to the couple, he dropped the ball at their feet and lied down on his stomach, looking up at them with hopeful eyes.

Pat jogged down the path and said, "Sorry. He's nuts." And when the woman started to reach down for the ball, he said, "Just leave it."

She raised her eyebrows, and Pat said, "You don't want to get slime all over your hand, and if you throw it to him once, he'll follow you guys home."

"Oh," she said and laughed. She rubbed Sully's head and then looked back at Pat. Almost immediately, her eyes darted over Pat's shoulder, and she stopped smiling. "No," she whispered.

Then Pat heard Grace say, "Dad?"

When he turned around, Grace was standing at the top of the narrow path, and a large coyote with a puppy in tow was standing right next to her. Pat took a quick step toward them, but the coyote arched its back like a Halloween cat and opened its mouth wide, showing its teeth.

"Don't move, Grace," said Pat quietly. He didn't want to spook the animal into a panic and have it snap at her. He held his ground and slowly reached down to grab Sully's collar. The coyote converted back to a more natural stance and stepped closer to Grace, who was frozen. No one made a sound. But Aretha Franklin was singing from inside Pat's pocket. It was a live version of *Precious Memories,* and, for a moment, it felt to Pat as if the cheering crowd was reacting to the coyote or Grace or both. But, of course, the cheering was for Aretha:

Precious memories, unseen angels. Sent from somewhere to my soul
How they linger, ever near me. And the sacred past unfolds

Pat was tempted to reach into his pocket to turn off the music, but he didn't want to move, and part of him thought the song might be a calming factor to the whole scene. To the animal. It was Aretha, after all.

The smaller coyote, about the size of raccoon, was sniffing around a gopher hole and didn't seem to notice the dramatic tableau unfolding just a few feet away. The larger coyote was staring down the path at Pat and the couple and Sully, who was surprisingly quiet and still. The larger coyote looked away from Pat's group and looked directly at Grace. It was literally two feet from her and closed the gap in one stride. Gracie didn't look. She was staring at Pat, who was ready to release Sully and run up the hill with the hopes that he could get Grace out of there unharmed, but something told him to wait for now.

Then the coyote licked Grace's hand.

Just like a big dog. And Grace didn't flinch. She let the animal lick her again, and Pat thought he might have seen her smile.

Sully didn't like it. He growled at this animal that could easily maul him to death in short time. But the coyote stopped licking Grace, looked down at Sully, and then trotted off the path into the trees. Grace melted a bit, and they all watched the little one scamper off after the big one.

"My God," said the man standing behind Pat, who had forgotten there was anyone there.

As Pat was running up the hill, he heard the woman say, "I got it! I got almost the whole thing." Pat didn't know what she was talking about. He and Grace raced toward each other and met in the middle of the hill. They embraced, and Pat squeezed her as tightly as he ever had. Sully was jumping up on both of them, trying to be a part of the hug.

"I got it, you guys," said the woman, holding her phone up and walking toward them. "Look," she said and held her phone up to Pat.

"I just saw it a few seconds ago," he said.

Grace said, "I wanna see it," and walked over to the woman, who tapped the screen and let her watch.

"This is the middle of a city," said Pat. "We shouldn't have to deal with this shit."

"It's their park, too."

"What?" said Pat.

"The coyotes," said this guy, wearing flip-flops in February. "It's their park, too."

"What kind of idiot are you?" said Pat and started walking toward the guy, not sure what he was going to do.

"Okay," said flip-flops. "Sorry, man."

~24~

When Grace was working on her laptop in her room, she could still feel the coyote's tongue on her hand. It was giving her the quivers but also making her laugh. It was so bizarre.

Alice was having pizza with the girls on her team tonight, so Grace decided that she wanted to use the rare privacy of her own room to contact "Sophia". Grace was still a bit nervous about online predators and other various creepos, but she was going to be cautious. She wasn't sure what the best form of communication would be, but she had to start with the email.

Subject Line: Message Board

Salutation: Dear Sophia,

Body: Thank you for reaching out on the message board. Did you direct that post to me because you can answer my question?

Valediction: Sincerely, Grace

Grace checked the email over several times. She was more used to talking to people on Instagram or Snapchat, so this was a bit of a departure for her, but since she didn't know anything about this person, she decided to be clear and formal. She still believed that the recipient might be a poser and that she was being catfished. But posing as what?

Send.

Once the email was sent, she clicked over to Netflix and searched for *Stranger Things.* She was sick of being behind everyone else who was already on *Season 2* , so she was trying to catch up by watching two or sometimes three episodes in one night. She knew it was stupid, and it was affecting her schoolwork to a certain extent, but she was sick of hearing Jill talk about it all the time at school. Just before she hit play, she wanted to take one quick look at her email to see if there was a chance that Sophia had replied.

She had.

Subject Line: Message Board

Salutation: Dear Grace,

Body: I think I can help you with your question. Let's chat on Insta. I'm SoMa_Ox1212.

Valediction: Love, Sophia Martini, Oxnard

Holy crap. This was really happening. Where's Oxnard? She Googled it. Southern California. North of Los Angeles. For all Grace knew, this person could be anywhere in the world, but if she wasn't from Oxnard, why would she say she was from Oxnard. So random.

When she clicked over to Instagram, she searched SoMa_Ox1212 and clicked. Only a few pictures. Sophia looked a little older than Grace, but not much. She was pretty. Long, dark hair and green eyes. Crazy long eyelashes. The pictures were at the beach and on boats. Very SoCal. But normal. A regular teenager.

And so Grace began her correspondence with Sophia:

Hi Sophia.

Hi Grace

You said you could help me with my question.

I can

Well ....

Grace was curious, but she didn't want to come off as naïve. She wasn't a tough girl, but she felt like she could play one on Insta if she had to.

Yes. You can get pregnant without sperm

How?

I don't know how but I know it's possible. Cuz it happened to me

Grace's stomach dropped, and she felt like her throat was closing up. If this were a live conversation, she didn't know if she'd be able to speak.

Her reflex was to totally believe this person whom she'd never met. She wanted to believe it because she knew it was true. She knew there was some way that this could happen to a girl, and Sophia from Oxnard was just further proof. Once there were two people saying the same outrageous thing, that made it true, right?

But she had to be careful. She had to figure out if this person was lying to her or not. It was hard to slow herself down when she DM-ed, but she would force herself to feel out Sophia by staying engaged but also being cautious.

OMG! Did you already have the baby?

No. Not until August. But I have a belly now and no one believes me

Okay. These seemed like normal responses.

Me either. Hey, why did you hit ME up on that message board?

This should explain a lot.

I've been trying to find other girls like me

Are there other girls?

Yes

How did you find them?

The same way I found you. Looking in chat rooms

How many girls?

A lot. But only two others will let me keep talking to them

Wow

Yeah. It's a trip

She was typing too fast, not being thoughtful. She couldn't help it. Maybe this girl—or woman—could help her find some answers. But she didn't want to get too excited and forget that this was a stranger. STRANGER DANGER! That's what they always said in elementary school. Stay cautious, Grace.

I get the SoMa_Ox. That's Sophia Martini from Oxnard. What's the 1212?

Oh, that's my birthday 12/12

Grace shivered. She felt like she sometimes did when she looked out over the ledge of a really tall building. It was as if her whole body was a tuning fork, and someone picked her up and struck her against a telephone pole. She became dizzy with the feeling.

That's my birthday, too

Yes. That's what I figured. The other girls, too.

WTF?

I know. Crazy.

Well what's next?

~25~

Pat and Emily usually went to bed at around ten, watched some of the Ten O'clock News on Channel Two, and then listened to a podcast on one of their phones after they'd turned off the TV. In addition to an infatuation with the meteorologist, Pat also had a bit of a crush on Heather Holmes, the tall, blonde anchor—not really his type, but she definitely had something going on. Maybe it was her confidence.

Pat believed she couldn't be rattled, no matter what the story. Whether it was the piece on Oscar Grant getting shot by the BART policeman or the tragic shooting of Kate Steinle at the hands of an illegal immigrant, Ms. Holmes kept her cool. The facts. She put them out there without editorializing and then moved on to the next story.

Pat wondered if she ever cried off-camera.

Tonight's local news was the standard fare: shocking images of homelessness, which didn't even seem shocking anymore, followed by interviews with homeless advocates blaming the problem on the tech industry or the Republicans or the housing crisis.

Pat didn't like the idea that homelessness was somehow related to the housing crisis in any way. He knew his notion was counter-intuitive—more houses should help the homeless—but the great majority of homeless people didn't have jobs. If there was, suddenly, a surplus of affordable homes, jobless-homeless people wouldn't be able to acquire them anyway. Teachers and cops would. And guess what? The homeless would still be homeless. And they'd keep showing up in San Francisco as long as the city kept providing tents and food and general assistance checks. To Pat, it was simple. It was human nature. It was even simpler than human nature.

He was thinking all this and losing track of the story as he tried to come up with an analogy to support his theory. He spent a great deal of his quiet time trying to come up with analogies and metaphors so that he would have them in his hip pocket if he needed them in the heat of an argument.

His brain was churning through ideas on the homeless crisis, and the first one that came to mind was the theory of the stray cat—or any kind of animal for that matter—that will continue returning to a location as a food source, especially an easy source provided by humans.

But he didn't like the analogy for two reasons.

First, he felt that if he used that kind of comparison, he would be dehumanizing these poor folks that he saw out on the streets every day. In some people's minds, to liken them to animals would be to *call* them animals, which was not his intention. And despite all the other old animal tropes that compare people to lemmings or snakes or weasels or chickens, the homeless champions would deem him a monster—even worse than an animal—if he were to consider the comparison when talking about those without homes.

The second reason he felt the need to abandon the analogy: it reminded him of this afternoon's coyote encounter, which affected him deeply.

And then *timing* scrambled into his bedroom. He was partly paying attention to the news and trying to push the insensitive analogy out of his mind, when he half-heard Heather Holmes say the words "coyote" and "Buena Vista."

He snapped out of his stupor and shouted, "Coyote."

"God damn it, Pat," said Emily, sitting up. "You scared the hell out of me."

He was having trouble coming up with the words. "It's us," he said. "Grace's coyote!"

He said it loud enough for Grace and Alice to come running into the bedroom and look at the TV. The girl from the park who shot the video was saying into the news camera, "These are beautiful animals. They're our gentle companions in the park."

"What the hell?" said Pat, and everyone shushed him.

Then he saw on the screen a fairly steady shot of his own back. He recognized his St. X hoodie. He was holding Sully by the collar and was in a kind of pseudo-athletic stance, like a guy at the starting line of an old-fashioned foot race—ready to go but waiting for the gun. Then the camera zoomed in to focus on Grace and the coyote, and Pat and Sully were just blurry apparitions in the foreground.

"Oh my God," said Alice and looked quickly at Grace before turning her eyes back to the screen.

The park girl was a good videographer.

The images were clear, and Pat couldn't figure out if there was no sound or if everyone in the scene was so quiet that it seemed like a silent picture. The coyote licked Grace's hand, and, yes, she smiled a little bit. Maybe it tickled. It was hard for Pat to believe the interaction was occurring even though he was present to watch it all happen live. There was just something about it that seemed staged, like these coyotes were simply actors playing out some director's vision. But this wasn't Snow White, and these weren't bunnies and deer. This was one nasty, unpopular wild dog, a prairie wolf. A scavenger. A predator. Pat was pretty sure that some states allowed citizens to shoot these things on sight.

But here was this mamma coyote licking Pat's daughter's hand on the Ten O'clock News.

And then Heather Holmes was back on the screen, and she looked a bit flushed. "So, there you have it," she said. "Humans and coyotes sharing Buena Vista Park." She was shaking her head slightly. Perhaps this was the first time she'd seen the clip. She continued, "But I wouldn't recommend this kind of interaction to anyone, as several dogs in city parks have been killed by coyotes in recent months. We've been told that you should avoid contact with these animals and never feed them."

She and co-anchor, Frank Summerville, moved on seamlessly to the next story about two men on scooters who caused a traffic jam on the Bay Bridge, but the Ryans weren't listening. They were all looking at Grace.

"That was really weird," she said and started giggling like she did when she was a little girl.

Grace

It has been a long day, and I easily drift off to the lady, though more and more, it feels like the she is with me always.

Today we're in a forest. There's something wild about it. Untamed. The trees and ivy and ground cover seem natural, untouched by people. And there's a light mist over everything.

There are also sounds today. Birds. Crickets. Cicada. And water. I can hear running water, moving over rocks somewhere in the distance. But when the lady speaks, her voice is clear like it always is.

"Did you see me today?" she asks.

"Were you with me?" I say.

"I was very close to you," she says.

I feel like she's always with me lately, but this time it seems like she's being literal. Like she means that she and I were actually together at some point in real life during this crazy day.

"Thank you for being with me," I say, but I'm still not sure what she means exactly. In school? At the park? At home?

"You're stuck with me," she says, and it sounds like a joke the way she says it, and I laugh. She hasn't been the jokey type up to this point. I'm happy. She gets me. She knows what to say when I'm scared. But tonight, I'm not scared about anything. My problems aren't eating at me. I feel really good. I was on TV.

The lady is usually there to comfort me. To give me advice. But right now, I feel like I'm okay for the first time in weeks. But that doesn't stop her.

"They're going to come for you," she says.

"Who?" I say.

"You need to remember who you are," she says. "You need to remember who to trust."

"I'll remember," I say, but I'm back to being scared again. She says something else, but I don't hear her anymore. Someone has turned up the volume on the crickets and cicadas, and I think I hear something moving in the undergrowth beyond the trees. An animal.

~26~

Alice and Grace were in the student center for only a few minutes before a couple of Alice's friends came over to the table. Toni from the basketball team and Melanie, a little blonde who was more a friend of a friend. Melanie was the first to speak. "You guys," she said. "This is crazy." She was holding her phone out to them and was smiling, excited that she was going to be the one to reveal this news, whatever it was. Alice always liked Melanie, so she wasn't anxious that it would be something negative, but she was surprised that Melanie seemed so eager to provide the report.

Alice didn't like to hand over *her* own phone to anyone because she'd dropped and broken a few over the years in exchanges. She didn't like to fully accept anyone else's phone either. Instead, she stood beside Melanie and cupped her hand over Melanie's like they used to in the movies when someone was lighting a woman's cigarettes. She changed the angle of the phone to correct the glare and watched a few seconds before she recognized the video of Grace that had been on Channel Two last night.

She released Melanie's hand and sat back down, saying, "Oh yeah. We watched it last night. My dad started yelling when it came on."

Melanie said, "Yeah, we figured that. But look who posted it?" Her eyes were narrowed, and she had a tight grin that looked like it was about to burst open and have confetti shoot out of it.

Alice said, "Who?" and reached back for the phone.

Melanie held the phone back out to her, and this time, Alice took it in both hands but accidentally touched the screen, and it ended up on Kylie Jenner's twitter feed. "Oh Shoot," she said and showed it to Melanie, thinking Melanie would have to help find the video again.

But Melanie shook her head and said, "Scroll up."

"Huh?" said Alice and began to scroll through a sea of cosmetics and skin care posts until she saw a thumbnail with a close-up of Grace's face. "What the fuck?" she said. "Is this real?" She touched the play button just to double check. Then she said, "Oh my God!"

"What?" said Grace.

And before Alice could respond, Toni finally spoke. "Girl," she said. "You're famous."

"Lemme see," said Grace.

Just before Alice passed over the phone, she read Kylie's simple caption: *Kylie Jenner Retweeted: Fierce!*

***

Pat had been in his office undisturbed for a good hour before he heard the tapping of his assistant's fingernails on the little window on his door. When he looked up from his emails, he saw her smiling face in the window.

He nodded, and she walked in. Hi Pat, I have Ms. Prattley here. She'd like a word."

"Send her in," he said and took off his reading glasses. Amanda Prattley was a young French teacher, maybe two years out of college, and was always nervous when she came to his office, but today she entered smiling and shaking her phone at him.

"This is incredible, Mr. Ryan," she said.

"New iPhone?" he said.

She paused a moment before she shook her head and said, "No, no. This thing with your daughter."

"Which one?" he said.

"I don't know," she said. "That's right. You have two."

"Yeah," he said. "Freshman and Senior. What's up?"

"Mr. Ryan," she said. "You need—"

Pat cut her off. "I've been telling you for about six months, Amanda. You don't have to call me Mr. Ryan. You're not one of the students."

"Yes, yes," she said. "You did. I know that. But this video. I think it's the younger daughter. Oh my God."

"Oh," said Pat. "Yeah. You saw the news last night?"

"No?" she said, not seeming to have any idea what Pat was talking about. Maybe not even knowing what news is. "I'm talking about the viral video."

"Okay," said Pat. "Just tell me what you want to tell me."

"Well," she said. "Your daughter is in a YouTube video with a coyote!"

"Yep," said Pat. "That's the one that was on KTVU last night. I already saw it. Crazy."

"Well, did you know that it already has a quarter of a million views?"

"Is that a lot?" he said.

"Yes," she said. "Kylie only posted it a few hours ago."

"Kylie who?" he said. "Does she go to St. Mary's?"

"No," she said. "Kylie Jenner. She's sis—"

"Yeah, yeah," he said. "I know who she is. Why the hell is she posting a video like that? Do people care about that?"

Amanda Prattley looked at him as if he had arrived in a time machine from the 1950's and didn't understand the complex ways of her society. "Now they do," she said. "Everyone cares now."

***

Emily had her last client of the day cancel, so she left the office early and went to Safeway to pick up something for Pat to make for dinner. There was no parking at the Taraval Safeway because of some construction going on in the lot, so she drove past it and decided to go to Diamond Heights. It was a little smaller, but it had a huge parking lot.

She'd been playing phone tag with Pat all day, so he didn't give her any suggestions for dinner. She was just going to walk to the meat aisle and see if there was anything on sale. She'd once seen a TV show warning against buying meat on sale. *60 Minutes* or *20/20*. They'd said that it could be that the meat was going bad, so the store was trying to get rid of it. It sounded reasonable to Emily, but if she could look down at a steak, and it wasn't turning grey, she could *see* that it was okay. And on a rare occasion, if she got home and pulled off the plastic packaging only to smell something, she could always dump it. She trusted her senses. The only sale items in the meat section she truly avoided were the ones that were slathered in some kind of sauce or marinade. She always felt that the store was trying to cover up something unsightly.

Today, they had a family pack of pork chops on sale. There were eight chops included, but she decided to grab them anyway, and figured they could eat the leftovers for lunch.

When she turned to drop them in with the cereal, the eggs, and the jar of olives that she'd picked up on the way to the meat section, Joan Ericson was holding the front of the cart with both hands. Joan always looked the same. She was wearing an ugly, expensive dress, had her hair teased up like a late 80s pop star, sported some pointy stilettos, and was wearing enough lipstick to make Ronald McDonald jealous. All this for a trip to the supermarket.

"Emily," she said. "You must all still be in shock."

Emily immediately thought this busybody had somehow heard about Grace's pregnancy. She just stared back at her, ready to run her over with the cart if she said anything close to slighting Grace or the family.

Joan waited for Emily to react, and when she didn't, Joan said, "I guess the Ryan family will be famous now."

It didn't sound to Emily like Joan was talking about Grace's baby, but she still waited to see what she'd say next. She didn't want to play her hand just yet. She had practiced a series of retorts for the myriad acquaintances she anticipated confronting her once the news was out. Everything from, *She made a mistake, but we love her and support her* to *This is none of your business; go fuck yourself.* She knew she wouldn't use that last one even on Joan Ericson, but it was fun to have it in her quick-reply-toolbox just in case the moment arose.

"The video?" Joan said. "This coyote thing?"

"Oh yes," said Emily. "Of course. We watched it last night. So scary."

Joan looked at her like she expected more.

"I've had sessions all day, so you're actually the first person outside the family that I've talked to about it. Did you see it on Channel Two?"

Joan said, "Channel Two? Honey, it's all over social media. I saw it on Facebook. Apparently, the Kardashians are talking about it. There're already some memes about it."

"Memes?"

~27~

Max's parents left this morning.

Tahoe.

His brother, Tony, took him to BevMo for supplies and picked everything out just like the last time. Everyone had a great time at the first party, so Max wanted to get the same drinks. Lots of beer and cheap vodka and stuff to mix with the vodka.

He'd tried to keep this gathering smaller, but it was only nine o'clock, and the house was filling up. Everyone was there. No crashers yet, but everyone else had shown, even people he invited but didn't think would come.

He was trying to have fun, but he was worried about Grace—all the things that had been happening to her.

This viral video was crazy. It already had close to a million hits because Kylie had retweeted it. Max also thought people liked to watch it because it was Grace. And Grace was beautiful. Everyone liked to look at beautiful people, especially when something crazy was happening to them, and the beautiful people were still beautiful while it was happening.

He'd viewed it at least fifty times. Every time he watched, he focused on something else. One time, he spent the whole 1:37 watching the dog, Sully. That dog chased after squirrels, ducks, other dogs, buses, whatever. Why didn't he chase that coyote? Grace's dad grabbed Sully's collar at one point, but not right away. That was weird. What made the dog stand there and watch like that?

The last two times he played the video, Max focused on Grace's face. She almost looked like she was staring at the camera, but her eyes were shifted just to the right at her dad. It wasn't a panicky look. She was just calm. She could have been waiting in line at the movie and watching her dad take out his wallet to buy the tickets.

At one point, she took a quick peak over at the coyote pup, and that's when she started to smile. The first few times he watched it, he thought she was smiling because the coyote's tongue was tickling her hand, but the timing wasn't right. She started to grin just *before* the lick and just after she'd turned her head slightly to the side, where the little one was sniffing around.

Max pressed pause when he got to that part and zoomed in on Grace's face. It was clear, but the coloring was slightly off because the sun must have been setting and there was a slightly orange glow on Grace's cheeks. But when he zoomed in to her face so that it took up the whole screen, he wanted that picture. He wanted to frame it and put it in his room. He wanted the girl who smiled like that. Smirked. Like she knew something was funny but no one else got it. It was a great smile.

But that's not what people were talking about when she arrived at the party. People were cheering and calling her *coyote girl*, which required zero thought. They should have at least come up with something more creative than that. Tarique just hugged her and said, "Glad you're alive, little lady."

Max only had two or three beers. Three. And he was giving her some space. Letting her try out her celebrity for a while. And she was handling it like Grace, telling people she was scared, but Max knew she wasn't. When someone asked her if she knew Kylie Jenner, she laughed. "Yeah right!"

Then he saw Tony walk up to her and put his arm around her. She didn't seem to recognize him even though Max knew they'd met at the last party. Jill was also standing there and seemed to be reintroducing them, and Max was pretty sure he could read Grace's lips: "Yes! I remember." But he still saw some hesitation. He was pretty sure that Grace had no idea who he was.

And that was good. Max remembered that early in the night at that first party, Tony seemed like he was hitting on her, and Max had to tell him to back off, that she was only fifteen. Tony had laughed at the time. "What?" he said. "Is she your girlfriend or something?"

And when Max was about to say *yes* just so Tony would leave her alone, Grace said, "We're just good friends."

He could hear it in his mind now as he watched Tony lead Grace and Jill into the living room. That's where Tony's two friends were sitting on the couch. Max barely knew them. They had both gone to public school but didn't finish. They said they were going to be coders, but they didn't seem smart enough. In fact, they seemed like idiots. They seemed like

Tony, who'd been sent away to boarding school because their parents didn't know what to do with him. He kept ditching school and going to the Dolores Park to smoke weed with people like the two idiots in the living room.

Grace was doing the thing where she had water in her plastic cup and was telling people it was vodka. Max watched his brother take her cup out of her hand and smell it and then start pointing at her and laughing. They were all laughing, even Grace. She was busted. And now Tony was walking toward Max.

"Where you going?" said Max.

"To get your girl a drink," he said. "She was drinking water. What kind of weak party are you having where hot girls are drinking water?"

"She doesn't want a drink," said Max.

"It's a party, Maxie. Everyone wants a drink."

"Tony," said Max. "She doesn't feel well. Seriously. Don't get her a drink."

"Max," he said. "Save that weak-ass shit for St. X. You sound like a total pussy right now."

Max looked over at Grace and Jill and the two idiots. He didn't want Grace anywhere near these guys. He followed Tony into the kitchen, where Tony was already pouring vodka into a red solo cup. He put in way too much. Then he opened a can of Red Bull and poured that in with the ice and vodka until it was filled to the top. He mixed it with his finger while smiling at Max and raising his eyebrows like a cartoon pervert.

When Tony started to walk out of the kitchen, Max stepped in front of him. "Don't give that drink to Grace," he said. "She can't drink."

Tony started laughing. "Well, there was a girl who looked exactly like her and did a lot of drinking last time you had people over." He turned his body and tried to slide past Max.

Max moved again so that there was no room for Tony to get by. If Tony wasn't holding the drink, he could have muscled past, but as it stood, he had only one hand to push Max's chest, and Tony didn't have enough leverage to move him.

"She can't have that drink, Tony. Stop." Max was leaning forward against the pressure of Tony's hand—the immoveable object and the unstoppable force.

"Get out of the way, Max."

Max could feel his shoes sliding on the tile beneath him, so he dug in and said, "Tony, stop!" But this time Tony quickly pulled his hand away and scooted to the side while Max toppled onto the kitchen floor. Tony, with the drink dripping on his hand and wrist, slithered out the door.

Max was looking at several sets of shoes. He felt the stickiness of the floor on his hands and knees, and he heard the laughing, but he bounced up quickly and shot out the door. Tony was almost in the living room when Max reached him from behind and knocked the cup out of his hand. Vodka-Red Bull splashed across the room and splattered on several guests.

Tony pivoted quickly and shifted his weight to throw a punch, but his back foot slipped on the wet floor, and he missed wildly.

At that point, Tarique from the basketball team handed his drink to the guy standing next to him and grabbed Tony around the waist, a reverse bear hug. "Chill, man," he said in a very calm voice.

Now the whole house was quiet except for the thumping of a bass line coming from the Wonderboom speaker perched on the mantle over the fireplace.

Tony didn't struggle against Tarique's hold. He settled himself, took a deep breath, and screamed from deep within his throat, "Everyone get the fuck out of my house!" It was high pitched and easily cut through the vibrating bass. It had the effect that Tony must have been looking for: people put drinks down on whatever piece of furniture was close and rushed to the front door. Tarique released Tony but remained between the two brothers.

Max watched Grace and Jill get swept up in the tide of partygoers. Grace locked her eyes on Max's as she floated toward the door. She didn't say anything. But she was sending him a message with her eyes—*sorry*. Or maybe it was *thank you*. Probably both. The way she was looking at him was meaningful, and he wanted it to last a little longer, but then the current pushed her toward the door, and she drifted out into the night.

~28~

Pat felt like he needed to talk to someone.

The family was handling everything really well and he felt like they were all on the same page. Gracie was going to be strong, and Emily and Alice were going to support Grace. Not that Alice and Grace had a lot of fights in the past, but neither of them had even raised her voice toward the other since the doctor's appointment.

But Pat needed to talk to someone outside the family.

Grace came home upset from a party last night, and he didn't know if it was normal teen stuff or if it had something to do with the baby. Did everything have to do with the baby? Could she separate her normal teen problems from her one colossal mistake? Was that possible? Or was the pregnancy affecting her every thought? Had the idea of the baby occupied an important province in her mind and claimed squatter's rights indefinitely? He didn't know. Couldn't see the world through Grace's lens no matter how hard he tried.

Of course, he and Emily had discussed these things and Alice had been really honest and helpful. But they were also seeing things as family. They all knew Grace so well and loved her so much that it was impossible for them to think intellectually about the situation. Outside of their conversations with Cindy the therapist, almost every discussion was controlled by emotions. Hearts were making decisions, and that was okay with some circumstances, but not necessarily certain important life-changing decisions concerning Grace.

He thought of calling his brother or one of his buddies from work or even Father Gilligan, who had always given him sound advice, but none of those people seemed right for this discussion.

He knew that contacting Jenny Daly wouldn't be fair to Jenny. It would clearly put her in a difficult position as Grace's principal, but he thought the two of them were good enough friends to weather that storm. They'd been through an awful lot together, and she'd confided in him things that he never wanted to hear. She'd dated one of his high school buddies for a while, and she told him details about bedroom oddities that he would have just assumed not knowing. Pat and Jenny were friends. And what are friends for if not to tell each other really uncomfortable things and have the other pretend that it was all totally normal.

So, he called her on a Sunday morning.

Emily was taking the girls across the bay to Corte Madera mall, so he was on his own anyway. And if Jenny didn't pick up, that was okay, too. He wasn't completely certain it was the right move, and he was fine watching college basketball if she didn't pick up.

But she did. And she was fine meeting him to talk as long as he didn't mind walking around Lake Merced with her. Of course, he minded. He was hoping to have coffee or, better yet, a beer. Or, upon further reflection, not talking at all and staying home to watch Syracuse play Gonzaga. But he called her. He was stuck.

He met her at the circular parking lot near the lake. The first thing he thought when he saw Jenny was that he was not dressed properly. Jenny was sporting yoga pants, new fluorescent running shoes, and what looked to Pat like the kind of shirt a competitive cyclist would wear.

He was wearing khakis, old desert boots, and a St. X fleece jacket.

When he got out of the car, she gave him the elevator eyes.

"I thought you said we were *walking*," he said.

"I did," she said, looking directly at his shoes now. "But you look like you're walking to a couch ... or a barstool."

"Yeah," he said. "I get it now. I saw some people walking by when I drove into the lot. This is like speed walking, I guess."

"It's not going to be a Sunday morning stroll," she said. "Do you have any sneakers in your trunk?"

"Just golf shoes," he said. "I'll be fine."

"Try and keep up," she said and took off toward the lake.

He had longer strides than she, so it wasn't hard to keep pace, but about a quarter mile in, he felt the sweat start to drip down the side of his face, and his armpits were getting chafed raw. He took off the fleece and tied it around his waist. He hated doing it. He felt like guys with sweaters around their waists always looked like dorks. But it was better than the frat boy look of putting it around his shoulders, and he couldn't keep it on. He looked for a garbage can. He was considering just throwing it away.

He was still working hard to keep pace with Jenny while he told Grace's story. They were cutting through Harding Park, the golf course, when he started to lose his breath, so he stopped talking for a moment.

"Pat," she said. "You can't stop now."

"I'm hyperventilating," he said. "Must ... stop ... talking."

"My God," she said. "You're a mess."

He just nodded and kept walking. He was taking deep breaths, and she was looking at him sadly. He knew his face was red, and he could feel the sweat pouring off his forehead. He was grateful when Jenny pulled him by the sleeve and led him to the bar and grill near the 18th hole.

She sat down at an outdoor table, and when he started to sit, she stopped him. "Wait a minute," she said. "If you're going to ruin my walk, at least go buy me a drink."

"It's 10:45," he said, still sucking air. "What do you want?"

"Get me that special bloody Mary they do here."

"The bloody Viking?" he said.

"That's the one," she said and reached back to fix her ponytail.

He came back from the bar with her bloody Viking, two glasses of water, and a pint of Lagunitas Pale Ale.

"I don't need any water," she said, smiling, happy that she'd worn him out after just over a mile.

"It's not for you," he said and downed the first glass of water then pulled the other one away from her and took a sip. He used a cloth napkin to wipe his forehead and then held the cold beer against his face for a moment before taking a sip.

"So, the psychiatrist said she's delusional?" she asked.

"She's just a therapist," he said. "And yeah, that's what she said. Partly because of the denial, but more because of these visions or dreams that Grace has been having."

"Visions? Like she's hallucinating?"

"I think they're just dreams," he said.

"About what?"

He finished off the water and took a sip of the beer before he said, "A lady."

"A lady?"

"Yeah," he said, squinting now as the sun was breaking through the marine layer. "She gives Grace advice and little pep talks, I guess."

Jenny paused for a minute, thoughtful, smiling now. "That sounds okay to me," she said. "I'd love to have dreams like that."

Pat smiled. Grace was unconsciously giving herself therapy. Daily affirmations with Stuart Smalley.

"I keep having the same crappy dream over and over," said Jenny. "I have to pass a calculus final exam in order to graduate from college, but I haven't attended any of the classes."

"Did you pass the test?"

"In the dream?"

"Yeah."

"I always wake up before it gets handed out."

"That's not so bad," he said. "At least you don't have actually take the test."

"No, Pat. It's terrible. I wake up the next day with anxiety. The stupid dream ruins my whole day."

"I'll tell Grace to send her lady into your dreams. Sounds like you could use the encouragement. *You're good enough. You're smart enough. And doggone it—"*

"*People* like *me*. Yeah, Yeah. Thanks," she said as she stirred her Bloody Viking with the celery stick before she bit the bloody end of the stalk and started chewing like a San Quentin inmate at feeding time, a little bit of the juice running down her chin.

"So, what do you think about all this?" he asked.

"At least I know why you were asking me about teen pregnancies a few weeks back," she said, still chewing and wiping her chin.

"Yeah," he said. "I wasn't ready to talk about Grace yet."

"Well, she has the right parents to make it through all this," she said as her eyes shifted beyond Pat toward the 18th fairway.

"What about school?" he said.

"You're doing the right thing, Pat. The archdiocese should be happy that you're going to help Grace care for this child."

Pat wasn't really thinking of himself. He was wondering about Grace and her place at St. Mary's. But Jenny's response had him thinking about his relationship with the superintendent. He got along with her really well, but now he was wondering about her reaction to one of her Catholic school principals having a pregnant daughter. That would not look good. That would not be sending a good message at all.

"I was actually asking about Grace," he said. "Will she be able to keep going to school?"

"We already talked about this when you pretended to be asking hypothetical questions," she said. "To expel a girl from school for getting pregnant would be to encourage other girls to terminate their pregnancies, right? And we don't want to do that."

"No," he said. "I was just double-checking."

"We will definitely have to sit down and come up with a plan once she starts showing."

We think it won't be until the beginning of next school year," he said.

"Oh, that's good," she said. "But in the meantime, you better make sure you meet with the superintendent or the Archbishop. They don't like to get blindsided by stuff like this."

"That's gonna be a blast."

"Do you want me to come with you?"

"Yes."

~29~

Ever since Grace had her Instagram conversation with Sophia from Oxnard, she was dying to talk to her again. Even though Sophia was a few months ahead of Grace in her pregnancy, Sophia never really gave her any advice or instructions on how to manage a virgin pregnancy. Sophia made Grace feel better that she wasn't alone, but Grace still needed help. She wanted to know if Sophia thought there was some purpose to their scenarios. Something religious maybe?

But when Grace started the chat today, Sophia jumped to a different topic altogether:

OMG, you're famous!

I know. Crazy

Were you scared?

It's hard to explain but no. I knew it didn't want to hurt me

My dad says he thinks you smile at one point. It does look like that.

Grace was having trouble remembering exactly what she was thinking when she saw the coyote. When she watched the video, she imagined what she should have been thinking, but she knew it wasn't right. It had been as if her mind just shut down for that one moment. She knew she saw the big one first. Then she called to her dad. And that's about all she remembered. She had zoomed in on the video many times, but it was hard to read her own expression. Yes. It did look like she was smiling, but she thought it was because of the puppy, not the big one licking her hand.

I know. It looks like that. Is that weird?

Totally weird, but cool too

Wait until people find out I'm pregnant and that there's no dad. Then they're really gonna think I'm weird.

At this moment it occurred to her that the reaction to her pregnancy was going to be so much more challenging than all the girls on *Teen Mom.* On that show, the real-life teenagers had problems like any other kids who got pregnant, but at least they knew who the dads were. Grace's situation was going to be different. People were going to think she was a weirdo.

That's true

What should I do?

The only thing that matters is taking care of your baby

I will

And you have to decide if you're going to keep saying you're a virgin

What?????

You can make up an anonymous father, but do you really want to deal with the mess of explaining to people that your baby is some kind of miracle?

Grace wasn't expecting this. She thought that Sophia had reached out to her so that she could help her figure out the best way to explain the situation to friends, family, doctors, teachers, and everyone.

No, I don't want to deal with the mess, but are you saying I should tell people that I had sex with a boy?

It's an option

Wait. You're showing now. Is that what you're doing?

Yes

Why????

It's just easier

Grace did want *easier*. For herself. For her mom and dad. For Alice. If she were just a regular pregnant fifteen-year-old, this whole thing would be so much easier. Not ideal, but easier. And since Sophia was now playing that role, she could be Grace's guide. And then Grace would be just like the girls on *Teen Mom*. And she would have a hard life, but at least it wouldn't be a crazy one. She wouldn't have to keep seeing the therapist.

But still, Grace thought she was special. She knew she was special. This had to be important. Maybe Grace and Sophia and the other girls experiencing this were supposed to be doing something different than other teen moms. Maybe these babies were coming into the world for a purpose. Could they all hide these virgin births and still have the babies end up doing what they are supposed to do? Or were the girls supposed to publicize what was happening to them so that the world would know?

Is easier better?

What else is there?

Grace didn't know. She'd been going about her last few weeks planning on the alternative—telling only the truth about her pregnancy when the time came—but she never thought it all the way through. She knew she was a good person. And she knew that she was an honest person. But now she was thinking about the fact that no one was going to believe her, and she didn't have any way to prove it.

Grace

It's dark this time. Not pitch black, but shadowy. At least it's not cold, but this is not like any previous visit. Shadow clouds seem to be floating all around me, different shades of black and grey and dark blues and maybe even greens—the colors of water at night. Blinking doesn't work. Eyes won't seem to adjust.

I know the lady is sitting behind me, but I don't turn around.

"You have doubts," she says, and her voice sounds like it always does. It actually makes me feel better, safer.

"Don't we all," I say and immediately think that I sound a little snarky, so I change course. "Sorry. Yes. I have doubts."

It's quiet for a long time. I have no real concept of the room I'm in, but it smells like a confessional. I almost feel like I should be kneeling. Unloading my most recent sins, but I can't think of any big ones.

When I was little, I used to have to make up the sins when we went to confession during school because I couldn't think of anything, and the priest would be waiting for me to say something. I would ultimately confess that I had fought with my sister or that I had lied to my mom and dad, and the priest would give me a few Hail Marys and an Our Father for penance, and I'd depart, smiling, knowing that I'd been forgiven even if I hadn't acknowledged any real sins.

Was I really such a good little kid? Or did I just choke under the pressure of reconciliation and resort to made-up stories? I had to have been sinning. I was just like everyone else. But I really could never think of anything. The term "sin" didn't really mean what it was supposed to mean back then. I knew people sinned, and I knew I sinned. And I knew the Ten Commandments. But I didn't really think about what the word meant until I was older.

It seems to me that it all really has to do with selfishness. All the bad sins come from people acting on their instincts to look out for themselves first. To get what they want regardless of how they get it. For primitive people, they had to be selfish in order to survive. Their collective reflex was to protect themselves first rather than worry about other people. Survival instincts, right? Aren't those just built in?

So, in order to avoid sin, you really have to fight against the instincts that God gave you.

No. That doesn't sound right. Could that be right? Why would God give us selfish instincts if he wants us to be selfless? Why would he make us natural savages when he wants us to be civilized? I think I learned all this at some point, but the questions seem odd as I sit here in the shadows. We want what's best for us. That makes sense. But in order to be good people, we have to ignore what we want so that we help others get what they want.

In my religion class, my teacher has a poster on the wall. It has a picture of a pile of different colored hands like at the end of a timeout in a basketball huddle. And superimposed over the hands, the famous line, "Love your neighbor as yourself." But what do you do when it's a tie? Wait. That's not the right question. It's more like this:

I get it when you have two pieces of candy left, and your friend asks for one. That's easy. You give one to your friend and take the other for yourself. But what if you have only one piece. My guess is that Jesus would say that I should give the last piece to my friend. But wouldn't that mean that the saying should really be "Love your neighbor more *than yourself"?*

That seems like a lot to ask. And it truly goes against your instincts.

I haven't been saying any of this out loud, but the lady asks, "Isn't there a scenario when a human's instincts are to sacrifice her own needs for someone else's?"

I think for a moment but can't come up with anything, so I offer, "There are lots of times when people think of others before themselves."

"Yes," she says. "But is there a time when a person's instincts *lead her to these acts of selflessness?"*

It feels like a trick question. My reflex is to say no. That people are naturally selfish. They often act with generosity, but it's not natural. It's not instinctual.

And then I think about everything. Like everything that's happening to me. I can't explain how that's possible, but something is going on. Sounds and pictures and smells are washing over me all at once, like I'm caught under water in the breakers at Kelly's Cove and have no control. I stop fighting it and let the undertow of images and conversations swirl around me in the snow globe of my little life.

And then it hits me. The answer to the lady's question. It's obvious. "Yes," I say. "Of course."

Second Trimester

"Life is always a rich and steady time when you are waiting for something to happen or to hatch."

– E.B. White, Charlotte's Web

~30~

By July, you could easily tell that Grace was pregnant. She was almost six months, and if she wasn't wearing loose clothing, the baby bump was clearly visible. She looked like herself everywhere else—her face, shoulders, legs—but she had this little rise where the baby was growing, and when she was in her swimsuit, it was obvious because the rest of her was so tiny. With her sunglasses on, she looked like she could be one of the young moms in People Magazine's *Celebrity Pregnancy Gallery.*

The Ryans were up in Guerneville visiting Pat's sister, Erin, at her place on the Russian River, just seventy miles north of the city. It was a short drive, and Erin had plenty of bedrooms and a little dock right on the river with beach chairs and an umbrella.

Grace was standing at the edge trying to talk herself into jumping in. She had already thrown an inner tube in the water, and it was starting to drift downstream. "It's gonna be too cold," she said and turned around for some kind of help.

"Don't lose that inner tube," said Erin. "It'll be down at Johnson's Beach soon if you don't get in there."

Alice was reading a book, but she put it down and walked toward Grace.

"No pushing," said Grace. And when Alice took another step, Grace said, "Oh shit!" and jumped in. She swam under water for about ten feet and came up through the bottom of the inner tube. "It's not bad," she cried and climbed up through the donut hole and after some contortions sat with her butt resting in the water, her arms and legs dangling over the sides, water dripping off her limbs back into the river. It was almost a hundred degrees, and the sun was shining on her belly. She looked like a black and white water bug, skimming across the water.

"I gotta go in, too," said Alice. "How do you live up here in this heat, Erin?"

"I love it," said Erin and took a long sip from her plastic tumbler filled with vodka, club soda, and loads of ice. There were four limes in there because she put a fresh one in every time she made a refill. "The other inner tube is under the stairs," she said.

"Thanks," said Alice, climbing down the ladder with the inner tube around her shoulder. Before she got to the bottom, she placed the tube in the water and dropped backward into it. Barely a splash. She pushed off the ladder with both feet and glided in the direction of her sister. She put her hands in the water and splashed herself.

"I love 'em both," said Erin.

"They're good girls," said Emily, who was sitting on a lounge chair next to Pat. She pushed her cat eye sunglasses down her nose, looked at Erin, and said, "Thanks for having us, E. We needed this."

"Any time," she said. "You know you guys are always welcome."

Pat loved the river, and he considered Erin one of his best friends. It was a welcome relief from the fog that blanketed campus all summer long. He didn't mind extreme heat, especially when he could take two steps, jump in the river, swim for a couple of minutes, then jump back out and grab a cold beer from the cooler that Erin kept fully stocked all summer long in case she had visitors.

He had done just that only a few minutes before Grace jumped in the water, and he was still dripping a bit when he said, "Do you think this is good for Grace?"

Erin was sitting at the end of the dock with her feet in the water. She looked over her shoulder at him like he was crazy. "Of course," she said. "She can be herself and be outside and not have to hide from anyone. Yes. This is absolutely good for Grace."

"I know it," he said. "It would be nice though if the baby was just here already, and she wouldn't have to go through whatever is going to happen over the next months."

"Or," said Erin, rising now, holding her cocktail and walking over toward Pat and Emily, leaving wet footprints on the dry dock wood, "you could all enjoy the next few months as a family and watch this miracle occur."

Emily did the thing where she lowered her sunglasses again. "When you say miracle," she said. "You mean in kind of a general sense, like *all* babies are miracles, right?"

"So you all don't believe her?" asked Erin.

Pat took off his baseball cap and walked down to the edge of the dock. He reached down and dipped his hat in the water and then put it back on his head. He'd been doing this every fifteen minutes for the past hour. The cold water felt great on his head and seemed to cool his whole body for about thirty seconds before the dry heat went back to work on him. "We believe that she thinks she's still a virgin," said Pat, nearly six months in and still trying to figure out how his daughter truly didn't seem to know who the father was.

"Yeah," said Erin, sighing a little bit like a spiritual medium talking to a non-believer. "You're choosing your words very carefully, but the fact is that you don't believe that this is a true miracle."

Emily sat up on the lounge now. "We really want her to accept what's happening. We're at the end of the second trimester. And Grace has been emotionally strong, but now that she really can't hide it anymore, we're entering a new phase, and she needs to come to terms with this."

"And you want her to tell you who the father is," said Erin, looking out at the river now, back in her spot at the end of the dock, her toes gently poking at the water.

Pat swallowed the last warm splash of beer at the bottom of his bottle. "It's not a matter of knowing who the father is," he said. "We just want her to come to the realization that this is a normal pregnancy." Without getting up from his chair, he reached behind him and dropped the empty bottle in a plastic trash bin. "That is to say, as normal as it can be when a fifteen-year-old gets pregnant."

"Well, I believe her," said Erin, still looking out at the water, a flotilla of kayaks passing by now.

"What do you mean?" said Emily.

"I mean that I believe what Gracie has been saying," she said.

"Why do you believe it, E.?"

"Because I want to," she said, and then leaned forward, hands extended, and plunged into the water. Only her plastic tumbler remained on the dock. She swam under water for a long time and emerged at least halfway out in the river.

The Russian River basin was an acoustic anomaly. In some parts, you had to raise your voice to talk to someone only a few feet away. In other parts, you could hear the full conversation of people eating breakfast on their deck on the opposite side of the river. You could hear the crinkle of their newspapers and the clinking of a fork dropped on a plate. It was strange and wonderful.

The current was strong this year because of the April flooding. When Erin popped up to the surface, with the midstream current rushing over her, she gasped for breath and simultaneously whispered, "Because I know it's true," and, in this auditory wormhole, Pat and Emily could hear her clearly from the dock.

~31~

After a barbequed chicken dinner up on the deck, Alice asked her parents if it was okay to walk into town for ice cream. It was still light out, and on Main Street, there was an ornate, old bank building that had been recently refurbished into an old-fashioned ice cream parlor. Alice and Grace had been there with their parents and Erin before, but they wanted to go on their own tonight.

Their dad told them to go straight there and straight back. He gave them a twenty-dollar bill and poured himself a bourbon and soda.

They were walking on Drake Road past the Pee Wee Golf and Arcade. Earlier in the day, Erin had shown them pictures of the area during the flood. The 6th hole with the smiling whale and the giant turtle were both completely submerged, which actually seemed kind of appropriate for those creatures. The T-Rex was chest-deep in the muddy water and looked like he was trying to escape extinction, if flooding was how it happened. Or was it an asteroid? Volcanoes? Whatever it was. In the pictures of the April flood, this big guy was running away from something.

Today as they walked past, they paused to look at a different hole, a really strange one. The 8th. It had two guys in togas leaning over a big pot and sitting in the pot was a naked man. Did people in toga times really cook people? It didn't make sense to Alice.

They were both leaning into the cyclone fencing, their hands on either side of their heads, gripping the rusty metal and looking through the fence into this strange pee wee golf universe. "Are they giving him a bath?" said Grace.

That hadn't occurred to Alice, but it seemed just as bizarre. "I think they're boiling him alive," she said. "Wow. This is supposed to be for pee wees. Should little kids have to ask their parents about why these Romans or whatever they are need to torture a guy like this?"

"Yeah," said Grace. "Little kids should be allowed to be innocent at least at a miniature golf course."

"True," said Alice. "Like I hope they're not showing porn at the ice cream store."

Grace laughed.

It was nice to hear her laugh. It was nice to see her having fun in the river today and laughing tonight. Alice wondered all the time if Grace was going to be a happy person. Grace always had been, and it was sad there was a chance that, in the later months of this pregnancy or after the baby arrived, it would be hard for her to be completely happy again. She might always wonder what her life would have been like if this hadn't happened to her.

Alice had these thoughts all the time. She was consumed by them, and it was affecting the way she looked at other things. Alice would always get a little nervous before big basketball games and sometimes a final exam, but what she was experiencing now had to be clinical anxiety. She literally worried about Grace all the time. Before the school year ended, she'd thought about going to her own guidance counselor to talk about it, but that didn't seem right. Alice didn't want anyone at school to know yet. They were eventually going to know, but if there was ever a time to procrastinate, this sure seemed like it.

She and Grace walked under Highway 116 and approached the walking bridge that led into downtown Guerneville. Just before the bridge, there was a public bathroom, and there were always people hanging around there. They looked a bit like the homeless people in San Francisco, but there was definitely a difference.

The group there tonight smoking and standing around a picnic table wore the dusty clothes and ragged shoes that you'd see in one of San Francisco's many tent cities, but these folks were dark. They were white people but so deeply tanned that their faces were like old baseball gloves. At first glance, they looked old to Alice—like forty—but they were listening to Post Malone, and one of them was wearing a t-shirt that said, *Trust Me, I'm A Millennial.*

Alice and Grace had to walk by them, but Alice wasn't scared because there were two girls in the group. One red head and one blond. The girls' faces also looked old, but they were wearing short shorts and flip-flops. They were so skinny they appeared tall, but when Alice and Grace got close, all the girls were about the same height.

"You pretty ladies want to join us for a party?" said one of the guys wearing a red baseball cap turned backward. The hat was the only thing that looked new. Everything else was covered in river dust except that hat and this guy's voice, which just sounded like a regular teenager's.

"No thanks," said Alice. "Going to get ice cream." She was immediately a little embarrassed and kept walking.

But then she heard one of the girls say, "That sounds good," her voice letting the words jump up at the end like a cooking show host.

Alice took a quick glance behind her to see which girl had said it, but they all had their backs turned now. Alice let her eyes linger on the group. From this angle, she could see that the leader's red hat had something stenciled on the front: *Make America Vape Again.*

Main Street was a bustling collection of townies and tourists—neither bothered by the other but careful to keep a safe distance. The ice cream parlor was all tourists.

After the girls had ordered their cones, Grace said, "Do you want to just eat here?"

Normally they'd walk and eat, but the place was so clean and shiny and cool that Alice said, "Yeah," and grabbed the corner booth by the front window.

Grace was careful with her ice cream, methodically licking around the edge of the cone so that nothing would drip down the sides. The result was always a light bulb shaped scoop that needed occasional licking on the top to keep it stable enough to balance on the cone.

"Do you think Erin's being a little weird?" asked Alice.

"What do you mean?" said Grace.

"I mean," she said. "She's walking around you like … I don't know. Like you're not you. Like she's treating you differently than she normally does."

"Well, I am pregnant," she said and did a full circumference lick around the rim of the cone and then a follow-up sculpting of the top.

"I know that, Grace," said Alice, "But it feels like she's acting even different than that. She's running around getting you stuff and staring at you when you're not looking."

"Oh," said Grace. "Obviously, I couldn't notice that."

"Grace," said Alice, and she knew it was going to get to this moment at some point. "Erin's treating you like she believes in you."

Grace smiled; a little bit of green mint chip smeared on her lower lip. "Isn't that good?" she said.

Alice had to figure out a way to enter into this discussion without hurting Grace's feelings. They'd talked about her pregnancy many times over the past six months, but Alice had been advised by her parents, who had been advised by Grace's therapist, to tread lightly on this subject and that Grace would eventually have a clearer understanding of what happened and come to accept it. There was always the chance that she would keep the identity of the father a secret, according to the therapist, but Grace would almost certainly admit, at some point, that the baby was conceived in the normal way.

"I don't think it's good, Grace."

"Why not?"

"Because we were all kind of hoping that you were getting closer to remembering or realizing or whatever transition is supposed to take place in order for you to move past this phase."

Grace was silent for a moment. Alice saw a single green, milky drop of ice cream drip onto Grace's wrist. Grace didn't move to wipe it. She wasn't looking at Alice. She had turned her head and was gazing out the window at pedestrian traffic moving in both directions. Alice was looking out the window now as well and was about to apologize to Grace for not believing her when the group from the bridge walked into their line of vision. They were all talking and laughing and looking west toward the Safeway parking lot. But then the red headed girl gazed through the big front window of the parlor. She looked at Grace or Grace's ice cream cone or her own reflection and said, "Oh," and pointed, but no one in her group broke stride, and she stumbled briefly, losing one of her flip-flops. She quickly retrieved it and smiled into the glass before catching up to her group.

Grace licked around the edge of her ice cream and then licked the sticky smudge off her wrist. "That makes me sad," she said to Alice. "I thought you believed me."

Alice hated to see Grace like this, especially after a day when she'd been so happy, so content. "I'm sorry," she heard herself say. "Let's just forget I even said it."

"Why don't we just talk about it?" said Grace.

Alice didn't immediately reply. She didn't know how to approach the subject. She'd tried to get Grace to come around several times in those first few weeks, but Grace was so convincing. So authentic. So believable that Alice just moved on, accepting the therapist's prognosis that Grace would have an epiphany, triggered by some external stimuli that couldn't be predicted. In a way, the therapist's strategy let them all off the hook. The whole family had stopped trying to help her remember. They'd all been told that Grace would have this self-discovery and that they'd have to be there to support her when it happened, but here they were all this time later, and Grace had a baby bump, but the idea of a virgin birth was still Grace's default mentality.

"Grace," said Alice. "I'm going to Cal Poly next year instead of Villanova so that I can be closer to you and the baby. I even considered USF, but dad talked me out of it. He said that I should have some distance even if I wanted to be closer to you." Grace was staring back with those blue eyes. God, she was a beautiful person, Alice thought.

"And I'll drive up to the city in a heartbeat if you need me for anything," said Alice. "I'll take a leave of absence from school for a quarter or two if you need me." Alice didn't expect this kind of emotion, but she felt herself starting to cry. She needed to finish, though, so she kept going with her voice cracking. "But it would be so much easier for me to help you if I knew what really happened."

"No," said Grace. "It would be so much easier if you would just believe me."

~32~

Pat was sitting in the living room with Emily, and Erin was shuffling around the kitchen looking for something to serve for dessert even though both Pat and Emily had said that they were full.

When Erin finally came out of the kitchen, she said, "Okay, I popped some cookies in the oven. They should be ready in a bit."

"Erin," said Emily. "We said we didn't need dessert."

"I just popped 'em in," she said. "No trouble."

"Oh my God," said Emily. "You're crazy, but thanks. I'll make some tea to go with the cookies."

Pat said, "Yes, I'll make another bourbon to go with the cookies."

Emily shook her head at him. "Why do you always have to have a drink in your hand when you're up here."

"That's the beauty of the river," he said. "Self-contained. No driving. No phone. No email." He smiled at the thought of it.

"Yeah," said Emily, "But that doesn't mean you have to be buzzed 24/7."

"Wait," he said. "That's exactly what it means."

"Let me show you guys the water mark," said Erin, who never liked bickering, even half-hearted bickering, especially when she was the one who'd made Pat his last drink.

"Water mark?" said Pat.

"Well, not a *water mark,*" said Erin. "But the line in the basement that shows how far up the water went during the flood."

To appease Erin, Pat said, "Okay. Lead the way." And to appease Emily, he left his drink on the kitchen counter before they got to the stairs.

"So when I came back to the house after the storm, I tried to come in the side door over there," she said and pointed across the basement, which seemed in pretty good shape. "But I couldn't open the door."

She paused for dramatic effect. "Was it locked?" asked Pat, as buzzed as Emily had alleged but still sharp enough to know that he had to prompt Erin, or she'd just stand there pointing at the door.

"No," said Erin. "The beer refrigerator'd come up off the floor, tipped over, and was blocking the door. Can you believe it?"

"Yes," said Emily. "We can believe it. You already told us that your picnic table ended up three houses down and that the whole apple tree was uprooted and probably ended up in Jenner."

"Well, believe it," she said and nodded.

"Where did you put the fridge?" asked Pat.

"Had to get rid of it," she said. "It got river water inside and smelled funky."

"Oh," said Pat as he nodded and looked around the basement for any lasting signs of damage. "You did a pretty good job of cleaning up. It kinda looks like it always has."

"Well," she said. "Joe from next door came over and Kevin from down in Rio Nido stopped by, and we had to really get to work. You gotta hose it down while the other two squeegee out the silt and dead fish and sticks and leaves and various debris. It's a process, but we got it all out."

"Impressive cleanup efforts," said Emily. "You got lucky compared to those lowland folks on the other side."

"I did," she said. "Here's how high the water came up." She was wearing green Crocs, and she shuffled to the far side of the space, where she got down in a catcher's crouch and pointed to a spot about two and a half feet above the floor. "I cut the drywall out because I was scared of mold, but I think everything is pretty clean down here." She stood up now and looked at Pat. "You don't smell anything, do you?"

"Nope," he said. "Like Emily said, you got lucky."

"Do you know the story about Ed Howden?" asked Erin.

Pat scratched his three-day stubble. "Old guy who lives across the river near the lodge?"

"That very one," she said. "You know what happened to him in the big flood back in '86?"

"I don't think I know that one," he said and looked over at Emily for help, but she just shrugged.

There was an old wine barrel a few feet away, and Erin walked over and leaned on it with her elbow and crossed her feet like some kind of old west raconteur. Pat could see that she was getting comfortable, so he walked past the kayaks and straddled Erin's Harley Davidson. He shifted his weight to get balanced on the cushioned seat and then nodded to Erin that she could begin.

"Pat Ryan," she said. "Do not screw with that bike."

"What?" he said, wishing he hadn't left his drink upstairs. "I'm just getting comfy."

Emily was sitting on a milk crate now and said, "What happened to Ed Howden back in the flood of '86?"

"So, Ed's wife Annie, had left him and stole the little girl, the daughter. Annie had a short fuse, so one day she got pissed off about something or other and packed up her shit and left while Ed was working trimming trees down in Sebastopol."

"That's cold," said Pat.

"Yep," said Erin. "And Ed didn't know this, but for months after, Annie and the little girl were just a couple miles up the river shacked up with Mervyn Withers."

"That can't be a real name," said Emily, and Pat laughed, but Erin was dead serious and stood there waiting until Pat stopped smiling.

"Do you want to know what happened in the flood of '86 or not?" she said. Pat did *not* want to know. He wanted to go upstairs and watch the golf highlights on ESPN. But he just nodded and gripped the handlebars even tighter, as if to relay to Erin that he was ready for whatever ride she was going to take him on with this story. If there had been a seatbelt, he would have buckled up.

"Mervyn's place gets swamped even during light flooding, but this was a big one." She raised her eyebrows for effect. "But Mervyn's out of town on business. Everyone thought he was a drug dealer, so I use the word *business* loosely." She winked at Emily and continued. "Annie thinks she has more time than she does, and she's trying to pack up any stuff of Mervyn's that she thinks is valuable, and while she's doing this, she loses track of the little girl and the dog. Mervyn had a mean old pit, but it was pretty good with kids."

"This doesn't sound good," said Emily.

"It's not good," she said. "The kid and the dog have wandered down to the dock, and they're watching all the debris float by. It doesn't look dangerous, so the little girl is just enjoying the parade of crap and doesn't realize what's going on."

"Wouldn't the dock be submerged in the flood?" asked Pat

"This is just the beginning," she said. "The water hasn't crested yet, but it's raining pretty good, and everyone knows it's going to happen. Except this little kid."

"I don't want to hear a dead kid story tonight, Erin," said Pat. "Let's just go upstairs and eat those cookies."

Erin looked at her watch and said, "Four minutes. If you shut up, I can finish, and then you can jam a bunch of cookies in your mouth and watch your sports."

Pat knew this was a good time to just listen. She was gaining some momentum, and the story would unfurl naturally now without his interruptions.

"So, the kid is out there with an umbrella when Mervyn's lousy old dock gets unmoored. It's one of those ones that sits up on floatation material, so now the kid and the dog are part of the parade, floating down toward Johnson's beach."

"Jesus," said Emily.

"Exactly," said Erin. "I've always thought He played a part in this." She's not leaning on the barrel anymore. She's walking around and using her hands to help create the picture. "The little girl and the dog go for a ride, and Annie has no idea. She thinks the kid is watching *Scooby Doo* in the back room where she left her, but now she's two miles down the river."

She gave time here for Emily to gasp before she said, "This is the good part. Remember Ed Howden?"

Pat and Erin nod.

"Well, he's out in his backyard throwing sandbags on the base of his storage shed, and he hears somebody yell, *Daddy*. So, he turns around and spots his daughter, who he hasn't seen in two months, but the kid is moving at a pretty good pace down the river. She's not crying. She's just waiving and calling her dad."

Pat wanted to call bullshit, but he knew that would just extend this yarn even longer than it already was.

"So, Ed drops his sandbag, tears down the back slope, and jumps in his canoe. He'd just stolen it from *Burke's Canoes* a week before and painted it red, and now he's in it and paddling like a bat out of hell to catch up to his daughter and the dog."

"Holy shit," said Emily. "Please tell me he gets her."

"He does," said Erin. "But not before he does battle with the pit bull that was trying to protect the little girl from this stranger that the dog had never seen before. The dog mangled his hand, but Ed got his kid back."

Pat pulled his leg over the Harley and smiled at Erin. "That's a good one," he said.

Erin must have seen something in his eyes. She said, "Believe it, Pat."

"Cookies ready?" he said.

She looked at her watch, nodded, and started to walk up the stairs. "Believe it," she said again.

~33~

When the girls returned from town, they were late and a bit red in the cheeks, so Emily said, "Everything okay?"

"It is now," said Alice.

"What happened?" said Pat. Slouched down on the couch, he grabbed the remote control and hit the mute button but left *SportsCenter* on.

Grace looked at Alice but said nothing. Alice was shaking her head now. "We got almost all the way across the bridge, but then we saw fire—"

Erin sprang out of the kitchen and shouted, "Fire?"

From the looks on the girls' faces, Emily knew not to panic, but she was curious what was going on and now a little angry that it was after dark, and Pat had specifically told the girls to be back at the house while it was still light.

"Yes and no," said Grace.

"Girls," said Erin as she led them over to the couch and made them sit on either side of Pat, who had slowed down the drinking and looked surprisingly sober at this point, though the back of his hair was standing straight up where he had been leaning back on the couch cushion.

"There was a fire," said Alice. "But it was controlled."

"What do you mean?" said Pat, leaning forward now.

Alice bent forward with him, her elbows on her knees. "It was in a garbage can," she said. "At the end of the bridge where those people hang out sometimes."

"Oh," said Erin, always a little embarrassed by the assortment of bridge folks that they'd encountered over the years. "Did they say anything to you?"

Emily was watching Grace, who looked like she wanted to jump in. "On the way over there," she said. "We saw some people who seemed okay, but on the way back, it was dark, and we couldn't really see who it was, so we didn't go close."

"They were kind of dancing around the fire," said Alice. "So all we could see was this pulsating gang of shadows."

"And some of them had horns," said Grace.

"Huh?" said Pat, over at the bar now, pouring in just two fingers of bourbon. "You mean like trumpets and tubas?"

"No," she said, laughing. "Like horns on their heads, antlers."

"I think they were wearing weird hats," said Alice. "We couldn't really see well from where we were, and, like I said, they were jumping around. And then me and Grace just got out of there."

"Did you just run past?" asked Erin, eyes wide open after the *horns* comment.

"No," said Grace. "We walked all the way back and took the other bridge. That's why we're so late."

"That was a good idea," said Pat.

"Yeah," said Grace. "And I think at least one of them was naked."

"Jesus, Mary, and St. Joseph," said Erin. "It's barely nine o'clock."

"I didn't see any naked people," said Alice. "I think a couple of the men just didn't have shirts on."

"Either way," said Emily. "I'm glad you're home." She didn't like the sound of any of it. These people got screwed up on meth and lost their minds. Who's to say they wouldn't do something violent to a couple of teenage girls?

"We're going out on the back porch for a little," said Alice, as she was pulling on the screen door. Grace followed dutifully.

Once the kids were both sitting on deck chairs facing the river, Pat said, "That was weird. Do you think they made it up so they wouldn't get in trouble for coming home late?"

"Are you drunk?" said Emily.

"I don't know," he said.

"Erin," said Emily. "Did that sound made up to you?"

"Let me tell you something, you guys," she said and sat down where Grace had been sitting. "I don't think these girls are liars."

They sat there for a while, the TV still on mute. Something had been on Emily's mind ever since they'd been sitting down at the dock earlier in the day, and she figured now might be the right time to broach the subject with Erin. "Do you really believe Grace?" she asked.

"Yep," she said after a moment. "Those details about the people at the fire were too specific, and the fact that they didn't agree on everything seemed pretty authentic to me."

Erin had been a junior high English teacher for thirty years and had very good instincts when it came to kids—a human lie detector. But Emily wasn't asking about the fire, and she was pretty sure that Erin knew that.

"I don't mean about the bridge people," she said. "I'm talking about her baby."

"I kinda figured that," she said. "But I'm surprised you're asking me. You all seem very sure of yourselves on this one. You think she's either lying or in some kind of denial, right?"

Pat and Emily both nodded.

"Well, *I* think she's special," said Erin and walked over to a broom closet near the bar. She poked her head in and rearranged some mops and the vacuum cleaner, and then bent down and pulled out a cardboard box. She brought it over, and said, "Move it," to which Pat picked up his drink. Then Erin placed the box on the coffee table.

"What do we got here?" said Pat, smiling a bit now like he did when Erin told her story about Ed Howden and the little girl in the flood.

"I know you already think I'm a little nuts, but this is really strange," she said and started lifting photo albums and framed pictures out and arranging them on the table. "But I needed to show this to someone."

"Okay," said Emily, looking over at Pat. She was ready to give him the evil eye if he started smirking again. They were guests in Erin's house.

"So I had a different box with all this stuff in it on top of the refrigerator in the basement," she said and nodded. "I figured no water could ever get that high. But, as you know, the old thing tipped over in the flood, so when I finally got in and waded through all the muddy water, I found all this stuff floating around with the dead fish and the tree branches."

"It's ruined?" asked Emily. "So sad."

"Yeah, most of it," she said. "But I want you to take a look through that photo album."

Emily pulled the album closer and opened it, and Erin shouted, "Pat, you need to get over here, too."

"Okay," he said and slid in close to Emily.

As they looked through the album, they could see that the photos were mostly of their own family, growing over the years, but the pictures were ruined almost beyond recognition. Emily was squinting to make out what they were doing in the photos, and she found herself remembering, not the moments, but the photos themselves. She'd seen this album before. Alice and Erin in the little boat. Grace sitting on Erin's Harley. The whole family in inner tubes at the annual Jazz and Blues Festival at Johnson's. She loved all those pictures and was sad they were gone. Erin took them the old-fashioned way and didn't have copies.

"Oh," said Emily. "So sad. I loved this album."

"Me, too," said Erin. "But do you notice anything odd about the pictures?"

"I know all these pictures," said Emily. "I never thought there was anything odd about them."

"No," said Erin. "Do you see anything strange about them now in their current state."

She turned the pages again but didn't notice anything except maybe the smell. The album held the earthy perfume of the river. She looked over at Pat, but he was looking at something else, something in one of the frames. "I'm not seeing it," she said.

"Look at your daughter," said Erin. "Grace."

And then she saw it almost immediately. The photos were all ruined. You could barely make out the images. But in some of the shots in which Grace was present—four or five of the pictures from when she was about age six to thirteen—she was clean. The parts of the pictures with her were perfectly clear, like they'd been taken yesterday. You couldn't even see the Harley, but there was beautiful Grace sitting on the blurred form of the motorcycle. You couldn't even tell they were in inner tubes. After the water damage, they were just black smudges, but ten-year-old Grace was as clear as she was when she was standing in this room ten minutes ago. And in one of the group pictures, every person except Grace was unrecognizable because of the water stains. But Grace's face was untouched, as if it had been protected by Vaseline or some kind of waterproof laminate. It didn't make sense. It was weird. Really weird.

But Emily didn't think it necessarily had some kind of *meaning*. "It's pretty strange," she said, still leafing through the album as Pat looked over her shoulder. He was oddly silent through the whole encounter. "It's some kind of fluke," she said and looked back up at Erin, who was standing with her hands on her hips.

"Would you say it's a miracle?" she asked.

"I'll say fluke," said Emily. "Pat?"

"I don't know what the hell it is," he said. "Some kind of crazy photographic anomaly, I guess." He put his hand over his mouth for a moment, and Emily tried to read his eyes. Nothing. "Are there any pictures in there where Grace's image *is* ruined by the water?"

"Some," said Erin.

"See," he said.

Erin folded her arms across her chest, a defensive move. "I think she's special," she said and nodded at the two of them, her mouth closed tight, willful. It almost seemed to Emily like a scolding. As if she and Pat had gotten caught talking in church.

Pat was still holding an old, framed newspaper article that was in the box with the albums. "What are you looking at?" asked Emily, ready to move on to a different topic until she could come up with a legitimate explanation for the pictures.

"The only other thing from the box that didn't get ruined in the flood," he said.

"Yeah?" said Emily.

"It's an old article from the *Stumptown Journal*."

"Is that from up here?"

"Yes," said Erin. "It's not around anymore, but that's the old Guerneville paper from the eighties."

"What's it say?" asked Emily, wondering why Pat seemed to be reading it for the third time now.

"Here's the headline," he said. "*Guerneville Man Reunited with Missing Daughter in Flood*."

"No way," said Emily.

"Believe it," said Erin.

~34~

Alice was in a regular patio chair, and she was watching Grace, who was in an old wooden rocking chair, her toes just barely pushing off the deck so that she was swaying gently, forward and back, in the warm river night.

They were both looking across the water at the dock connected to the Guerneville Lodge. A couple of families had set up tiki torches and a limbo stick. They were listening to Harry Bellefonte, and everyone was taking a try at limbo.

Grace was smiling.

"What are you thinking about?" asked Alice.

"Nothing," she said, and Alice thought she could see the torches dancing in Grace's eyes.

"C'mon," said Alice. "You're smiling about something. Did you really think you saw naked people at that bonfire?"

"That's not what I'm thinking about!"

"Did you?"

"I thought I did," she said. "That whole thing was so weird. They must've been on drugs."

"Most definitely," said Alice, looking across at one of the dads, totally cheating at limbo. The little kids were pointing at him and screaming, and he was pretending that he'd made it under, even though he clearly moved the stick with his hand. "What *were* you thinking about?" she asked turning her attention back to her sister.

"I'm thinking about how Erin believes me," she said. "I think Erin and this girl I met online are the only two people in the world who believe me."

"A girl you met online?"

"Yeah," she said. "The same thing is happening to her, and she says there's others."

"Other girls who have supposed virgin pregnancies?"

"You see," said Grace. "You said *supposed.* Sophia never says *supposed.*" She pushed hard with her feet to get the chair rocking, and then she pulled her feet up under her, held them with her hands, and let gravity do its work.

"I didn't mean it," said Alice, feeling really bad now. "I know you want me to be on your team, and I am. And I'm not saying you're lying. But I think something happened to you, and for some reason, you can't remember it happening or you didn't ever know it happened to you, or your mind is so traumatized by it, that it won't let you recall any of it. Like your brain's trying to protect you."

Grace was still curled up on the old chair, and the rocking was slowing back to a gentle sway that Grace was controlling by shifting her weight slightly. She was looking over toward the family at the lodge, and she said, "What do you think happened to me, Alice?"

Alice was looking at the tiki torches dancing in Grace's eyes again, but Grace was staring blankly across the river. Alice didn't know what to say. In fact, her mom was going to be pissed that she was getting into this without a therapist or one of her parents there to moderate. She wasn't equipped to say the right things. But she wanted to help her sister. Grace's eyes were wet, but she wasn't crying. She was shimmering.

"What do you think happened to me, Alice?" she said again.

"I don't know," she said.

"Do you think I was raped?" she asked.

"Tell me about the girl you met online," said Alice. She could feel herself shaking a little bit and heard her voice falter. This was an obvious deflection, but she was hoping Grace would just let the conversation roll in that direction before either of them said something that would ruin this otherwise wonderful day.

Grace glanced at Alice for a moment before turning her attention back to the dock on the other side of the river. The dad who'd cheated at limbo was holding a little boy by the feet and dangling him out over the water. The kid was screaming and laughing at the same time. "Sophia from Oxnard," she said.

"Huh?"

"Her name is Sophia Martini, and she lives in Oxnard."

"Oxnard?" said Alice. "How did you guys find each other?"

Grace got up and stood in front of the railing. She rested her forearms on the splintery two-by-four and then rested her chin on her forearm. Her voice sounded different when she said, "We were both on the same message board about teen pregnancy."

"Do you trust this person?" said Alice. "Because there's a lot of crazy people out there."

"I guess," said Grace. "Y'know, we both have *supposed* virgin pregnancies."

Alice didn't reply.

"I trust Erin," said Grace and spun around to go back inside.

Alice kept her eyes on the tiki torches as she listened to the screen door rattle behind her.

***

The good thing about Aunt Erin's was that she had four bedrooms, so Grace got her own room. The other good thing about Aunt Erin's was that she had excellent Wi-Fi despite being out here in the sticks.

Grace hadn't talked to Sophia in weeks, but she felt like she wanted to DM her tonight. Back around the time of the coyote, Sophia had told Grace that the safest way to handle the situation was to avoid any mention of the fact that she was a virgin. The reasoning was that it would be a mess. People would think she was a mental case.

Sophia was only a few weeks away from delivering her baby. She hadn't posted any new pictures since the two of them had first started talking, but that made sense. Since Grace's belly started to swell, she stopped posting pictures as well. For Grace, it was still a secret. They hadn't even decided what to do about school yet, though Grace wanted to start the school year with her class and be at St. Mary's right up until she had the baby. The family was still forming a plan. Her dad still needed to work this out with Ms. Daly. But that was what Grace wanted to do.

Sophia had stopped attending school but planned to get her GED after she got settled with the baby.

Grace was curious to see how Sophia was doing this close to her due date.

How are you feeling?

I'm about to burst. I'm as big as a house, and my back is killing me, but I'm ready.

Are you expecting anything unique in the delivery room?

Grace wasn't sure how to ask the question. This was not a normal birth or a normal baby. It was a miracle, so what happens in the hospital when a miracle baby comes into the world?

Do you mean am I expecting angels to come down and pull the baby out of me?

No! Haha! I'm just wondering if you think it will be like all the other babies who are born that day.

Trust me. Both of our babies are going to come out just like all the other babies.

How do you know?

Not to get too religious, but Jesus was born in a barn.

She was right, of course. And that was fine. Grace didn't want anything special to happen when her baby was born. She just wanted the baby to be healthy. That's what everyone wants. But she also thought it was their duty to recognize the fact that these two babies were special.

Yeah, but Jesus also had three kings come visit him in that barn.

Haha! That's true.

So you'll tell me if any kings show up?

Absolutely! Haha!

Grace liked the fact that Sophia sounded so relaxed only weeks before she would be bringing a new person into the world. She seemed happy, and that was good. She should be happy. Grace was nervous, but she wasn't sad. She was curious why she had been chosen, but she wasn't angry.

Well, good luck. Hopefully, we'll talk before your day, but if we don't, I want to thank you for supporting me through this.

Thanks, Grace. I love you.

Maybe the hormones were affecting her. Sophia was never the mushy type. *I love you*? That didn't really sound like her friend. But it was nice. Grace knew she would sleep well tonight.

Love you, too!

~35~

Pat knew he'd put this meeting off too long, so he was glad to be sitting in Jenny's office with Emily and Grace. Jenny knew the situation, but they had to go over some of the details.

Summer school had ended last week, so the campus was a ghost town except for the Finance Office and Jenny.

Jenny's office was unadorned except for a portrait of the Blessed Mother behind her desk and large bookshelves on the two walls that didn't have windows. The bookshelves had many volumes on educational theory, but the shelves were also crammed with contemporary fiction. Pat knew she read a book a week, so she was constantly rotating out books and replacing them with her newest favorites. Her window looked out on the St. X campus. In fact, Pat could see his own office window if he leaned back in his chair, which he did.

"What? Are you a twelve-year-old?" asked Jenny. "You're gonna break that chair."

"Pat," said Emily.

"Sorry," he said and saw Grace try to stifle a smile. "That's my office next to the two trees and …" He felt all three women looking at him, so he let the rest of the sentence drift off into the stacks of books with the other more meaningful compendia.

Jenny had a couch and two chairs in front of her desk and the four of them were sitting around a small table as if they were equals at this summit. Jenny probably organized the room this way so that the group didn't feel like this was some kind of disciplinary matter with the Principal sitting in the big chair behind the desk. But even Pat felt a little nervous being in another Principal's office.

"So, let's get right to it," said Jenny. "Are you at about five or six months?" She was looking directly at Grace rather than having the parents answer for the child.

"Almost six," said Grace.

"And the baby will come sometime in October or early November?"

"That's right," said Grace, confident, even smiling. Proud?

"Okay," said Jenny. "Then today is just a way for us to sit together and go over the options and figure out which ones will be best for you and your family. I know this is a very challenging time for you guys, so I'm here to help."

"Thank you, Ms. Daly," she said.

Pat's mind jumped the tracks at this point. He didn't know why it hit him just now, but he suddenly felt very sad for Jenny. She was just past her childbearing years, and he wondered if she regretted never having children. She was so wonderful with kids that it would seem natural for her to have some pangs of longing for a child of her own, but here she was dealing with one of her freshmen, who was about to have a child, yet it seemed that she would never have one. Pat also knew that Jenny would hate him for even thinking these thoughts.

"Pat?" said Emily.

"I'm here," he said. "Just thinking over the options."

Emily raised her eyebrows at Jenny, who smiled and said, "The first option is that Grace begin school in a few weeks with the rest of her classmates, and when she gets really close to her due date—that should be after quarter break—she takes a leave, and we figure out a way to get her caught up before the second semester starts."

"That's what I want to do," said Grace.

"Okay," said Jenny. "Then let's look at the possible challenges." She got up out of her seat and took a few steps back to grab a hardcover notebook off her desk. She returned to her chair, put on her reading glasses, and flipped through pages until she found what she was looking for. "Ah, here we go," she said. "Being on leave while you have a broken leg or mono is one thing. You would still be able get your assignments online and get your work done. But being on leave while taking care of a baby is something entirely different. Do you think you're ready for that?"

Grace didn't rush her answer. She was thinking.

Before she responded, Jenny asked, "Unless you're planning on putting the child up for adoption. In that case—"

"No!" Grace blurted. And then in a more subdued tone, "I think I'm supposed to keep this baby."

"Okay," said Jenny, smiling. Keeping things very warm. She was a natural problem solver, and she was going to get this done. "If you're keeping the baby, it's going to be really tough to do the first option." Jenny stopped. She wasn't smiling now. She closed her eyes for a moment. She was problem solving. "But I think we can make it work. We can waive a couple of St. Mary's requirements that aren't required by the UC system. At the very least we can drop P.E." Then she stopped again and closed her eyes. "We can have you do project-based assessments for a few classes." Then she flipped some pages in the notebook and read for a moment before saying, "But I think you'll need to do at least your math through an online course, and you might want to skip language for sophomore year and then pick it up for your junior and senior years. Do you take Spanish?"

"No," said Grace. "Latin."

"Even better," said Jenny. "That will be easier to pick up after a year off, but you'll have to do some review next summer to make sure that you're not too far behind for Latin II."

"So, you think it's doable?" said Pat.

"Those are the things I can do," said Jenny. "But you guys have to decide if your family can handle it." She was looking right at Emily now. "I know Alice won't be around much to help, so it will really be just you three, and you know better than I how much work a newborn can be."

Pat thought he saw just a hint of pain when she said it, but he probably imagined it. Emily and Grace were nodding.

Emily said, "I'm going to take a leave of absence for a few months. Pat's sister, Erin, is going to come down and live with us for a while, and my mom has said that she'd like to help out as much as she can."

"That's great that grandma can help," said Jenny.

"It'll actually be great-grandma," said Pat.

There was a moment of confusion before Jenny said, "Of course! Even better."

Pat knew that Grace wanted to try to stay in her class and graduate on time, but he thought she should listen to the other options as well. "What about Plan B?" said Pat.

"Right," said Jenny. "Another option is to simply take this coming year off of school and spend it with your baby. You could come back the following year as a sophomore."

In Pat's mind, this was certainly a viable option. Who cared if she graduated at eighteen or nineteen? In the wider scheme of things, did it really matter?

"I know that one makes sense," said Grace. "But here's why I'd prefer to stay on track." She was just barely sitting on the edge of the couch, and her posture was perfect. While wearing her jacket, you'd never know she was pregnant. "For me to care for this child, I'm going to have to set up a routine that allows me to continue with school. If I don't get an education, I'll never reach my potential as a mother, and my baby will suffer for it." She sounded a bit like she was giving an oral presentation for one of her classes, but everyone in the room was listening. "For at least the next seven years, I'll be attending school, so I don't know why I'd wait a year to start that routine. I think it's best to begin as soon as possible. If anything, I think I'd prefer to do that gap year between high school and college rather than now."

"I see," said Jenny, still warm. "If your family is willing to help you, I'm willing to help as well."

"By the time I finish high school," said Grace. "My baby will be three. If I take a gap year after graduation to take care of him, then I'll be able to go to SF State or USF, and I can work my school schedule around my child's pre-school schedule, and I won't have to rely so much on mom and dad and Alice if she comes back to San Francisco after graduation."

"Well," said Jenny. "It sounds like you've got it all figured out."

"I know it's just a plan, and things don't always work out," she said. "But I'd like to try." She paused for a moment before she said, "And I know how lucky I am to have parents who are supporting me through this." Her voice broke just a bit at the end, but she pulled it back together and nodded as if to say *That is the end of my presentation.*

"How about the father and the other set of grandparents?" said Jenny. "Will they be helping as well?"

Pat had told Jenny the whole story, and they'd discussed it many times, so he was surprised that she asked this question. Maybe she was trying to trap Grace into revealing the father.

But Emily intervened before they could find out. "Grace believes that this child was conceived without a father," she said, her cheeks flush as she reached over to hold Grace's hand.

"Yes," said Jenny. "Pat had told me that months ago. I didn't know if you'd remembered anything since then."

Grace just smiled and shook her head.

"The other options of doing only online coursework for a year or transferring to a different school don't seem to be in the mix here," said Jenny. "So, I'll just ask you to do a few things before we start in a few weeks. Is that okay?"

"Yes," said Grace at the same moment that Emily was saying, "Fine."

"Okay," said Jenny. "First, I'd like you to talk to a therapist friend of mine who has helped many girls get through difficult challenges while they were students at St. Mary's."

"You mean Ms. De Castro?" asked Grace.

"No," said Jenny. "This isn't a school counselor. It's someone I trust very much who is in private practice."

"Oh, okay," said Grace.

"And second," said Jenny. "Your dad has to go check in with the Archbishop or the Vicar or the Superintendent to make sure this plan is okay with the Archdiocese. He probably should have done this months ago."

"I'll make an appointment today," he said. He could feel Emily's eyes penetrating him, and he was not happy that Jenny had thrown him under the bus on this. However, in Jenny's defense, she'd told him to set up the meeting at least three separate times.

"The last thing, Grace." Jenny said. "Is that you need to be ready for however these girls are going to treat you when you're at school. It might not all be supportive. I don't believe we've ever had a pregnant girl at St. Mary's before, and the girls might not know how they feel about it."

"I'm ready," she said, but to Pat, she looked tired. Like she needed a nap.

Grace

More and more, the lady has been sitting behind me when we talk, but today we are walking down a narrow path in a forest, and she's in front of me, leading. The sun slants down in beams between the branches. It feels like afternoon, comfortable. The path itself is smooth dirt, no tree roots or rocks or gopher holes on which to stumble, and when there are branches or ivy obstructing the path, the lady pushes them away so that it's easy to pass.

"Not much longer," she says.

"Where are we going?" I say.

Her voice is clear, sounds like it's coming to Grace through ear buds. "To the end," she says.

The dust particles in the rays of sunlight look like tiny dancing fairies, but as we get into the denser sections of the forest, it's dark and cool. It almost feels as if we're walking in a cave, but it's really just a thick canopy of branches and leaves, moving gently in the breeze. The forest almost looks like its breathing.

We've walked a long way, but I'm not tired. I don't mind that she isn't talking much today, but I decide to break the silence with a riddle. "How long can you walk into the forest?" I ask.

The lady is quiet for a few steps before she replies, "Half-way. Then you're walking out *of the forest."*

"Ah, you know that one," I say.

She keeps walking the same pace and doesn't turn around. "I know all of them," she says.

"You know every riddle?" I ask, incredulous now, as we start up a somewhat steep grade with sandier soil.

"I know all the ones you know," she says and keeps her constant stride despite the fact that the sand and the hill are making me slide backward with every step.

I focus my attention on the ground and try to step in her footprints to get more traction. And it works. My foot fits perfectly, and the tamped down sand makes for easier walking. "Is there anything I know that you don't know?" I ask.

She likes to pause before answering my questions, so I just keep watching the ground, using my natural stride to step directly into her footmarks and then springing out as we approach the top of this rise. When she doesn't answer after a few paces, I look up, but she's gone. I'm still about ten feet from the crest, so I assume that she's just on the other side. However, when I get to the top, she's not there.

It's a cliff. Nowhere to go except back through the tracks I took to get here.

~36~

Pat went to meetings at The Chancery a few times a year, but those were all with the Superintendent of Catholic Schools, as well as the other principals and presidents of local archdiocesan schools. Today, he was here alone to meet with the Archbishop, himself. The only other time he'd had a one-on-one with His Excellency occurred years ago when Pat interviewed for his current job.

Pat really liked the man.

But this time, Pat was meeting with Archbishop Dolan to talk about Pat's pregnant daughter. It was difficult to think of a more embarrassing topic than this one.

When people hear about *The Chancery* they tend to think of an old gothic building with tall ceilings and stained-glass windows. Statues. Candles. The whole nine yards. But the Chancery in San Francisco is new. It's an oddly shaped office building downtown, on a sneaky street called Peter Yorke Way, tucked between Geary, Gough, Franklin, and Post. If you live in the city, you've passed by it a thousand times but probably never knew it was there.

Pat parked down at The Cathedral and walked up to the Chancery, rehearsing his lines the whole way. When he got there, they buzzed him in and told him that the Archbishop would be right with him. While he sat in the lobby, he picked up a copy of *Catholic San Francisco Weekly* and skimmed through some articles about priests who had passed away, an organist who played at two parishes, immigration as a moral issue, and the Mercy sisters celebrating jubilees. The same old ads adorned the bottoms of the pages: death services—hospice care, mortuaries, and cemeteries—and senior living, Irish help at home, Catholic cruises. Between Pat's and Emily's families, he'd patronized all these businesses except for the cruise line.

After about ten minutes, the receptionist told him to go on up. Although most of the rooms looked like they could be in an insurance building or a law office, the Archbishop's was different. While the other offices were sterile and plastic, his Excellency's was all mahogany and leather.

Pat knocked on the door as he was opening it. When he looked inside, the Archbishop was sitting on a small wooden chair in the middle of the room across from another wooden chair about two feet away. No table in between. All the beautiful furniture and curtains and scents seemed to surround them. "Patrick!" he said. "Please sit."

Pat pointed at the small chair across from the Archbishop, who nodded. Pat sat down, his knees nearly touching His Excellency's. They were in this enormous space together, but Pat was close enough to see the pores on the man's nose.

"So, it looks like you're in a bit of a pickle, Pat."

"I am," he said.

"What is it I can help you with?"

Pat really just wanted the Archbishop to tell him it was cool if Gracie wanted to continue to attend school while she was pregnant. That was the decision they'd made with Jenny's blessing, so it would happen if the Archbishop gave it the okay.

"As you know," said Pat. "My girl is pregnant out of wedlock, and she's a student at St. Mary's. We would like to keep her in school, but we wanted to ask your permission, especially since I'm principal across the street at St. X."

Jenny told Pat that she'd already talked to the Archbishop about this complicated scenario, but today His Excellency looked almost surprised by the query.

"Has she confessed her sin?" he asked, hand on his chin like an old professor.

For some reason, Pat wasn't ready for this question, so he started with, "Um." The Archbishop did not look intimidating. It did not seem that he was trying to ask a trick question. He was generally concerned about whether or not Grace was prepared to seek reconciliation for what she had done. However, the question had stumped Pat, and he was still trying to formulate an answer.

"Patrick?" he asked.

"Yes," he said. "Still here." Then a terrible fake laugh before, "This is tricky because Grace does not believe that she has sinned."

"Pat," said the Archbishop. "If she doesn't believe that pre-marital sex is a sin then—"

"It's not that," Pat blurted. "She very much believes in the teachings of the church." He scratched his head now. He must have been starting to perspire although the room was cool and dry. "But Gracie has no recollection of ever being with a boy. She doesn't believe that she has ever had sexual intercourse, so it's going to be hard for her to repent for her sin."

"Pat," said the Archbishop and then put his hands together in front of his lips like a small child does when he says his nighttime prayers on his knees next to his bed. "Patrick," he mumbled under his breath and closed his eyes the way Jenny had done in her office when she was trying to provide the best options for Grace.

"We've tried to get her to tell us how this happened," said Pat, but she has stuck with this story for nearly six months."

"Has she talked to anyone else about it?" he asked.

"She's spoken to Jenny Daly," said Pat.

"How about a professional?"

"She had several sessions with a therapist," said Pat.

"And?"

"The therapist says she's a perfectly sane teenaged girl," said Pat. "No depression or bi-polar or schizophrenia or anything like that."

"So just the denial?" said the Archbishop.

"Yes," said Pat, frustrated by the thought that he and Emily and Cindy couldn't prompt a breakthrough in all this time. "But Jenny Daly has given us the name of a different therapist that we're going to try next week."

"Do you think your daughter might just be lying?" he asked.

"Your Excellency," said Pat. "She doesn't really have any reason to lie at this point. She knows we don't believe that this is a virgin pregnancy, and we've loved and supported her through the entire ordeal. We can't figure out a motive for her to continue to lie. It's only made things more difficult for everyone."

The Archbishop shook his head slowly back and forth, but his eyes remained on Pat's. "I'd be more comfortable with her coming back to school if she recognized her sin and attended a reconciliation service."

"I understand," said Pat. Pat would be more comfortable as well.

"Let's see if the new therapist can help her, and then she can get on with the business of her contrition and her new life in Christ."

~37~

Grace liked Cindy a lot, and Cindy really helped her get through those first months of the pregnancy. But, apparently, Ms. Daly gave Grace's mom and dad the name of a different therapist to help with the transition back into school, which was only a few weeks away.

The office was in very familiar territory for Grace: West Portal. In fact, it was in the same building as Grace's orthodontist's office, right next door to *Squat and Gobble* and across the street from *Lemonade*. A streetcar was screeching its way into the tunnel just as she entered the building with her mom and dad.

It felt kind of weird for Grace to walk by Dr. Walton's office. She felt like she wanted to go in and show him that she'd been wearing her retainer. Unlike Alice, whose teeth were already getting crooked again.

But she didn't do it. The therapist's office was down at the other end of the hallway. The door didn't even have a nameplate. It was just a plain door with the number 12 on a frosted glass square to the right of the trim. She put her hand on the doorknob, but before she could turn it, her dad said, "Wait."

Grace let go of the knob as if it were on fire. "What?" she said, angry that her dad had waited until now to say whatever he had to say. She was nervous enough without him playing games.

"Sorry," he said. "I just want to warn you that Jenny said this guy might seem a little eccentric."

"What does that mean?" said Grace.

Her mom said, "Like quirky ... a little weird."

"No. I know what the word means, mom," she said. "I'm asking what *kind* of weird? Is he going to be wearing a wizard's hat or ask me to sit on the floor? What are we talking about here?" She was anxious and was surprised how much she sounded like her dad when she was in this state.

Grace was looking at him now, but he was looking up at the ceiling. "It doesn't matter," he said. "I don't know. I'm just saying he might be different from Cindy." He paused for a moment and then said, "But maybe he's not."

"He's not what?" asked Grace, but it was too late. Her dad was opening the door.

The waiting room looked like a normal waiting room—some magazines on display on a coffee table, more magazines on a wall rack, plain cushioned chairs lining three of the walls. A man sitting in one of the chairs reading *Sports Illustrated.* No fish tank. And also, no receptionist window. In fact, there was seemingly no door leading to a back office either.

Her dad sat down and examined the magazine selection on the coffee table, but Grace and her mom just stood there for a moment, looking at each other. Her mom said, "I think this is the wrong office," and started to move toward the door.

The man reading the magazine closed it and said, "This Serena Williams is really something, huh?"

In the few seconds they were in the room, Grace had almost forgotten that he was there. He had curly hair that was too long, a messy beard, and a pair of wire-rimmed glasses that nobody really wears anymore. "She won a grand slam event while she was pregnant!" he said and smiled like this was one of the greatest things he'd ever heard.

Grace's mom said, "Oh, were you reading an article on Serena?"

"No," he said. "Just thinking about her. Amazing woman."

Grace thought this was funny and laughed a little bit even though her mom seemed very confused still.

"You all must be the Ryans," he said, rising and extending his hand toward Grace. "H.P. Cooper, but all my clients call me Coop." They shook hands, and Grace had to tilt her head back to look into the man's eyes. He had to be at least six foot five, maybe taller, but really skinny. His hand had long, slender fingers that made her feel tiny, but they were smooth and dry.

"H.P. Cooper," he said to Grace's mom as he extended his hand to her.

"Nice to meet you, Coop," she said. "Emily."

Grace's dad was still sitting, looking around, like he'd landed in one of Willie Wonka's factory rooms and was afraid he was going to be baited into doing something stupid and getting kicked out.

"You're Jenny's pal, right," said Coop to Grace's dad from across the room.

"I am," he said and finally got up. "Are we actually in the office?" He was still looking around but standing very still like he thought he might step through a trap door if he moved. "Or is this like a waiting room, and we have to go back outside to find the office?"

"No, no," said Coop. "This is it, but I don't really use it except to wait for people to show up. Parents wait in here, but I usually walk with the clients. It's just how I work."

"Got it," he said, and then her dad did something weird with his mouth that Grace had never seen before. The corners of his lips turned down just slightly as if to say, *Okay, buddy, but I'm watching you.*

"So, are you up for a walk, Grace?" said Coop.

"Sure," she said.

Coop then looked at Grace's mom and said, "You guys can either wait here or go get some coffee or ice cream across the street. We should be about an hour." He looked at his watch. "That should get us back here around five. That okay?"

"That's fine," said Grace's mom. Her dad nodded and did the thing with his mouth again.

***

"What the hell was that?" said Pat as soon as the door had closed.

"Pat, be quiet," Emily yell-whispered and walked over to the door. She opened it, peaked out, and then closed it again. She had a thing about whispering when they were talking about other people even when the people were in different houses or in cars with the windows closed or in other countries.

"Guy looked like skinny Hagrid," said Pat.

"I was thinking Joaquin Phoenix when he went crazy for a while."

"Good call," said Pat. "But way taller."

"Do you want to wait here?" she asked. "Or go somewhere for a while?"

"I only like to wait in waiting rooms when there's an actual office somewhere," he said. "This is bizarre."

"Okay," she said. "How about the Dubliner for one?"

"Really?" he said and looked at his watch. Just past four. A lot of the regulars would be there. They all knew Emily, but she didn't make many appearances except when she picked him up, or when they went in for a drink before seeing a movie up at the Empire.

"Sure," she said. "It'll take us a few minutes to walk down there, and then we can have a beer and make it back before they're done."

The smells on that side of the street were familiar. *Squat and Gobble* and then the pizza place and then popcorn wafting out the open door of the theater.

"Do you think this guy will help her?" asked Emily.

"No idea," he said. "But it'll be different than the Cindy sessions."

"If Coop gets her to realize who the dad is, then what?"

"After I beat the kid up," he said, "then we can move on, and if the kid is still alive, Grace will at least know who the father is."

"C'mon, Pat."

"Fine," he said. "But Grace should know who the dad is."

"Will that make it better?"

"Are you just playing devil's advocate?" he asked as they walked past the Wells Fargo, and Pat nodded to the security guard waving a car into the parking lot.

"No," said Emily. "I'd like to know why you think things will be better."

"It's better because kids should know who their dads are," he said. "That's why it's better." He looked over at her, but she was looking at the street.

"Let's cross here," she said, and they jaywalked toward the Walgreen's, simultaneously jumping the low divider in between the streetcar tracks. Every time Pat jumped that curb, he remembered tripping over it during a fistfight when he was in his early twenties. He was winning, but he was back peddling because there were two guys, and then wham! He was flat on his ass, and the two guys kicked the crap out of him.

It was hard to judge Grace when he'd done so many really stupid things in his own life.

"Would it be that bad if we never found out?" she asked.

"I guess it wouldn't be any worse," he said, and paused outside the door to the Dubliner to let Emily step in first.

There was a pretty good crew sitting around the corner near the entrance. When they saw Emily, they let out a loud cheer as if she were a favorite regular or a celebrity. When Pat walked in behind her, they all booed.

***

Coop led her across the street toward *Sub Center* and *Burrito Loco* tucked in next to the station entrance, and then they crossed the street again in front of the tunnel and over both sets of tracks before taking a right at the library and walking up Lenox toward the park and the middle school.

It was mostly small talk for these first few minutes. Coop asked about the coyote incident. He'd seen the YouTube video and recognized her as soon as she came into the office. He was cool about it, though. He didn't push too hard for details.

Then, just as they were passing the library, he said, "So let's get to it."

"Okay," said Grace.

"Lemme make sure I have this straight," he said. "You're almost six months pregnant. Your parents want you to tell them who the father is. But you're a virgin, so, technically, there is no father. You're going to start school in a few weeks. People will be asking questions. You need to have a strategy. Is that about it?"

He was tall, so he took long strides, but he wasn't moving fast. Grace was keeping pace as they made their way up the hill toward Taraval Street. "In a nutshell," said Grace, happy that this guy seemed to be cutting through the bullshit.

"Great," he said. "So please bear with me. I have a few questions before we get to a strategy."

"Okay," said Grace as she peeked over at the park. It was foggy and a little wet, so she didn't expect to see anyone, but there they were.

Max and Jill.

Because it was wet, they weren't sitting on the grass like the three of them usually did. They were sitting on the bench on the far side near the chain link fence. It was pretty far away, but she recognized Jill's jacket and Max's hair.

Coop had been talking for a few moments, but Grace missed it because she was so surprised that her two friends were together and had left her out. She caught only a couple of Coop's words—*lying* and *forgot.*

"I'm sorry," she said. "Can you repeat that?"

"Sure," he said. "Are you all right?"

"Yeah," she said. "I just saw a couple of my friends at the park, and my mind started to wander."

"Do you want them to see you?" he asked.

"No," she said.

"Okay, just stay on this side of me," he said and made sure that she was camouflaged by his skinny frame.

"Thanks."

"So, have people accused you of lying about all this or suggested that you have some memory loss perhaps associated with trauma?"

"Yes," said Grace. "All that."

"But you're not lying and don't believe that you have memory loss?"

"No," she said. "And no memory loss."

"Got it," he said and looked over to where Jill and Max were sitting on the bench. They weren't sitting close, but they were leaning in, like they were telling each other secrets. Grace wondered if they were talking about her. Coop turned back toward Grace and said, "How do you know that you don't have memory loss?"

"Oh," she said and laughed. "You're right. How does anyone know? I guess I could have forgotten something, but I'm not aware of it."

"If you were aware of it, then you'd probably be able to remember."

"Right," she said, her head spinning a little bit.

"Do you believe that you're special, a chosen one, who's carrying out a miracle?"

Grace had to think about it. She didn't like the word miracle because it sounded religious, and she didn't want to sound too religious because she'd seen a lot of people lately treating overly religious people like they were crazy. And Grace wasn't crazy.

"I don't think *I'm* special," she said finally. "I think the *baby's* special."

Coop didn't look at her, but she could see he was smiling. "But don't you have to think of yourself as at least a little special, if you've been picked to be involved in the miracle."

She quickly answered this time. "I guess," she said. "But I don't want to sound like I'm cocky or like I think I'm better than other people. I really don't think that."

"Well, if you care about what a weird, skinny old guy thinks," he said. "You don't come off as that kind of person."

They had passed the park now and were at West Portal School. Grace was happy that Coop said that. She knew there would be girls at her own school who would think she was on her high horse, and they'd want to knock her down, but she just wanted to try to be as normal as possible and not cause a commotion.

"So how do you think I should handle school?" she said.

"I think it's actually quite simple," he said. "When people ask you about your pregnancy, you have to be very consistent. You can have only one answer, always. No variations, or people will try to pick at the inconsistencies and try to expose you as a liar or a lunatic."

"Okay," she said, feeling nervous all of sudden. "That makes sense. But what's the answer?"

"The answer to what?" he said as they moved up Taraval and walked toward the turnabout.

Grace looked over at him to see if he was messing with her. "The answer when people ask me about the baby."

"Oh," he said, as they approached the corner and started to walk down Claremont back toward West Portal. "I think you just say, *I consider it a really personal family matter, and I promised my parents I wouldn't talk about it with anyone.* Then just leave it at that." He nodded down at her and looked pretty confident in his answer. "It's a totally boring response," he said. "So, if you just keep on saying it over and over again, high school kids will get bored with you and move on."

"Okay," she said, thinking that it sounded as reasonable as anything she'd considered. Her parents and Alice would probably support this approach. "Now are you going to try to get me to remember an event that may or may not have happened six months ago?"

"Haven't they been trying that for six months?" he said.

"Yeah."

"Then I'm not going to waste your time," he said. "Unless you think I can help you remember something."

"I know you can't," she said.

"Then let's just focus on making sure you're feeling okay about everything that's happening to you."

"Okay," she said, and then just blurted out, "Do you believe me?" She really thought he might.

"No, probably I don't," he said. "But who cares? I'm a natural skeptic. Most people won't believe you. But I still think I can help you."

"Sounds good," she said, somewhat taken aback by his honesty but also impressed by it. "Do you mind if we talk about my two best friends a little bit?"

"Fire away."

~38~

It was Grace's turn to take Sully out. The Ryans had a schedule.

When Grace asked Alice to accompany her on the afternoon dog walk, Alice didn't really want to go. She was tired. But she was really trying to support Grace as much as she could now that Grace's body was changing so fast. Also, ever since the river trip, there was a part of Alice that believed Grace's condition might actually be some kind of supernatural phenomenon, and Alice didn't want the bad mojo of being a virgin birth denier of her own sister. Also, Grace had told her that the therapist had made her walk during their session earlier in the day. Alice felt bad that Grace would have to walk again.

Alice said she'd go on the walk with her. In fact, Alice said she'd just do it herself, but Grace wanted to come with her.

When they neared the ramp on Buena Vista West, Alice asked, "Is this the first time you've been back since the coyote?"

"That was months ago, Alice," she said.

"I know, but I thought maybe you'd be scared to go up in here and that you'd been just take him down to the dog park at Corona Heights."

"I like it here," she said.

"Me, too," said Alice. "People down at the dog park always want to talk. Just because I have a dog, and someone else has a dog, doesn't mean we're supposed to have a conversation about dogs."

"C'mon, Alice. Some of those people are nice."

"Yeah," said Alice. "I'm just saying. Just because me and some other person both have cars or lawn mowers or big screen TV's, that doesn't mean we're automatically supposed to be friends and have to talk to each other."

"You're nuts," she said.

"Seriously," said Alice. "Two people owning dogs should not be a conversation starter. *You do your thing, and I'll do mine, dude.*"

"Okay," said Grace. "That's healthy."

She sounded like a sarcastic psychiatrist chiding a stubborn patient.

"How was the new therapist?" said Alice as they reached the top of the long grade, and Sully took off to the patch of grass just around the turn.

"Weird," she said and threw the tennis ball to Sully, who caught it in his mouth after one bounce and ran back toward the sisters, where he dropped the ball at Grace's feet. She picked it up and threw it again. There were no other dogs up there this late in the afternoon.

"Did he help you remember anything?" asked Alice.

"Didn't even try," said Grace, who picked up the ball again and started walking toward the coyote path. "I ended up talking to him a little bit about Max and Jill."

"Why them?" said Alice as they walked right past the spot where the coyote licked Grace's hand. Grace didn't even pause or seem to notice where they were.

"Um," she started. "Well, the therapist and I actually saw them when we were walking past West Portal Park."

"Yeah?"

"They were sitting on a bench together."

"And?"

"Well," she said. "I wonder if they're like dating now or something since I'm probably not going to be able to hang out as much anymore."

Alice and Grace were in the shadows now as they moved to the paved walkway under the tallest trees in the park. On the right, there was a *Don't Feed the Coyotes* sign, and on the left, a steep slope covered by low ground cover. Alice pretended to examine the sign even though she'd seen it a hundred times. She felt like she knew the coyote in the photograph. Sully barked once at the sign and kept trotting down the path.

"I talked to those guys together once," said Alice. "And they didn't seem to have that kind of relationship. It seemed like Max had a mad crush on you, and Jill knew it."

"Maybe," said Grace. "But things are different now."

"Yeah," said Alice. "But I think you guys will all still be friends no matter what."

"Hopefully," said Grace and then jogged down the hill after Sully, who was now rolling on his back in the high grass at the bottom of the hill. For some reason he liked to do this in the most disgusting possible places—in stale puddles, on dead vermin, in mounds of fertilizer.

Today, they were lucky. It was a gopher hole. Grace had to wipe some soil off of Sully's black coat, but nothing too gross today.

As they navigated the curve at the bottom of the path, they were treated to one of the great views in the city. It was overcast, but St. Ignatius Church, Lone Mountain, and the Golden Gate Bridge were still bursting out of the sightline with the dark, rolling hills of the Marin Headlands in the background. It was awesome, and Alice always paused to look.

"The church looks the coolest," said Grace.

"Hard to beat the bridge," said Alice, who always loved bridges and was spoiled in the bay area, where they were all over the place. Bridges connected things but they also took you places. She only had a few weeks before she left for school. She'd be driving in the only direction that didn't require her to cross a bridge—straight down the coast. "You know, I won't be that far away," she said.

"Huh?"

"When I'm in San Louis Obispo," she said. "It's actually pretty close."

"Can we talk every day?"

"Yes, ma'am."

"And you'll come up when I'm having the baby?"

"Of course," she said.

"I'm pretty sure Max and Jill will be there for me, too."

"I can guarantee it," said Alice. "Especially Jilly-bean. You guys have known each other forever."

"I wonder how Sophia's doing?" she asked as they moved toward the rotting wooden stairs that would lead them back to the street.

"Sophia who?" asked Alice.

"The girl I met online who's also having a baby that doesn't have a dad."

"There are lots of girls like that," said Alice.

"You know what I mean," said Grace. "She got pregnant without having sex."

"When's she due?" said Alice, not trusting this Sophia person at all.

"Like within the next few weeks."

Grace was watching her footing on the old steps, but Alice could see she was smiling. She seemed genuinely excited for her online friend, but Alice's instinct was to protect Grace. "Maybe this girl's for real. But maybe she's not," said Alice. "That's all I have to say."

"She's been helping me, Alice."

"I'm glad about that," she said and whistled for Sully to come over before they got to the street. Sully scampered out of the bushes and sat in front of Alice, who put his leash back on. "But I want you to be skeptical of this person, okay."

"My new therapist is a natural skeptic," said Grace.

"He said that?"

"Yeah."

"Why?" asked Alice. "What was the context?"

"I asked him if he believed me."

Alice paused for a moment, put her arm around Grace, and said, "Well, I believe you."

Sully didn't like to be left out when members of the Ryan family showed affection, so he immediately started jumping on the two girls as they walked away from the park toward home.

~39~

It was almost seven o'clock, and neither Jill nor Max had texted her all day. Grace had never really been jealous about anything. It just wasn't her thing. She had other selfish flaws like resentment and vanity and impatience. But Grace was feeling something else tonight. Maybe it was loneliness. And maybe loneliness was just a different way of being jealous of people who weren't lonely ... if that made any sense. Whatever it was that she was feeling, it was confusing to her.

Coop had helped her a little bit this afternoon simply by being an adult who listened to her and didn't judge her, despite the fact that he didn't believe her. And Alice had told her that she did believe her now, but Grace wondered if she meant it.

When Grace had asked Coop about her relationship with Jill and Max, he'd told her that they sounded like good friends, and she always believed they were. She had lots of other friends, and so did Jill and Max, but there were things that she'd never tell anyone else besides these two. There were things that she'd tell Jill and Max that she couldn't even tell Alice. Alice could be judgy.

But she felt herself drifting away from her friends. She, herself, probably wouldn't want to hang out with anyone who had a baby. Why would Jill and Max want to hang out with her? And she didn't want their pity either. That might even be worse. She didn't want them pretending that they wanted to stay friends when they really wanted to distance themselves from the girl with the baby. Or even worse, the *crazy* girl with the baby.

When she got on Instagram, there was already a DM from Sophia.

What up, girl?

Grace was excited to hear from her. She wanted to know if strange things were happening as she got closer to her due date. Grace wanted to know what was in store for her in a few months. She wanted to know if it would be different from other pregnancies. If there was anything she needed to prepare for.

How you feeling?

Like a cow!

Any weird things going on?

Weird things?

Yeah, like maybe something that's making you think your baby will be different

You sound like you think I might give birth to an alien ...

I was actually thinking of something more spiritual.

Grace had been trying to squeeze something out of Sophia for weeks. Something that suggested that Sophia thought her predicament at least had the possibility of being a miracle—an act of God. But Sophia was handling it differently. She didn't want any attention, and Grace understood that. But when it was just the two of them talking? Why not just admit that this was special? Something extraordinary?

Grace, I have something to tell you.

Grace didn't like the sound of it. In fact, her stomach tightened when she saw the words, and she waited. She didn't know what to say. She just didn't want this to be something bad, and maybe in the back of her mind, she thought that if she didn't respond, then nothing bad could happen. She could manufacture a kind of time warp, a cryonic vacuum, and everything could just stay as it was right now. But Sophia didn't want to indulge in this fantasy. She sent another message.

I'm not a virgin

You mean you had sex after you got pregnant?

She typed it so fast that she didn't realize how ridiculous it sounded until she saw it on the screen.

Grace, are you serious?

I don't know what the fuck is going on!!!

I'm so sorry.

Grace was hyperventilating. She went back and read from the beginning of the thread, hoping that she somehow got confused and misinterpreted Sophia's message. Then she stood up and walked around her room. She needed to catch her breath and calm down. She took deep breaths until she felt less agitated. Four seconds in, then four seconds out. Then she had a moment when she felt like she might faint, so she sat down and closed her eyes. Once she got it together, she opened her eyes and looked at Sophia's last post: *I'm so sorry.*

Now Grace really was alone.

Why did you do this to me?

Grace was crying now and staring at the screen. Waiting. She needed to know. Freakin' catfish. These people had mental disorders. Why would someone do this to her? She waited for five minutes. After the first two minutes, she got control of her breathing again and considered all the consequences of her being tricked by this person. She was assuming now that Sophia was not even the real name.

The longer she sat there staring at the screen, scrolling through the pictures, the harder it was to find the negatives involved in this online relationship. Yes, it was based on a huge lie. But it really helped Grace get through these past few months. Yes, Grace felt manipulated. But she also felt supported. The relationship and the emotions associated with it felt so real. Better to have been catfished and lost than to have never been catfished at all? Did that sound right?

On about the sixth minute of staring at the screen, Grace received another DM.

I'm so sorry.

Why did you do it?

Too hard to explain. Maybe I have something wrong with me.

Grace decided to send at least one message with a little attitude.

You can do better than that.

No I can't. I'm sorry. I love you.

Not good enough. Tell me why. Who are you?

This time, Grace waited a full ten minutes. Nothing.

Grace

This is the first time she comes to me and there's actual weather. It's raining. Early evening. Familiar streets, but they're dream streets. Just when I think I know where I am, there's a weird house with awnings over the windows or cars from a different era or the lady's wearing my jacket and my shoes, and I'm wearing shorts and a t-shirt even though, as I said, it's raining. That's how she works. Whenever I'm with her, I love our connection, but I always feel like I could lose my balance at any moment. Like I'm totally myself, but not quite feeling like me. Rather, I'm watching me from a few feet away. Like I'm split between two selves.

"Why did you leave me on that path last time?" I say.

"I never left," she says. "I was always there."

"Well, when I got to the top, you were gone."

"That wasn't the top," she says, and I know she's being mysterious. She likes to keep me guessing.

"I'm feeling a little lost," I say. "My friend lied to me."

"Was she really your friend?"

This kind of throws me off. What is a friend? To me, it's someone who tries to help me. It's someone who wants the best for me. It's someone who would do something for me even though it would make her life more challenging. A friend is someone who laughs with me. But also laughs at *me, and when she does, that's okay. I feel like good friends should laugh at us when we're stupid, and that should help us not be stupid anymore. You know what I mean? When other people laugh at me, it's terrible. I get that no one likes that. But when a good friend laughs at me—not with me—it's actually a good chance for me to learn something about myself and grow from it. No one should be above being laughed at by friends. Jill and Max laugh at me all the time. Sophia did too, but not about anything serious. I don't think she was laughing at me in the end. I think she knows how absolutely fucked up that all was. But she did let me know when I was being weird or stupid or sensitive. That's what friends should be able to do.*

"Yeah," I say to the lady. "She really was my friend."

"Did she help you?"

"Yes."

"Good."

The lady has an umbrella, but I'm getting pretty wet. I want to walk up and get under the cover with her, but we've given each other so much personal space up to this point that it would feel weird.

So I just follow. It's the first rain in a while so the water has revitalized all the oil on the street. For some reason, we're walking in the middle of the road, and I'm wearing sneakers, so I start sliding on the asphalt like I did when I was little. And the next thing I know, I'm working my feet like I'm ice-skating. I'm just goofing around, but I skate right past the lady. I'm not usually any good on ice, but this is different. I feel stable, and I'm moving fast, using my arms to pump as I gain traction when I push off my right foot and then my left, gliding, really free for the moment.

When I look back, the lady is there, but she's under the umbrella, and I can't really see her face, but she's laughing. I can hear it.

Third Trimester

"How strange when an illusion dies. It's as though you've lost a child."

— Judy Garland

~40~

Jill was worried about Grace. The summer was pretty easy for her. Well, relatively speaking. When she started to show, she just kind of kept to herself or hung out with Jill and Max. But now she was going to be walking around school. If Alice was still here, it would be easier. People respected her, and honestly, were kind of afraid of her. She was a badass.

Jill wanted to be a badass for Grace, but she knew she didn't really have it in her. They were only sophomores. Alice probably didn't become a true badass until at least her junior year. Jill was ready to stick up for Grace if any freshmen or sophomores tried to pull anything, but she wasn't sure how she'd react if a junior or senior tried to mess with her.

Grace asked Jill to meet her across the street in the St. X parking lot so that the two of them could walk in together. For some reason, Grace wasn't worried about the boys. It seemed like it never crossed her mind that the boys might taunt her or try to embarrass her or ask a bunch of stupid questions.

And maybe she was right. Grace had power over boys, and she didn't even know it. It was hard to explain how beautiful she was, but the fact that she looked like she did without even trying and that she didn't seem aware of her beauty made her even more fascinating to boys. For the last couple of years, Jill had seen popular boys their own age freeze in front of Grace as if they didn't think they were worthy. Grace was the kind of girl that other girls would be jealous of if she wasn't so nice to everyone. She really was nice to everyone. Everyone.

One time last year, a senior girl who'd been a model for the Macy's catalogue came up to Grace and said, "I'm obsessed with your face."

They were all in the cafeteria at the time, and Grace had just taken a big bite out of her sandwich, so she was chomping on a sour dough roll, and she had a little mayonnaise on the corner of her lip when she said, "Thank you?"

Jill and the rest of the girls at the table had laughed when the senior walked away. Grace didn't seem to understand what had just happened. None of them did.

Jill was thinking that today might have some moments like that—interactions with people they didn't really know. But everyone was going to know Grace now.

When Mr. Ryan pulled into the parking lot, Grace was smiling out the window at Jill. This was earlier than Jill was used to coming to school, but she told Grace she'd do it for a while until Grace was comfortable.

Mr. Ryan smiled at Jill and gave a little salute. Then he said to Grace, "I have my cell phone. Call me if you need anything. The first day might be weird."

Then the two of them did kind of a half-hug, like they weren't used to doing hugging at all, but Grace was smiling when they walked in opposite directions.

"Thanks for coming early," she said to Jill. "Alice and I used to ride in with my dad, so we were usually the first ones in the cafeteria in the morning. I just didn't want to be alone on the first day."

Jill put her arm around Grace as best she could with their backpacks making it awkward. "I know," she said. "We went over all this last night. I don't mind coming in early"

Jill stepped back from Grace and said, "Let me take a look at you."

Grace twirled once and then stopped like a dancer and snapped her head around so that she was looking at Jill. It was dramatic and funny because she did it with a straight face, as if she'd been waiting for someone to give her the cue for this particular move. Jill looked her up and down. Grace's boobs were a little bigger, but her shirt was untucked, so it was kind of hard to tell that she was more than six months pregnant.

"How did you fit into that skirt?" asked Jill.

"My mom replaced the waistband with an elastic one," she said. "Look," and she lifted her shirt to show her protruding belly.

Just then, three junior girls were getting dropped off across the street. Once all the doors to the car closed, one of them, Stacy V., screamed, "Oh my God!" and pointed at Grace.

"Oh shoot," said Grace, dropping down her blouse while the three girls came running across the street. It was Stacy V. and the two Claires.

The taller Claire said, "Isn't that Grace Ryan?" as she hurried behind Stacy V.

Jill whispered, "Are you ready for this?"

Grace just shrugged.

When they got to the other side of the street, Stacy said, "Grace Ryan, are you like ... pregnant?"

Stacy seemed to be smiling but not mocking. She looked kind of hopeful, like she wanted it to be true, but not so that she could make fun of Grace. It was maybe more that she thought this was something new. It wasn't boring. This would make school interesting to her.

That's what her face and her voice and her gestures told Jill.

Grace said, "Yeah. Just over six months."

"Oh my fuckin' God," said the taller Claire. "Can I ...?" She was walking closer to Grace and had her hand out in front of her as if she were reaching out to test the ripeness of a melon.

Grace didn't move, and Tall Claire actually did it. She put her hand on Grace's belly and said, "This is so unbelievable."

The other Claire was just staring at Grace's tummy and shaking her head. Finally, she said, "Grace, are you like in trouble for this?"

"What do you mean?" asked Grace.

The shorter Claire finally looked up from Grace's stomach and then moved her eyes back and forth from Grace's to Jill's. She said, "Like at school. Is the school mad at you? I mean, are they going to punish you? Is there something in the handbook about this?"

"Ms. Daly knows," said Grace.

"What about Sister Margaret?"

"She knows," said Grace. "But I haven't talked to her yet. Ms. Daly told her, and they told me to come to school."

Stacy was still smiling and hanging on every word that came out of Grace's mouth. "What do you think Sister's gonna say?"

Grace shrugged again.

Stacy lost the smile and revealed a sterner look now—a Rhonda Rousey sneer. "Well, we got your back, Ryan. Let us know if anyone messes with you."

"Thank you," said Grace. "I will."

And then Stacy V. and the two Claires walked across the street. Jill and Grace watched them without speaking, and just before they got to the door, Stacy turned and started running back across the street to where the two of them were standing.

She was out of breath when she said, "Is the father a St. X boy?"

Grace delivered her practiced reply. "My family and I consider this a private matter," she said. It was short, but it seemed to do the job.

Stacy said, "Oh."

~41~

When Jenny Daly got to Sister Margaret's office, Sister was sitting behind her desk, but she was facing the side window and holding a set a rosary beads with one hand and massaging her temple with the other. Her mouth was moving as she whispered her prayers.

Jenny had tapped on the door twice before entering the room, but Sister must not have heard, as she continued to pray. Jenny made a move to leave so that Sister could finish the decade on which she was working, but before she was all the way out, she heard her say, "Please come in and sit down, my dear."

Sister Margaret was nearly eighty, but Jenny still felt that she was a beautiful woman. She no longer wore a habit, and her white hair was cut short, almost like a boy's, but not. More stylish, like Mia Farrow in *Rosemary's Baby.* She had soft features, and when she smiled, it changed her face. It was the kind of smile that could be used to manipulate people, but she never did.

"Well, do we know how we want to handle this, Jenny?" she asked once Jenny had taken a seat and had her hands folded on her lap.

"I thought we decided that we wanted to support her anyway we can."

"Yes," said Sister Margaret. "How do we do that?" She moved her hands gracefully when she talked, and the rosary beads rattled gently with every sentence. They sounded like wooden wind chimes.

Sister Margaret flashed the old smile, and it had the effect it always did on Jenny. She breathed in, let it out, and found herself in a more relaxed state. "That's a good question," she said. "I've briefed the admin team, and some of them feel that we should have an assembly and send a message home to our parents about the situation."

"Yes," said Sister. "I suspected as much."

Jenny nodded and felt herself chewing on the inside of her lip. "You can guess who wants to broadcast Grace's dilemma to the public."

"Yes," said Sister. "But we don't need to get into all that." She opened her top drawer and dropped the rosary beads in without much reverence and said, "What do *you* think we should do?"

"Protect Grace," said Jenny. "And I don't think we'd be doing that if we made a production out of this and tried to turn it into some kind of teachable moment."

"Yes," said Sister Margaret. "Everyone already knows the lesson. We're going to have a girl walking around our campus who looks like she has a volleyball in her shirt. That's the lesson. Make a stupid mistake with a boy, and your old life is gone."

"But if we do nothing," said Jenny. "Are we going to be accused by people of endorsing Grace's behavior?"

"Well," said Sister. "That's the quandary, isn't it?"

"And then there's the added hurdle that Grace does not know who the father is."

"That's not a hurdle, Jenny," she said. "The hurdle is that she believes that she is still a virgin." She smiled again, but it wasn't the one that could light up a room. This one was strained. Her lips were closed tightly as if she were trying to suppress a toothache, and her eyes didn't have their sparkle. "We cannot use this as a cautionary tale if the girl doesn't believe that she's done anything wrong."

"I agree," said Jenny.

"And they've tried everything to get her to remember?"

"Yes. And I believe she can't remember that she doesn't have any idea how this happened to her."

"Is that because of your close relationship with this family and Mr. Ryan in particular?"

"Jeez," said Jenny. "I hope not." She thought about that question for a moment. If Grace was putting on an act, then they should consider renaming the theater after her. The performance has been a masterpiece.

"Because the alternative is not a pretty one," said Sister.

"The alternative?" said Jenny.

"Yes," said Sister. "If she's not lying, and she can't remember how this happened, then this girl was quite probably subjected to something awful. Something unspeakable."

For some reason, it sounded so much worse coming from a nun. The words stung Jenny because she did want to protect Grace and the family. They were good people. "I've thought about that," said Jenny. "And it makes me question whether or not the family should even be trying to help her remember. If this is some kind of psychological defense mechanism for Grace to protect herself from an ugly truth, maybe we should just let the mechanism do its work at this point."

"Interesting," said Sister Margaret. "So, you don't believe all that about the truth setting us free."

"I almost always do," said Jenny. "But in this case ...." She didn't finish the thought. If the memory loss was only temporary, then she was all for getting to the truth as soon as possible.

Otherwise, they were all just procrastinating.

But if this was permanent, why not relieve Grace from having to fight the demons for the rest of her life. Would it be good for her to have trust issues with men forever? Was that healthy? Jenny had gone back and forth on this for months. She had her own issues with men and didn't wish that on anyone.

"Have you ever heard of Charles Spurgeon?" asked Sister Margaret.

"I don't think I have.

"That's okay," said Sister. "He was a *Baptist*." She laughed a little bit. "But he was a pretty good eighteenth century preacher, and he once said, *A lie can travel halfway around the world while the truth is putting on its shoes.* I always liked that."

"Wow," said Jenny. "And Ol' Charles said it before the Internet."

"He did," said Sister. "No Twitter. Very prophetic for a Baptist."

"And sometimes," said Jenny. "The truth never catches up."

"And in this case," said Sister Margaret. "You'd prefer that it never did?"

"Probably not," she said.

Jenny still wasn't sure how she wanted to handle this. She knew she didn't want an assembly, and she didn't want to send out a missive to all stakeholders reiterating the school's stance on abstinence. She just didn't think that would do any good, and she knew that both would be hurtful to Grace.

"The Archbishop told Mr. Ryan that he would appreciate it if Grace at least admitted she had intercourse with someone."

"You can say *sex,* Jenny," she said. "I'm a nun. Not a five-year-old."

"Sorry," she said, a little upset by her own awkwardness on the subject. "So Pat, Mr. Ryan, has told Grace that when people ask about the baby's father, she will simply say that it's a personal matter and just leave it at that."

Sister Margaret had her chin in her hand now, but she didn't respond.

Jenny continued, "That way, she doesn't have to say anything about the idea of a virgin pregnancy."

"Yes," said Sister Margaret. "That should appease His Excellency." She leaned forward in her chair now and looked over at the door, which was shut. Then the smile. The big one. The powerful one. "Do you think there's any chance she's telling the truth?" she whispered.

~42~

Pat's day wasn't bad, but he was glad to be home.

At the opening faculty meeting, he'd explained to the faculty and staff that Grace was pregnant but that she was going to remain at St. Mary's until she was ready to have the baby.

No gasps. Nobody fainted. A few people frowned. Some tried to smile.

A long-time Religious Studies teacher had raised his hand and asked, "What's the Archdiocesan policy on this issue?"

Pat just smiled and said, "Life."

No one else said a word, and they moved on to some housekeeping items regarding lunchtime supervision and the new platform for online grading. And that was it. At least in a public forum.

Pat assumed that the meetings after the meeting contained the real conversations—in the photocopy room and behind the theater and in offices all over campus, in groups of two and three and four, they were judging. And Pat didn't mind. As long as no one did anything to Grace, he could withstand the sideways glances and the fake smiles. It wouldn't be fun, but he was going to be okay.

After lunch, the Dean of Discipline, Russell Pyne, had walked right past Pat's assistant and into the office. He closed the door behind him and took a seat on the couch. He was a big man, and he was sweating a bit just above his eyebrows. If he were a southern gentleman, he might have dabbed his forehead with a handkerchief, but, alas, he was not a southern gentleman, so he wiped at his head and face with the sleeve of his jacket and said, "Please tell me it's not a St. X kid."

"Russell?" said Pat. "What's up?"

"Is the father one of our guys?" he asked.

Pat said, "It's a personal matter, and Grace would prefer that we kept it private."

"Tell me his name, Pat."

"Russell," he said. "Settle down."

"Pat—"

"I'm serious, man," said Pat. "We're not going to talk about this."

Russell walked up to Pat's desk and took a Werther's Caramel out of the bowl. He sat back down on the couch and struggled to unwrap the candy. It must have been difficult for Russell to work on tiny tasks like this with his enormous fingers. This was like watching a bear try to send a text.

He eventually got it. He popped it in his mouth and started to work it around aggressively.

"Russell," said Pat. "You gotta calm down, brother."

Russell slowed his breathing and said calmly, "Sorry, Pat. I got a little worked up." He wiped at his head again, this time with the palm of his hand, and said in a really quiet voice, "When you're ready to tell me, please let me know." He smiled like a bouncer who is about to punch a drunk. "And then I'll pull the little bastard out of class, take him into the wrestling room, and—"

"Russ!" said Pat. "Enough. We're handling it. Gracie's doing fine. This is what she wants, and you and I are going to honor that."

"If that's what Gracie wants," he said and stood up. Before leaving, he grabbed a handful of caramels and stomped out the door.

***

Pat was smiling about Russell now as he was chopping onions and celery and green bell peppers to put in the chili he was making for dinner. Cornbread was baking in the oven, and the TV was explaining the layout of another mass shooting.

Emily was standing in front of the TV mounted across from the kitchen island. It was just about eye level, and her face was about eight inches from the screen.

"This has to end," she said, as she walked over to the kitchen table and let herself fall into one of the chairs.

When Grace walked into the room, Emily said, "Let's turn this off."

Without even looking at the screen, Grace pushed the off button and continued to the table where she sat next to her mom, who said, "How did things go today, sweetie?"

"Not as bad as you might think."

"Well, that's good," Emily said and looked over at Pat, who was leaning on the counter now, waiting for the oil to heat up. He nodded at her and offered a half-hearted smile. This was still going to be really hard no matter how well the first day went.

"All the girls treated me really nice," said Grace. "And the teachers, too."

Pat liked hearing that. He really didn't know how anyone would react. This was kind of a big deal, and St. Mary's was very traditional. "How was your meeting with Sister Margaret?" he asked.

"I like her, dad," she said. "She gets me."

"Really?" said Emily.

"Yeah," said Grace. "She had a sister who got pregnant when they were teenagers in Boston, and the family had to hide her away while she was pregnant, and then they put the baby up for adoption. It was really sad." Then she stopped and put her hands up to her mouth. "Oh my God," she said. "I wasn't supposed to tell anyone, and I just told you guys."

"That's okay," said Pat. "We're not going to tell anyone."

"But I promised," she said.

"Okay," said Emily. "That's it. We won't mention it again in this house. It's in the vault," she said and pantomimed the locking of her lips.

"But just to clarify," said Pat. "Was it a *sister* or was it *her sister*?"

"Are you serious, Dad?"

"Well, you said sister, and I—"

"Her *own* sister, her family," she said. "God."

"Okay," he said.

"She's a cool lady though," said Grace. "She never tried to get me to talk about the father, and she seemed really supportive. I was nervous before I went in, but she made me feel safe. And Ms. Daly was there, too."

"What did Ms. Daly have to say?" asked Pat, who was using a large knife to push vegetables off a cutting board into a large pot that was crackling with olive oil. He spilled some of the onions under the back burner, but just left them there. He'd burned himself enough times trying to retrieve his choppings that he didn't even attempt the rescues anymore until everything had cooled.

"Ms. Daly just handled the academic stuff," said Grace. "What time are we eating?"

"Give me twenty minutes," said Pat.

"Who did you sit with at lunch?" asked Emily.

"Just the normal girls," said Grace. "Jill, of course, and then Jaime and Kim, and also a freshman that Kim knew who didn't know anyone yet, so we let her sit with us."

"Well, that was nice," said Emily.

"She was a little weird, though," said Grace. "She had like a hair style from the sixties or something, and her socks were pulled all the way up."

Emily didn't respond, but Pat was thinking that maybe it was healthy for Grace to see another kid as weird when Grace was the one who was pregnant in high school. Maybe that meant she didn't consider herself weird. Or was pregnancy in a different category? What were the kids going to think about her? Or even worse, what were they going to say to her?

If the other girls knew that Grace believed this to be a virgin pregnancy, that's when things could get difficult. If she stuck to her story, they could make it through this. *It's a personal matter.*

"Did anyone ask you about the father?" Pat asked.

"Yep," she said and stared back at him as if this were some kind of challenge.

"And?"

"It worked," she said. "In fact, after I said it, girls looked like they were embarrassed for asking."

"That's a relief," said Emily. "Maybe word will get out to not even ask you."

"Hopefully," she said.

~43~

Max had been at Jill's house a couple times before. They were in her room, and they were trying to pump themselves up to send a DM to Grace.

Max was making her nervous. He was looking at all the pictures on her bulletin board and asking annoying questions: *Who's this? Where's that? You know this girl?*

That's my cousin. Tahoe. She goes to St. Mary's.

Once they'd gone through every picture, and he'd read out loud the titles of all the books on her shelf, he said, "So where did we leave off last time?"

"Are you serious?" she said. "You can't remember?"

"I remember it was dramatic and terrible, but I just want to review the exact words."

"These aren't the exact words," she said. "But you were typing, and you told her that you weren't really a virgin, and then you said, *I love you.*"

Max tilted his head down and scratched at his curly hair. He was a mess. He'd been a mess for a couple of weeks now.

"Remind me how you started this hot mess of a plan in the first place," he said, looking up at Jill.

"*You* know how it started, Max," she said. "Don't pretend that you're not a part of this."

"Jill," he said, his eyes bugging out at her now. "I admit to being a part of it, but you started it, and I just want to know what we're dealing with before we send anything tonight."

If Jill didn't feel sorry for him, she would've kicked him out of her house, but they both had the same goal. They were trying to help Grace.

One night several months ago, after Grace had read Jill some posts from a virgin birth website, Jill found the site and reached out to Grace, who had posted on the message board. Jill did it without enough thought. She made up a fake identity on Insta with pictures of her cousin from Oxnard. And then tried to make Grace feel better about her crazy situation.

Jill tried to make her feel like she wasn't alone.

But then it went too far.

And that's when she brought in Max to help. He knew all this. And it was his idea to put a stop to it. To try to help Grace face reality about her pregnancy. To try to help her stop thinking she was a saint or something.

But Grace didn't handle it well.

And Jill and Max didn't handle it well either. They went for the ripping off the Band-Aid method rather than trying to slowly wean her off the idea of Sophia Martini from Oxnard.

And now they were in damage control. They wanted Grace to still have Sophia, but they'd dropped the *ordinary* pregnancy bomb, and now they had to try to rebuild the friendship despite the lie. That is, the lie within the lie. They didn't know if they would eventually tell her the catfish truth. They didn't know if they would eventually use the weaning method. But they knew they wanted to help her, and Grace really did like Sophia. She seemed to believe the new narrative that Sophia was just a pregnant teen. Nothing special. Just another girl who was about to have a baby.

"I just tried to make her feel like she had a kindred spirit," said Jill. "She totally thinks she's a virgin, and I wanted her to know that she wasn't alone." Jill didn't like the sound of her voice. She sounded like a fool. "I know," she shouted. "It was stupid. I told you all this before."

"Okay, okay," he said. "Sorry."

"And then you were supposed to help me, but you kept saying *I love you* at the ends of the posts. Are you crazy?"

"Yeah," he said. "I know. I got caught up in it."

Jill walked over to where he was sitting on her beanbag chair. She crouched down so that they were looking eye-to-eye. "You think?" she said.

"I was like you," he said. "I was trying to help her deal with this."

"And," said Jill, "you're in love with her." Jill stood up and walked back over to her desk, but she didn't sit down at the computer. Max had taken over this duty, and Jill thought it was best to stay consistent.

"Did we leave off with us—I mean Sophia—telling her that she just couldn't explain why she lied?"

"That," said Jill. "And you telling her that you love her."

"Okay," he said, walking over to the desk chair. "Are we going to give her a reason or just keep saying that we can't tell her why we—she—did it?"

"We have to come up with a reason," she said. "Or she's gonna block us."

Max was in front of the computer now, opening the account. "Can we tell her that Sophia hadn't told her parents that it was her ex-boyfriend, and she was just trying out the virgin thing to see how it felt?"

"That's not bad," said Jill, pulling her suitcase out from under her bed so that she'd have something to sit on. "Then Grace will feel bad for her maybe?"

"Maybe," he said.

"What about saying that she'd been date raped and was embarrassed to tell anyone the truth."

"I don't like that one," said Max. "Too depressing. Aren't we still trying to cheer her up?"

"You're right," said Jill. "So is that what we're going with?"

"What?"

"The ex-boyfriend knocked her up story?"

"If that's what you think," he said. "Or we could just delete this account and let Grace move on from the whole thing."

"You don't think we can help her through Sophia?"

"I do," he said. "But I don't want to screw it up again. I just want her to know that this online *friend* supports her. Do you think we can do that without messing up?"

"Yeah."

"Are we going to make a pact that we never tell her?"

"Is that what you want to do?" she asked and got up to open a window. It was humid in her room. Uncomfortable.

"Yeah," he said. "I don't want to ever tell her we did this. Seriously. Even though I think we're helping her, she might not see it that way."

"Okay," she said. "It's a pact." They were sitting close. The screen was waiting for a DM. They both took deep breaths. Then Jill said, "And don't tell her you love her anymore."

~44~

Grace had been watching Alice pack for college for the past two weeks—pulling out sweaters and replacing them with different sweaters. Working out a strategy for the shoe dilemma. Boxing up framed pictures, shot glasses, her crucifix.

The early packing was probably a habit inherited from their mom, who would employ a similar practice and still find out, once they'd gotten to their destination, that she'd forgotten several important items. Their dad would wait until the morning of a trip and scramble around throwing random articles into inappropriately sized bags, and he would also forget several important items.

They just weren't good packers.

Alice didn't look like she had much talent in this area, either. "Do I bring these?" she asked and held up a pair of striped sox with little toes built in—like gloves for the feet.

"Please don't," said Grace. "You want to have friends, right?"

Alice threw the socks in a pile next to her bed with her basketball jersey, a summer camp t-shirt, a fake leather jacket, and several pairs of underwear that she'd had since grade school. "How about this?" she said and held up a long purple wig.

"That might come in handy," said Grace. "Halloween? Maybe a wig party? I'd take it."

Alice nodded and put it in the box with the pictures. "How was school?" she asked. "Anything weird yet?"

"Totally normal, actually," she said and pulled the fake leather jacket out of the pile. "Can I have this?"

"What?" she said, looking up from the work she was doing untangling her ear buds, her charger, and an external drive.

"This jacket?"

"Take it," she said as she got at least the phone charger out of the twisted nest of wires. "Any kids bug you about anything?"

"Not really," said Grace. "Except maybe people who are being overly nice. It's weird."

"That's good," said Alice.

"PE was the only awkward time," she said. "Not that I couldn't do the yoga or anything like that. It's just that with my regular school uniform, I can kind of hide my stomach, but in my PE uniform, I look like a joke. My shirt just barely fits over my belly."

"At least it's only for an hour a day," said Alice. "And at some point, you're gonna be able to just say you can't participate. Then you won't even have to dress down."

Grace nodded and walked over to her desk, where she opened her laptop and logged on.

There was a notification from Sophia.

She looked back at Alice, but Alice was still tangled.

Grace had made up her mind after the last exchange with Sophia that it probably wasn't healthy to maintain the relationship. Although Sophia seemed like a nice person who was trying to help Grace, she was also a liar. But a liar who eventually came clean on her own. That had to count for something. But still a liar.

Grace had her friends at school, and she had Max and Jill and Alice and her parents and Coop. But none of those people understood her situation as well as Sophia. She had been there with Grace from the beginning.

And there was a good chance that Sophia had the baby already or that she was about to have the baby. Either way, Grace needed to talk to her.

Sophia's message was brief:

Hi

Grace replied without even thinking. Then she decided that she was going to be careful about the rest of this conversation. Be guarded. Maybe even let Sophia know that Grace was not going to be able to fully trust her again.

Hi

Grace looked over her shoulder to see what Alice was doing, but she was gone now. Grace could hear her upstairs talking to Mom and Dad.

She waited for a reply, and when it didn't come immediately, she clicked over to Spotify and put on her daily mix. First song: Billie Eilish. *All the Good Girls Go to Hell.* No way! She turned it up. Thought it was hilarious. What did it even mean?

All the good girls go to hell'Cause even God herself has enemies And once the water starts to rise And heaven's out of sight She'll want the devil on her team

It sounded like nonsense to Grace, but she liked the song. Thought Billie was crazy cool—she didn't give a crap about what anyone thought. She dressed like a rodeo clown but still looked good.

Hills burn in California
My turn to ignore ya
Don't say I didn't warn ya

Maybe Grace just liked the way the words sounded together even if she didn't know what they meant. She looked at the clock at the top of her screen, and out of the corner of her eye saw a message pop up.

Grace, I had my baby.

Grace felt her heart getting warm, and the heat rose through her throat and up to her chin until her whole face was warm. Then she felt the tears running down her cheeks. She wasn't much of a crier, so this feeling was somewhat foreign to her. She wasn't making any sounds, but there was a steady stream of tears.

The Kleenex box on her desk was empty, so she grabbed one of Alice's striped socks—foot gloves—and wiped her whole face. She had control of her breathing, and her nose wasn't running. It was just those big tears running down her face. And they'd stopped now. Grace wasn't even sure if that was really crying. It was more like something was leaking.

I'm so happy I can't even explain how I'm feeling.

You don't have to, Grace. Just telling me that makes me feel better about everything.

Grace had a list of questions that she would have asked if Sophia's experience was a virgin birth. Since it wasn't, all she could do was ask the basic questions. *Boy or girl? Name? How big?*

Dominic Anthony is almost 8 pounds. His little face is red all the time. As soon as he's a little bigger, I'll send you a picture.

I'm praying for you, Sophia.

I'm praying for you, too, Grace.

I thought you weren't religious

I'm not

?????

But you never know ...

~45~

Alice had only been down at Cal Poly for a week when Trisha, her roommate from San Diego, must have seen her walking out of the rec center. Alice had just gotten off the elliptical and was still sweating when she walked out of the complex. The sun was out, and she was squinting. She couldn't tell who was coming at her because the girl was wearing a baseball cap pulled down low, and she was moving fast.

She sprinted right at Alice, and Alice, who had also been taking a boxing class on Tuesdays, put her hands up in a fighter's stance. When Trisha finally darted out of the glare, she did an old-fashioned basketball jump-stop two feet in front of Alice.

Alice finally recognized her and said, "What the hell?"

"Sorry," said Trisha, out of breath. "I've been looking for you. Have you seen this?" Her face showed concern but also excitement. Can those two emotions coexist?

Trisha blinked and held out her phone.

Alice wiped her sweaty hands on her shorts and grabbed it. She saw a twitter post and immediately recognized a picture of Grace, a nice shot of her profile. Cheek a little pink and glowing. A half-smile. She was wearing her St. Mary's PE uniform, and she was leaning back a little with her hands on her hips.

Her pregnant belly seemed even bigger than it did just a week ago. Maybe it was the way she was standing. Either way, it was a very clear photograph of a very pregnant Grace Ryan in a St. Mary's t-shirt.

"That's your sister, right?"

"Yeah," she said. "What *is* this?"

"Somebody posted a picture of *Coyote Girl,*" she said. "She's pregnant?"

"Yeah," said Alice and gave the phone back to her roommate. "I gotta go."

She ran back to her dorm so that she could look at this by herself.

***

Pat was standing on his desk chair. He was adjusting a crooked picture that he had hanging in his office behind his desk. It was a framed, enlarged photograph of former Red Sox first baseman, Bill Buckner, with a ball rolling through his legs during the '86 series against the Mets. Buckner was an incredible baseball player, who had an outstanding career. But after this epic error, nobody remembered how good he was. No one remembered his all-star appearances or his 2,715 hits. The way he assaulted second basemen when he broke up double plays. His headfirst dives into third. The fact that he played in the bigs in four different decades.

But everyone remembered the error. New Englanders blamed the curse and hated this good man for nearly twenty years until the Sox finally beat the Cardinals in the series in 2004, and the curse was lifted.

Tragic story. But Pat liked the picture. Especially since Buckner had signed it for him for free at a spring training game in Scottsdale in '07.

Pat thought it was a perfect conversation starter when students got sent to his office for making some kind of stupid mistake. When kids would get upset, he liked to talk about Buckner. Not many kids knew the story of how Billy Buck made an error that cost the Sox their first world championship in over 70 years. They didn't know that he'd made that epic mistake in one of the most watched televised baseball games of all time.

Pat would often have boys in his office who'd gotten into fistfights or stolen things from the cafeteria. They'd be upset. Scared that their parents were going to send them away to military school. So Pat would explain that their stupid mistakes were small compared to Bill Buckner's. Pat didn't know if the story helped anyone, but he liked to tell it. And he had the signed picture right there as a visual aid.

One of Pat's favorite poems was called *Forgiving Buckner,* by John Hodgen. The first line said it all:

The world is always rolling between our legs

Didn't that capture it? Our essence as humans? Our egotistical feelings about our own mistakes? To us, screw-ups always felt colossal, like the end of the world. But we always seem to get the opportunity to make another mistake. It was hard to get kids to understand this concept and be accepting of it, but Pat still tried.

He'd heard all the different iterations: *epic failure, shit the bed, major screw up, FUBAR, whoops!* But *dropped the ball* always seemed the most illustrative to Pat, and Hodgen carried that metaphor all the way to the end of the Buckner poem. He described that slippery, bouncing ball…

…as if it had come from before you were born
to roll past your life to the end of the world,
till the world comes around again, gathering steam,
heading right for us again and again,
faith of our fathers, world without end.

Pat was balancing on the chair, straightening the picture, and thinking about the poem when he was startled by a loud voice coming from the doorway, "Mr. Ryan!"

He meant to just turn his head to see who was there, but he was standing on a swivel chair, and when he moved, the chair moved. He immediately tried retain his balance by countering the initial swivel; however, the result was that he swiveled back violently in the opposite direction. Any sane man would have simply jumped off at this point, but Pat continued to do the twist while waving his arms like a Tourettic surfer. After about five seconds of this dance, he gave up. *It's in God's hands now,* he thought as he toppled over the backrest and smashed his elbow into the bookshelf. He ultimately landed on his back.

When he looked up to where he'd been, he saw that the picture was still, indeed, crooked.

While he was lying on his back, he simultaneously tried to assess any physical damage while he reviewed the last few seconds of his life. The one thing that was coming back to him was the voice that had called his name and then had cried out, "Ooh, ooh, ooh," as his body was jerking back and forth spasmodically before his eventual demise.

Amanda Prattley.

He closed his eyes for a moment, and when he opened them, he was looking up at Amanda, whose whole face was a collection of O's. Her eyes, her nostrils, and especially her mouth, wide open. Speechless.

"Didn't I tell you to stop calling me *Mr. Ryan*," Pat asked without making any effort to move from his supine position.

"Are you okay?" she said and extended her hand.

"I'm just gonna stay here for a moment, thank you."

"Are you sure?" she said and knelt down near his head.

"What can I do for you, Amanda?"

"It's just this," she said and handed him her phone.

When he touched it, however, whatever she wanted to show him disappeared, and an ad for fake eyelashes materialized on the screen. He didn't say anything. He just handed her back the phone.

"Oh, here," she said after a moment and handed it back.

This time, he made sure to hold the phone around the edges. He was still on his back, so scrolling was slightly more difficult than normal, but he found what Amanda wanted him to see—his Grace and her pregnant belly.

He didn't know if it was the fall or this photograph of his beautiful daughter with child, but he felt the overwhelming urge to weep. He felt his hand start to shake, so he decided to sit up quickly. This made him feel dizzy for a moment, but at least it seemed to prevent him from crying in front of Amanda.

He took her hand now and let her help him to his feet, but he immediately walked over to his chair and sat down. "What am I looking at, Amanda?"

"That's Grace, Mr. Ryan."

He looked at her but didn't change his expression. He exhaled out of his nose and said, "I know who it is, Amanda." He tried to scroll but didn't really know what he was looking for. "Where is this picture posted?"

"Okay," she said. "This is Twitter. Just like the last time."

"Got it," he said. "And have a lot of people seen it?" He looked up at her, and she nodded, her face sad, like she wanted to help him but knew she couldn't. He didn't ask for numbers. The last time, millions of people had watched that Buena Vista Park video.

"Who posted it?" he asked.

"No one seems to know," she said. "It was an anonymous account."

"Oh."

"But it has been retweeted by so many people," she said. "Including Kylie again."

"Why would *she* care?" he asked, suddenly angry.

"She actually jumped in to try to defend Grace."

He handed her back her phone. He needed to get over to St. Mary's and get Grace home. "From what?" he said.

***

Emily was sitting in her car in the parking lot of Stonestown Mall. Her phone had been blowing up while she was paying for a pair of shoes at Aldo. Ten texts in about thirty seconds. When she got into her car, she scrolled down to the one from Alice. Without even having to click, she could read the partial text: *Total Bullshit!*

When she clicked on the full text, Alice had written *They're going after Grace* and copied a twitter post. Grace looked cute in her PE gear, but she looked really pregnant. Who would take this picture and post it? *Coyote Girl*? That was the title.

As she scrolled down to look at the twitter comments, she became more and more appalled. These people were savages. Yes, there were people who were supporting her—including, apparently, the youngest Kardashian girl, the one who did the makeup line and made Grace famous after the whole coyote thing. But Emily couldn't get all these savage digs out of her mind.

I wonder who the father is?

I thought Catholics were supposed to be abstinent.

Maybe the coyote's the father!

You people suck. Give this kid a break.

I'll be the father...

You perv! She's sixteen!

That'll work!

Sick puppy!

But she's so fine, bro

Brave girl! She's got guts.

Fierce!

What was the Billy Joel line? Catholic girls start much too late? Do they?

Why didn't St. Mary's kick her out?

Why would they?

They kicked a girl out for vaping. Isn't this worse?

Do you think every girl who has ever had sex should be kicked out of St. Mary's?

She's fine. Total babe.

She gonna be a MILF soon! Haha!

No. But the ones who get pregnant should get the boot.

Catholic girls the horniest

What about Muslims?

Don't bring religion into this

This whole thing 'bout religion, homie!

And on and on and on and on. Thousands of these. Emily had heard Alice call the commenters *keyboard warriors*—losers, sitting at home thinking they're living life but really wasting away in their rooms. Feeling power. Fake power.

Gracie had real power.

~46~

Jill was worried that St. Mary's was going to have to make some tough choices about Grace now. Some really conservative Catholics had seen the picture of Grace online and were calling for her expulsion. Jill liked being a Catholic because one of the main principles was forgiveness. Kicking Grace out would seem like it was the opposite of forgiveness. What would that be? Vindictiveness?

Jill didn't even know if that was a word, but these online jerks who were picking on Grace seemed like they were being vindictive. Unforgiving. Jill was positive that if these people knew Grace, if they even spent ten minutes with her, they would change their minds.

Jill could hear her mom downstairs talking to Grace and Max now. Although they didn't usually come to her house, she thought this was an important day. Grace needed their support. This was different from when the coyote video came out, and everyone just thought Grace was so beautiful and cool. This new pregnant post had trolls creeping around the edges of every comment, nibbling away at the supportive ones and cackling loudly at the mean ones. Jill didn't know how much Grace had been reading, but some of these people were so nasty.

There was even a group of pro-choice trolls, who were calling for Grace to have an abortion. They were saying that she was being forced to keep the baby by the Catholic Church and her dad, who worked for the Archdiocese.

Jill didn't quite understand the logic. She knew that lots of people felt that a woman should have the right to control her own body. And that made some sense to her. But she didn't get why anyone would try to convince someone else to terminate a pregnancy. That just seemed weird and intrusive. She wondered how that was supposed to be empowering to women and if she was missing out on some important knowledge in this regard because she went to a Catholic school.

The whole situation made her think of that Hemingway story she'd read in freshman English. *Hills Like White Elephants.* It was really short, but good. For basically the whole story, the man is trying to talk the girlfriend into having an abortion, but the story never says the word *abortion*. You're supposed to figure it out on your own. And he keeps doing it. He says things like *I know you wouldn't mind it. It's really not anything.* And he's pretending to be nice and that he wants this for *her*. For the both of them. For their relationship. But Jill really felt like this guy is just selfish. He doesn't want a baby because then they won't be able to travel around Europe anymore trying new drinks, and instead they'll have to settle down and have responsibilities.

At one point the man says, *You don't have to be afraid. I've known lots of people that have done it.*

And then the girl says the most important line in the story. At least for Jill. It's the line Jill always thinks of when she remembers this story. After the guy says that he's known lots of people who have done it, the girl says, *So have I. And afterward they were all so happy.* And Hemingway doesn't write *she said sarcastically* or anything like that. But it's pretty clear that she's being sarcastic. And when Jill first read the story, she kept reading that paragraph over and over. To her, it said everything.

She thought, if women felt bad afterward, didn't that mean they believed there was something important inside them? Otherwise, who cares? Just a simple operation like the man kept saying.

So, Jill didn't like these trolls trying to say that Grace should get rid of this baby. Not now. She was like seven months pregnant. And Grace never once said that she didn't want to have the baby, so why the heck would anyone tell her that she should have an abortion. Again, that just seemed so weird to Jill.

And when Grace and Max walked into her room, she was tempted to say, "Don't listen to these assholes on social media," but she didn't know how much Grace had read. So instead, she said, "How are you feeling? You look really good."

Grace smiled. "Yeah, right," she said. "What part? The huge stomach or the chubby cheeks?"

"I guess the cheeks?" said Jill. Grace really did have lovely cheeks, and for the last few weeks they seemed to be shiny all the time.

Jill noticed that Max had his hand on the middle of Grace's back, but he wasn't saying anything.

"Are you doing okay, Max?" asked Jill.

"Not really," he said. "But this is a hard day for Grace, so let's not talk about my messed up life."

"It's okay," said Grace. "Tell us. Maybe it'll make me forget about my own messed up life." Grace was smiling when she said it, which made Jill feel like Grace really didn't consider her situation a bad one at all. She still felt that this was some kind of blessing.

"I think my brother is gone for good," he said.

Grace sat down on Jill's bed, and Max sat on the floor near her feet with this back up against the bed. Grace put her hand on his shoulder and said, "What happened?" It came out as a whisper even though the door was closed, and Jill's mom didn't really care what they talked about.

"I'm not sure if he ran away or if my parents kicked him out, but he's gone."

It looked like Grace was squeezing his shoulder now, maybe just to let him know that she was there.

"Do you know why?" asked Jill.

"My parents found a stash of drugs in his room," said Max. "Like a big stash. They think he's dealing drugs out of our house."

Grace and Jill said nothing.

Max craned his neck to look at Grace's face behind him. "I also heard my mom and dad talking about some kind of robbery, but no one will tell me the details. My brother was into some bad shit."

"Was it weed?" asked Jill, who had just last week tried her first hit from a vape pen and kind of liked it.

"Much worse," he said. "He either left the bag, or my parents took it from him, but I saw all the bottles lined up on the kitchen table. A couple of different kinds of pills with oxy-something on the label. Rohypnol. GHB. Ketamine. I don't know. A whole bunch of stuff."

Jill was fascinated by this discussion but felt bad for Max, who was clearly struggling with all this. "So no cocaine or like, heroin? The really bad ones?"

"These were all pills," said Max. "But I think they're all really bad. Opioids."

"Have you heard from him since he left?" asked Grace.

"He called me."

Grace leaned over so that she was looking at Max's face upside down, her hair cascading down to make a veil over his face. "Is he okay?"

"I think so," said Max. "He's staying at a friend's house in Santa Monica. This guy Henry."

"Is that good?" asked Jill, while Grace leaned back on the bed again.

"I don't know," said Max. "The guy's a complete jackass. One time he slapped me across the face because I didn't have matches." His voice was trembling a bit. "I would have rather had him punch me. The slap really stung, and it was humiliating."

"Well maybe this will be better," said Grace. "For a while at least until he gets his life together."

"He won't," said Max.

Then it was really quiet for an uncomfortably long time. Jill thought about breaking the silence, but the only thing she could think to talk about was Grace's twitter picture, and that didn't really seem like a good topic to end this awkward moment. She'd heard the expression to *fight fire with fire.* But trying to reduce awkwardness with more awkwardness didn't seem to fit that theory. So Jill didn't say anything. She watched Grace sigh and stand up.

Grace walked around the room looking at the junk on Jill's desk. She picked up a pair of sunglasses and tried them on. Then she walked over to a bulletin board with photographs all over it. There must have been fifty pictures, but Grace zeroed in on one and yanked it off the board. She stared at it for a long time and then looked over at Jill. Grace had no expression.

"You know this girl?" asked Grace pointing aggressively at the picture, tapping the middle of it with her index finger.

Jill lost her breath. She didn't have asthma, but she imagined that this was what an asthma attack felt like—lungs deflating.

"Is this Sophia Martini?" she asked, shaking the picture at Jill. "This picture is on her Insta page. Do you know her?"

They'd made the pact to never tell her, and Jill was not ready for this. She couldn't believe how stupid she was for having that picture up.

She couldn't talk.

She couldn't even come up with a bad lie. Her brain wasn't functioning. To stall, she was going to ask Grace if she could hand her the picture so that she could get a better look, but before she could get any words out, Max said, "We're so sorry, Grace."

~47~

When Pat asked Jenny if she wanted to meet somewhere off campus, she said sure, but she didn't want to go to the Dubliner or any other West Portal bar. Too many familiar faces. Just enough people who have Twitter accounts. She'd heard about Pat getting in fistfights in high school and college, and she didn't want the wrong guy to make a comment and push him over the edge today.

He didn't sound good on the phone. His voice was thick, tired.

But when he walked into Finnigan's Wake on Cole street, just down from the N Judah Line, he looked fine, maybe even a little wired. Aside from his tie being crooked, he looked like he always did.

Jenny didn't like to sit at the bar. She thought bar tenders were nosey, at least some of them, so she was seated at a small, round table near the dartboard. It wasn't a tall table like you see in most bars these days. Finnigan's was old school, and the little table was accompanied by two short chairs. Emily was sitting in one and watching Pat look for her.

When he finally saw her, he gave her a *what the hell?* shrug. Why didn't she call him when he was wandering around? She just smiled.

"What do you want?" he said.

"805," she said and leaned back in the chair.

Pat maneuvered his way between what looked like two regulars sitting on stools and monopolizing the bartender with Trump talk. Both patrons clearly hated the president, and the bartender was trying to convince them that they just hated his personality but that his policies were making America better, not necessarily great again, but better.

When Pat leaned into the bar, they all looked at him as if he might settle the argument.

"Are you serious?" he said. "You guys know I won't talk politics with you. Try something less controversial like homelessness or the Middle East."

The bartender smiled and said, "What'll you have, Pat?"

"Two 805's," he said and whispered something to one of the regulars, who laughed so hard that he snorted a little bit.

When the bartender came back with the beers, he said, "What's the big joke? You guys talking about Hillary?"

"God bless America," said Pat and placed his money behind the collection of pint, shot, and cocktail glasses that had accumulated in front of this small group. "Tommy, get yourself something."

The bartender nodded a thanks to Pat and swiped the twenty off the bar.

When Pat put the two pints on the table, Jenny said, "Do you know every bartender in town?"

"Just the one," he said and nearly stuck his whole face into his glass to take a drink. He came up with a bit of froth on his lip, and he wiped it off with the back of his hand.

"I thought we'd come here so that we wouldn't have to see anyone you knew," she said.

"Who?" he said. "These guys?" Then he shook his head. "They barely talk to me. They think I'm a Republican because I'm nice to Tommy."

"Well, are you a Republican?"

"Shhh," he hissed. "It's not really safe to say that word around these guys. I'm apolitical. I hate almost all politicians."

"Yeah," she said. "I'm sure you have some leanings though."

"Don't we all," he said and raised his glass.

She tapped it with hers, but she hadn't taken a sip yet, so she spilled some on the table. He didn't even flinch at the mess. "Well," she said. "Regardless of whether or not you're political, aren't we here to talk about politics?"

"I guess so," he said and lost a bit of the playful twinkle in his eye.

"Have you decided how you want to handle it?"

"I have not," he said and peeked over Jenny's shoulder at the Giants game playing on the TV behind her.

"What's the score?" she said.

"Giants still down by two."

"Church politics might even be more complex than national politics," she said and sipped at her 805.

"To me," he said. "There's nothing complex about national politics anymore." He nodded toward the three still arguing at the bar.

"Conservatives think Liberals are stupid, and liberals think conservatives are evil."

"That sounds about right," she said.

"Which is ironic," he said.

"Why?"

"Because even though the liberals are supposed to be the stupid ones in this scenario, they're on the smarter side of the argument."

"Why?"

He smiled. "They might have just lucked into this," he said. "But it's a winning strategy because people don't generally hate stupid people, but they do hate the evil ones. And any time you can get some good old-fashioned hate going, you can win elections."

Jenny didn't really smile with her mouth, but she could tell that her eyes were betraying her because Pat started to laugh before he said, "Unless you go too far, of course, and make up a bunch of irrational shit about the other side. Then the whole strategy could backfire."

He sounded so confident that Jenny had to smile. "So, I guess you've got it all figured out," she said.

"I do," he said.

"Then what do you need me for?"

"That's national politics," he said. "I need help with the archdiocese."

"Why don't you just tell me what you're thinking right now?"

"I'm thinking I should pull her."

"Why?"

"Because she's a distraction."

"Not good enough," said Jenny. "What else?"

"She's making it hard on you, Sister Margaret, and the Archbishop," he said. "I don't want that. You all have been very good to me."

This made some sense to Jenny, but she wasn't sure if this was his complete rationale for taking Grace out of school. "You sure that's all of it?"

"I think so," he said. "And I just think it will be easier. What's the rush? Who cares if she graduates college as a twenty-two-year-old or a twenty-three year-old? It really doesn't make a difference."

Even though he seemed to be talking the whole time, his pint was empty. She didn't even remember seeing him take a sip after the first one. "You make a good point there," she said. "The age is arbitrary." Then she paused for a moment as a piece of information from some educational journal rose to the surface and revealed itself. "There's a high percentage of girls who take a year off for whatever reason, and they plan on returning to high school at some point, but they never do."

"Are you telling me you think that could happen to Grace?" He had a smirk on his face now, like he'd caught her playing Devil's advocate, which he had.

"Just sharing data," she said and got up to get him another beer even though she still had more than half in hers. "You want the same thing?" she asked.

"No" he said. "I'll get it." Then he made a pretty good act of pretending he was going to get up even though he knew she wouldn't let him.

She pushed his shoulder down and said, "805?"

"That would be grand," he said in a fairly decent Irish brogue.

Jenny walked to the same spot at the bar that Pat had ordered the first round, right between the two Trump-haters. "Can you bring me one 805?" she said. "I lost a bet to my friend over there." All three looked over at him, but Jenny kept her eye on the bartender. "He was able to give me the first names of all the Trump kids. He even knew some cousins. Seems like a big fan."

"I knew it," squawked the one on Jenny's left. "We don't want you in here anymore, Pat."

"She's jerking you around, Rick," said Pat.

"Is that true?" he said and looked at Jenny, but she just smiled and walked back to the table.

"Why do you do things like that?" he asked.

"I need a little fun sometimes, Pat."

"I guess you do," he said. "Thanks for the beer."

"And I think you're right about pulling Grace," she said. "And I'm not saying this because I think it will be easier on me." She caught Pat looking over her shoulder again. "Score?" she said.

"Posey just hit a two-run double," he said. "Tied up."

"I'm not telling you this because I want to take the easy way out," she said. "Sister Margaret's going to be pissed. I think she wants to make a statement. I think she wants to fight for Grace."

"I guess they have a connection," he said. "But I'm not really sure what we're supposed to be fighting for."

"Could it be forgiveness?" she said. "Isn't that what we're asking from the Arch? From the community?"

"I wish it were that simple," he said. "As you might recall, my daughter does not believe she has anything to be sorry for. So, going about the business of offering an apology is complicated." He moved as if he were going to take a sip of his beer, but he stopped and took a deep breath instead. "She's doing really well emotionally for a kid who's going through all this. I think her blocking out of whatever happened to her must be helping her. It's a fragile situation. A delicate ecosystem, as the scientists say."

He seemed very serious for the first time today. Jenny wanted to help. The educator in her wanted to try to guide him to the right decision, but he was making her doubt any course of action that she'd considered before. "So, you're scared that if you disrupt some small part of the psychological construct that she has assembled, the effects on her emotional state could be emotionally devastating."

"That sounds about right," he said.

"It sounds good," she said and laughed a little. "But I really don't have any idea what I'm talking about."

"Sure you do," he said.

"Thanks for the support."

"I could go the tough love route and *force* her to face the fact that she doesn't really have a miracle growing inside her."

"Didn't you try that?"

"For months," he said.

"Do people ever hold onto some scrap of denial for their whole lives?"

"I don't know," he said. "I think that in a situation like this one, she'll have to eventually be able to explain to the kid the …," he looked up at the ceiling. "… the *details* of the conception."

"You're telling me that your parents told you about your conception? Kind of creepy."

"You know what I mean," he said, not laughing. "I know who my dad is."

"I think you're trying to say that the child is eventually going to ask about the father."

"Yeah," he said and took a long drink. "We have this new therapist that Grace really likes …." His eyes looked like there was nothing going on behind them.

"Are you thinking about using him yourself?"

Pat's expression didn't change, but he yelled over to the two politicos at the bar, "This woman just said that she voted for George W. Bush … twice!"

Tim Reardon

Grace

It's raining again. It's almost always raining lately. The lady is sharing her umbrella with me, and we're standing so close that, from far away, we could look like one person.

We walk for a long time before she says anything.

"This doesn't mean they don't love you," said the lady, her voice sounding younger than normal, softer.

I'm not in a great mood, and when I feel like this, I'm almost always sarcastic. "You're right," I say. "Catfishing someone is probably the best way to say I love you."

As soon as I say it, I feel like a jerk, but I keep walking. The lady and I have the same stride, so keeping pace is natural, easy.

She doesn't say anything for a long time. The rain is steady. There's a flash of lightning and then a distant rumble of thunder. Even though it's far away, I can feel it in my chest, like a heavy base line, a deep vibration.

All the streetlights are out, so I can see the sidewalk right in front of me, but everything else is dark, muted. But when the lightning bursts the night sky, I feel like I can see the whole city for a fraction of a second.

Then we're right back to the blind leading the blind.

I wonder where in the city we are that I can see so much of it during the flashes. Everything seems to be within one freeze-frame. The bridges are the borders, and the rest of the city is in the middle—Coit Tower, Transamerica Pyramid, Salesforce, Saints Peter and Paul steeple, Mount Davidson Cross—everything squeezed into a compact panoramic cluster.

We must be high up.

"Are you aware that you can love someone without knowing how to love them?"

Are you aware? *she says. She sounds like my mom. This is her way of scolding me for being a wiseass earlier. "I suppose," I say. Giving it right back to her.*

Another flash of lightning, but this time, all I see are trees, and I notice for the first time that the sidewalk has crumbled into a gravel path that quickly smooths itself into a tamped down dirt trail.

The lady is quiet again. Probably not happy about my participation in the conversation so far. The ground has a strange texture, and I don't even hear our feet as we walk, but I hear movement in the forest that surrounds us. Squirrels in the trees, maybe. I'm not scared. The lady is with me. I should be more appreciative. "I guess you can be bad at love," I say.

"Explain, please."

The trees around them go quiet. No wind. Maybe even the rain has stopped, but the lady still holds the umbrella above us. "If a person loves someone, let's say a really good friend, but that person does things that make the friend unhappy, that's bad love. Even if the original person was doing whatever she was doing for the right reasons. Right?"

"Say it again in a different way," she says. "You don't sound confident."

I'm confident in the idea. I'm just having trouble with the wording. The lady wants me to get the language right even though she knows what I'm saying. "Okay," I say. "Let's work with a boyfriend and girlfriend."

The lady says, "That should be fine."

"The boy sells his watch to buy the girl a beautiful set of combs, and the girl sells her hair to buy the boy an expensive watch chain."

"Grace," says the lady, and she sounds like she's getting impatient.

"What?" I say. "Does this example not illustrate my idea?"

"Do you even know what a watch chain is?" she asks.

"I guess not," I say. "But that's an example of bad love."

"In the end, those two people knew how much they loved each other," she says. "But I'd like you to come up with one on your own."

"How about if a big sister tries to stick up for her little sister by intimidating kids who pose a threat, but those kids spread the word about the older sister, and no one wants to hang out with the younger sister anymore because they're intimidated by the older sister?"

I feel good about my example.

"Did that happen?" asks the lady.

"No," I say. "But it could've."

"Is there something that really *happened recently that could be an example of what we've been talking about?"*

I'm not going to say it. I get to be mad for a few days. I deserve it. "I can't think of anything," I say.

This time the flash is longer, and I look over at the lady, but I can't see her in the flash of light.

~48~

Pat stopped short when he walked into the kitchen. He felt his toes mash up against the fronts of his loafers. His sister Erin was leaning against the kitchen island, and she looked emotional.

Erin almost always held it together.

Emily was at the kitchen table with her phone and a cup of tea in front of her, but she didn't even look up at him.

"I'm so sorry, Patrick," said Erin. "I had no idea."

Pat was coming home from a very, very long day at work. To end the day, he had a half hour meeting with a mom who felt that her son's grades were miscalculated. All of them. She believed it was some kind of computer glitch. And she thought that, for some reason, the glitch only made the boy's grades lower. Never higher. Apparently, some kind of malicious glitch. She wanted the grades fixed immediately because her boy was applying to Dartmouth.

Earlier in the day, Pat found out that a long-time English teacher had been instructing her classes that all men were the products of toxic masculinity. At an all-boys' school.

Also, the football coach was being accused of recruiting a player to transfer from a rival school.

And the Dean of Students was being accused of racism because he was enforcing the no dreadlocks rule.

And two sophomores were airdropping pornography in their biology class.

Also, a department chair had ordered the wrong digital textbooks and the school was going to have to eat the cost.

And finally, the Dean of Academics informed Pat that he was retiring at the end of the year.

And here was Erin in his kitchen telling him that she was *so sorry.*

Before Pat even asked why Erin had driven all the way down from Guerneville, he turned to the refrigerator and pulled out a Corona. He drank half and placed it on the counter. "Go ahead," he said to his sister.

Erin took a deep breath and said, "I was at the River Inn Grill." She stopped and swallowed. She looked back at Emily, but Emily was either looking at her phone or her cup of tea. Pat couldn't tell which from where he stood.

"Keep going," he said and felt like they were kids again, and she'd lost one of his G.I. Joes or something.

"Well," she said. "I was having breakfast with Virginia Tunney. She's ninety-four. I can tell her anything and know that she won't repeat it. She forgets whatever I tell her before we even pay the check."

Pat looked past Erin now, and it was clear that Emily was scrolling through something on her phone.

"I was telling Virginia about Gracie—"

"What about Gracie?" he said.

"Everything," said Erin. "It's a good story. I was just passing the time."

"And this old lady told someone?"

"No," said Erin. "I told you. She can't remember anything."

"Then what's the problem?"

Erin took a deep breath. "There was a gentleman sitting in the booth behind us," she said.

"Jesus Christ."

"And I had to talk loud because Virginia doesn't hear so good."

"Unbelievable."

"After I was finished with the story, the man spun around in his booth and said *Are you Erin Ryan?* So I told him I was, and then he said *I'm from the Santa Rosa Press Democrat. Would you be able to answer a few questions?"*

Emily sighed, and Erin turned around to look at her. Emily looked up, startled to see that she had drawn attention to herself. "I'm sorry," she said. "I'm just reading some of these posts."

"What posts?" asked Pat.

Emily was looking back at her phone now. "Just let Erin finish," she said.

"So I say to the guy *Questions about what*? And he tells me that he'd like to know if I'm Grace Ryan's aunt. Then I tell him that I don't want to talk to him. I'm sorry."

"Was the guy going to write a story about Grace in the paper?" asked Pat. "It doesn't really seem like newspaper material."

Erin was in storyteller mode now, and she didn't seem to like being interrupted. She just wanted to get it out. "Not in the paper," she said. "This guy does some writing for the paper, but he's more popular as a blogger."

"So now some obscure Santa Rosa blogger is doing a story on Grace?" he said. "Don't worry about it, Erin. You didn't do it on purpose."

"Hon?" said Emily. "The guy *is* obscure, but the headline has *Coyote Girl* in it, so the article did pick up some traffic."

"Really?" he said. "These people need to get lives." He drank more of his Corona, but it didn't taste right. Sour. He poured the rest down the sink.

"The virgin part is getting the most attention in the comments," said Emily. "Lots of comments."

Erin said, "I'm so sorry, Patrick."

"And you're not going to like this part, Pat," said Emily.

"What?"

"Lots of the comments are about you," she said and looked up from her phone. She shook her head and frowned. "This is crazy."

"What about me?"

Emily scrolled through some of the comments, scowling at the phone. "The story talks about the fact that you don't believe her, Pat." She looked over at Erin, who must have divulged this fact to the old lady at the River Inn Grill. "And this is the part that still seems so odd to me. Grace actually has a fan base, and they're all mad at you for not believing your daughter."

Pat suddenly felt tired. Like, if he closed his eyes, he could fall asleep while standing.

Emily started to read: "Grace's dad should get his head out of his—"

"Please don't read anymore," Pat said. He had his eyes closed now, and he was feeling a bit dizzy. He put his hand on the counter.

When he was coaching, there were message boards on which parents would post complaints about anything they wanted. Much of the content was based around the idea that Pat was a mental case. That he couldn't coach a third-grade team. That he couldn't see talent if it dribbled up and dunked on him. That this team would be undefeated if they just had a better coach.

Pat had seen all these anonymous messages. His first year. Then he never read another one again. And he wasn't about to start doing it again now. "We're not going to get caught up in this shit," he said. "And I don't want Grace reading this stuff either."

"You gonna take her phone away?" asked Emily.

Pat knew it was impossible to stop her from reading about herself, about the family. But he did want to tell her how to interpret it. He needed to explain to her that this stuff moves really fast and that people won't be talking about her for very long. Something else is going to come up, and she'll be a distant memory, an overexposed, faded Polaroid from a different era. And it might only take a couple of days.

The Coyote Girl was out of school now, and no one was going to take her picture. She was going to rest and prepare for being a young mom. This blog post was another unfortunate turn, but it would pass.

He was running through this in his head when he heard the side door open and close. Grace was home. She didn't stop in her room. She walked straight to the kitchen, and before she got to the door, she said, "Hey Dad, everyone hates you."

She walked into the room with her eyes on her phone. She wasn't smiling, but she didn't seem sad either. When she finally looked up and saw her aunt, she said, "Erin," and ran around the kitchen island for a hug. "What are you doing here?"

Erin looked over at Pat before she said, "I had to come down to say sorry to your dad. And to you. too."

"For what?" said Grace.

"The latest online stuff about you is my fault."

"How?"

Erin's eyes started to well up. She wiped at them before there were any actual tears. "I was talking too loud about you to someone I trust, and someone I don't trust heard me."

"And now the virgin story is out there," said Grace and held up her phone. She didn't seem angry. Like Pat, she seemed more amazed at the sheer speed at which a story could travel.

Erin nodded first then started shaking her head—*yes, I did this; no I didn't want to hurt you.*

"It's okay, Erin," said Grace. "I love you."

"I love you, too, sweetie."

"So, you must have said something about my dad not believing me?" asked Grace with the hint of a smile at the corners of her mouth.

"I did," she said.

Pat smacked his hand flat on the kitchen island and said, "And now I'm the bad guy."

"I still love ya, Dad," she said. "You'll eventually come around."

~49~

Saturday was warm. Indian summer in the city.

Jill and Max called Grace and asked her if they could meet to talk about the Sophia Martini online relationship hoax. It all sounded so terrible to Jill now as she thought back on it.

But Grace said yes. In fact, she didn't even seem angry. When Grace had originally figured it all out in Jill's room that day, she didn't yell at them. She didn't tell their parents. She probably didn't even tell her own parents. She didn't throw anything. She simply dropped the picture of Sophia on the desk and walked out of Jill's room.

She didn't answer texts or calls for the next couple of days, but today she said yes, she'd like to meet. How about the beach?

It was an extraordinary day. The city didn't get many like this. Jill was wearing a tank top and shorts, and there was actually a crowd on the L Taraval streetcar as they moved west toward Ocean Beach. Usually, if you saw three kids with beach towels on the L, you'd think they were tourists who didn't understand that, while San Francisco is in California, it isn't really much like California. But today, they fit right in with the rest of the passengers headed for cooler temperatures near the water.

After they passed The Tennessee Grill, Parkside Tavern, El Burrito Xpress, Nick's Tacos, White Cap, and The Rip Tide, they got off at the last stop on 47th Avenue. As soon as they took a few steps toward the Great Highway, they saw surfers everywhere. Men were changing into wet suits next to their cars and trucks. Some guys were running with their boards across the Great Highway. Others seemed content to just stand around half dressed and talk about surfing. When Jill's group walked past some of the surfers, they sounded to Jill like they were speaking a different language. *Barrels, Bennys, and bombs … goofy foot, grubbing, and green rooms… macking, mullering, and mushburgers.* They sounded like words right out of a Dr. Seuss book.

Jill tried to collect all the lingo like sea shells as they made their way to the top of the bluff before heading down to the beach, but every time she eavesdropped on a new group, she'd forget all the jargon from the last group.

They walked on a sandy path surrounded by ice plants, and Jill stopped as soon as they could see the water. "Doesn't look like there's any barrels today," she said, pointing out at the sea. "Only mushburgers."

"What does that even mean?" asked Max.

"Not really sure," she said. "But it sounds cool, I think."

"It does," said Grace. "I was trying to pick the perfect moment to say *goofy foot*. I guess I just did."

They all laughed, but Jill was a bit anxious. She just wanted to spread their towels out so that they could sit down and have an actual conversation about what happened. She wanted to explain to Grace that she never wanted to hurt her. She wanted to tell Grace that she was so sorry to put their friendship in jeopardy. She wanted Grace to trust her again.

She also wanted to know how Grace felt about the fact that the virgin part of her story was now a thing that people were tweeting about. Jill was thankful that she didn't have anything to do with this development.

Maybe that was why she didn't seem so mad at Jill and Max. She had someone new to be mad at now.

The whole ride down on the streetcar, they talked about school and TV and movies. That was it. Nothing of substance. So Jill felt like she was about to explode. She didn't want to talk on the L because there were so many people, and she thought things might get emotional.

The beach path snaked down toward the Pacific. The surfers in their black wet suits were bobbing beyond the breakers. The long stretch of dunes was colonized by every kind of San Franciscan you could imagine. Every shape, color, and size. But it wasn't like a SoCal beach or even Santa Cruz for that matter. There were no professional beachgoers. There just wasn't enough opportunity in the city, so most of the folks besides the surfers and dog walkers were amateurs, just happy to feel the warm sand beneath them.

Jill, Max, and Grace decided to set up camp next to a cute family—a mom and dad and two little boys. The only thing strange about them was the fact that they were all wearing black jeans and black t-shirts. It was about eighty degrees out. They were doing all the normal things a little family might do at the beach—plastic buckets and shovels, an umbrella, beach chairs—but they were dressed as if they were going to a Metallica concert.

When Jill looked on the other side, she saw two skinny men in nothing but Speedos. One was old with bushy grey hair and the other looked to be about twenty years younger and was as bald as an egg. They had a cooler between them, from which the younger man pulled out a White Claw. He offered it to the older man, who waved it off. The younger man smiled and opened it himself.

Grace was wearing one of her dad's St. X t-shirts. It was several sizes too big, but it had the extra room she needed. She set up her towel between Jill and Max, and once they were settled, she said, "So … Sophia Martini."

Jill's reflex was to immediately start explaining herself, but she hesitated. She wasn't sure why, but she didn't blurt anything out. Grace's face was so calm that Jill decided to wait and see. She looked over at Max, and he appeared to be taking the same strategy.

"Do you guys want to tell me why you did it?" she said. "Or do you want me to tell you why *I* think you did it?" Grace leaned back so that Jill and Max could look at each other, but neither answered immediately. Jill could see in Max's eyes that he needed help, but Jill was the one who birthed Sophia, and she still felt so guilty about it that she was paralyzed.

It was a chickenshit standoff.

"Okay," said Grace. "I guess I'm going to tell you why I think you did it." She was smiling and looking back and forth between her two friends. "And at the end, you two don't even have to talk since it seems like you're having problems with that skill right now. All you have to do is either nod at me or shake your heads *no*. Can we do that?"

Jill and Max nodded.

"This is a weird configuration," said Grace. "Because we're all looking over each other." The three towels were lined up in a straight line so that they were all facing the ocean.

"Should we form a triangle," asked Jill, happy that her voice still worked.

"Sure," said Grace. Then, "Wait … no. Let's just lie back and close our eyes so none of us has to look at each other, and I'll tell you guys what I think happened."

To someone up on the bluff gazing down, they must have looked like three sunbathers enjoying the day. But Jill knew this was more. It was a pivotal moment in a friendship that meant everything to her. It was one that she wanted to have for the rest of her life. It was that kind of friendship.

"This is probably why you guys catfished me," she began, and Jill cringed, her eyes shut tight against the sun. It almost hurt physically to hear that word. People who catfished other people almost always did it for selfish reasons—sometimes revenge, sometimes jealousy, and sometimes because of their own insecurities. But Jill didn't really think of herself like that. At least she didn't want to.

"You knew I was kinda messed up because of everything that was happening to me," she said. "And you wanted to help me because you're my friends. And you maybe even thought I was losing my mind a little bit because of the fact that there's no father involved."

She paused for a moment, and Jill almost sat up to respond. She felt the tightening of the muscles in her abdomen and neck, as if she were going to pull herself up, but she didn't. She relaxed again and let Grace's voice cradle her back into the sand.

Grace continued, "So you guys thought that if only I had someone else who was going through the same thing, I would be able to cope a little better."

Jill heard Grace moving around next to her, but she didn't look over. She was just sunbathing, listening to a story.

"Even though I thought I was doing pretty well—" she said.

"You were," Max interrupted.

"It speaks," said Grace in her best monster movie voice. "So, I was doing pretty well, but not great, so you guys gave me another friend who could relate. Ooh, that rhymes."

A general stillness came over the beach for a moment, and Jill heard only the crash of the waves and calls of the seagulls. A peaceful instant in the middle of all the craziness of the past few weeks.

"And then," said Grace. "You guys got too deep into it and didn't know how to get out. You had no exit strategy." She started to laugh now, a full-bellied laugh that Jill hadn't heard in a long time. "I can just picture the two of you trying to figure out what to say. It's hilarious, actually."

Jill was tempted to peek to see how Max was reacting to all this, but she didn't. She stayed in the moment like Grace wanted.

"Maybe you thought if Sophia was admitting that hers wasn't really a virgin pregnancy that I would have some kind of realization that mine wasn't either. I don't know about that part. It'll be interesting to hear what you guys were thinking there. Maybe you just thought the online friendship would end because there was no connection anymore." She sighed loud enough for Jill to hear it over the crashing of the waves. "But there was still a connection. Because it was you guys. It *was* a real friendship. Get it?"

Jill couldn't figure out if Grace was coming up with stuff on the fly, or if she'd studied the scenario from all angles and determined that this is what must have happened. Grace had done a pretty good job. They all knew each other very well. At this point, it was hard for Jill to even remember exactly how the Sophia Martini story evolved—what parts came out of her mind and what parts came out of Max's.

"Can we open our eyes," said Max.

"Yes."

They all sat up, and Jill and Max were both nodding at Grace. Jill leaned over to hug her best friend. "I'm so sorry."

Max looked so shy over there on his towel. "I'm sorry, too, Grace."

"So what did I get wrong?" Grace said, smiling like they were playing some kind of party game.

"First off," said Jill. "Max shouldn't take as much blame for this. I was doing the first few on my own. I didn't call Max until things got out of control."

"Oh," said Grace. "Okay. That makes sense. What else?"

"What else do you want to know," said Jill.

"Why you took away Sophia's virgin status?"

"Max can answer that one," said Jill. "I think he wrote that whole exchange."

"You mean you guys went back and forth?" asked Grace.

"Most of the time, we weren't even together," said Jill. "There were times when I was typing while talking to Max on the phone, and times when Max was typing while talking to me on the phone."

"Two-headed catfish," said Grace. "Max? Do you want to tell me why you wanted to take away Sophia's virginity?" Then she burst out laughing again. "I'm sorry. That sounded funny. But you know what I mean. Why not just let me continue to have a friend who gets me?"

Max looked normal for a second, and he even opened his mouth like he was going to say something, but then he just jumped up and started running toward the water. He jumped over towels and coolers and zigzagged through sandcastles and beach toys until he got to the water where he actually started to run even faster. He was still wearing a shirt, but he high stepped through the shallow undertow and dove into the first breaker.

"What the hell?" Jill finally said.

Grace stood up. "What's he doing?"

Max was splashing out past the casual swimmers toward the flotilla of surfers and boogie boarders. He disappeared under the swells a couple of times and then popped up again and aggressively clawed at the water like he was trying to hurt it, like he was going to paddle his way all the way out to the Farallon Islands.

Grace was holding her belly and walking very quickly now. Jill scampered behind and felt on her shins the sting of sand that Grace was kicking up as she stomped toward the waves.

When they got to the wet, squishy sand, Jill felt her feet get suctioned in with every step. Each time her feet hit the film of water over the mush, it produced a slapping sound as she chased after Grace, who was knee deep in the water now.

When Jill looked back out to sea, she couldn't find Max.

He had to be somewhere in the maze of bobbing surfers, but she couldn't find him.

Grace was in up to her waist now, and she was screaming, "Max. Max!"

Jill got in deeper with Grace and pulled her back just as they got hit in the shoulders by the next roller. Now they were both yelling, "Help! Help!" But the surfers couldn't hear them. Jill was a terrible swimmer, and Grace was pregnant. Jill's feet were sinking into the spongy sand, and she was starting to lose her mind. She looked down the beach for one of the rangers that patrolled, but she knew they'd be nowhere. They're never ready for a day like this in the city.

Jill looked the other way and saw Grace talking to three surfers on the beach. She was waving her arms around and pointing out toward where they'd last seen Max. Two of the surfers dove in and started paddling out. The third stayed with Grace and put his hand on her shoulder.

Jill felt like she was in quicksand. Why wasn't she doing something? Why couldn't she move? Maybe it was a panic attack. She looked back at the water and thought she saw him for a second. Then she saw some surfers clustered together and thought they might be helping someone, but they dispersed a second later. She screamed one more time nonsensically. "Max!"

Then she ran back up to the towels, pulled her phone out of her bag, and called 911.

***

Before Max had left the house for the beach that morning, he'd gotten up early and wrote out what he was thinking. Like a journal, but he just did it on a piece of notebook paper. He thought if he could get it down in writing—all of it—he'd be able to share it with Grace at some point. In many ways, he'd never really accepted all that happened. This would be a way to document the event. He needed there to be a record of what happened and why.

Max

None of this is easy to talk about. I'm only sixteen, and I already know that I will never make a worse mistake as long as I live. You're probably thinking How does he know. *Believe me. I know.*

And the worst part is that I absolutely never wanted to hurt anyone. That's a fact. And this is the worst kind of mistake. A haunting mistake.

My parents were away, and I decided to have a party at my house. Our group of friends had met up with St. Mary's girls near the backstop at Aptos playground and in the Reservoir across the street from City College. But we'd never had a real party. With my parents gone and my older brother, Tony, willing to buy up for us, there wasn't going to be a better opportunity.

I also thought it would be a good time to find out if Grace liked me.

I was in love with Grace.

I know you're thinking that I'm just a teenager and that I don't really understand love, but it's true. A lot of people don't believe in love at first sight or soul mates or any of that stuff, but I'm here to tell you that it's real. Maybe not for everyone, but it was for me.

Now I'm not saying that Grace loved me or even liked me more than just a friend. And I'm also aware that lots of other boys might have been in love with Grace because she's that kind of person. The only thing I'm sure of is that I was in love with her. I could go into all the reasons I knew it, but you've heard all these kinds of things before, and I don't want this to sound like a Hallmark card. All those old clichés won't help you understand what was going on in my heart and in my mind. Try to just trust me for the sake of it.

I wasn't going to tell her about my feelings at the party. I didn't want to freak her out, and I was still trying to play it cool, to maybe earn her love by letting her see me as a great guy. Not sure if that makes sense, but that's what was going through my mind when I decided to have the party.

Once the party started, everyone was having fun. It really was a good party. A few people didn't know how to drink and were acting like fools, but at least they were happy fools, and they weren't breaking anything or spilling beer on my mom's couch or throwing up yet. A few people did later, but for most of the party, people were cool—my buddy, Tarique, was a great DJ and the neighbors weren't complaining, and my brother was a generous bartender.

I probably had too much to drink, but not so much that I couldn't keep an eye on things and make sure the party didn't get out of control.

I hung out with Grace and Jill off and on for the first couple of hours, but then I lost track of them for a bit. At one point, Jill was hanging with Tarique, and Grace wasn't in the kitchen or the living room. I didn't think much of it, but I did do a quick check around the house. I got sidetracked a couple of times, but then I saw Grace come out of the bathroom. She was smiling but unsteady.

My brother had turned the bar into self-serve and was there to help her. It was almost as if he was waiting there for her. He took her hand and walked down the hallway. I thought he might have been bringing her to the kitchen to sit down, but they walked right past, and then Tony opened the door to the stairs. His room was in the basement. Grace was holding his hand and walking with him.

This is where things get really embarrassing.

My first instinct was that I was hurt. Sad for myself because the girl I loved was walking away with another guy. I was drunk and a little emotional, and I stood in the hallway and felt sorry for myself for a minute. It should have been even worse because she was with my brother, but I wasn't thinking about that. I was really just thinking that she didn't like me.

Then my brain started to adjust the focus of what I had seen. Grace was drunk, and Tony was nineteen. This was bad on many levels. So I ran down the stairs and saw Tony in his room with his hands on Grace's waist. It almost looked like they could be dancing, but the only movement was Grace, trying to get her balance.

I stepped into the room and said, "What's going on?"

"Max!" said Grace like she was glad to see me.

My brother said, "I got it."

"What do mean?" I said.

"She drank too much," he said. "I'm gonna take care of her."

"She's my *friend," I said. "I'll take care of her."*

"Max," she said again.

"Get the fuck out of here," said Tony, and he let go of Grace's waist. He must have really been holding her up because as soon as he let go, she fell back on the bed. She must have been in a lucky spot because she landed like she was going to sit down, and in some drunken way, she pretended that she did it on purpose. Like she was taking a seat to watch this prize fight between two creeps.

"Tony," I said. "I'm not leaving you down here with her."

Right then, there was a tapping at the side door. Tony's room was really an in-law apartment, and it had a door to the alleyway. The door's window looked out at a small tree and the side of the neighbor's house, but right now it framed the faces of two of Tony's asshole friends.

They opened the door, and one of them said, "We came. Where is she?"

Tony looked like he was going to kill me. He stared at me and had both hands clinched into fists. Then he looked at his friends and said, "Forget it. Let's get out of this lame party."

I watched them all walk out the side door, and I walked over and locked it. I was shaking. Tony had punched me in the face a couple of times before for lesser crimes. To be honest, I'm still surprised that the three of them didn't beat the crap out me right there. I think Tony was so mad he couldn't even function. The three of them probably went out and smashed windows or started dumpster fires or something.

After I locked the door, I stood at the window for a minute to see if they were coming back. Then I heard Grace.

"My knight in shining armor," she said. "Come over here."

She didn't sound like herself, but when the girl you love says Come over here, *you go over there. And I did.*

I sat next to her, and she didn't say anything. She just took my face in her hands and kissed me. I closed my eyes and got dizzy almost immediately. Remember, I'd been drinking, too. So we both lost our balance and fell back on the bed.

She was whispering nonsense in between kisses, and things kept progressing. I want to tell this truthfully, but I don't want to be too graphic, either. So, yeah, it kept progressing, and I didn't really know what I was doing because I hadn't really gotten this far before. Not even close.

But neither of us had pants on now, and I was on top but kind of sideways. And not even really moving or anything but still kissing. And then it was over before it began for me.

The two of us were still virgins, and, to tell you the truth, I was actually relieved. I didn't want the first time—if there was ever going to be another time—to be while both of us were drunk.

I told you this was embarrassing.

So I said I was sorry, and I went into the bathroom to get a towel to clean up. And when I came back, Grace was asleep. I mean really asleep. Where I couldn't wake her up. I cleaned her off down there and put her pants back on, but she was still asleep.

I was really scared at this point. She was breathing normally. I knew that because I kept checking. Then I was scared that maybe the party was getting out of control, so I told Grace I was going to check upstairs. She didn't respond, but I had to check.

When I got upstairs, Tarique told me he'd keep an eye on things but that two girls were already throwing up in my parent's bathroom. Jill was helping them.

This went on for over an hour—me running back and forth between upstairs and downstairs. Eventually, I came downstairs and Grace was sitting up. She said that she had too much to drink and felt weird still, but she was able to go upstairs and sit on a couch for about a half an hour.

The party broke up, and I eventually walked her home.

It wasn't until a few days later that I realized Grace didn't remember any of it.

And when she ended up pregnant, I didn't think it could be possible. I knew what had happened. But the more I read the timing all pointed to me—the one in a million fluke. And I was off the hook because no one knew. Not a soul.

And then Grace told me that she believed this was a virgin pregnancy, and, in a way, it was. But not the way she thought.

And eventually, when I found my brother's stash of drugs and saw what kinds he had, I knew what Tony had done and what he planned to do that night.

You can imagine how my brain was handling the whole thing. One part of it was telling me that I had saved Grace from an unspeakable atrocity, and the other part was telling me that I had taken advantage of her, too. I was a savior and a tormentor.

The only thing that kept me from killing myself was that I knew in my heart that I never would do anything to hurt her. And that barely kept me going. I was hanging on by a thread.

It felt good to expose Tony's stash to my mom and dad. I hate tattletales, but my brother was out of control. He was going to end up in jail. Maybe that's where he should be.

So that's what I've been going through. And believe me, I don't expect anyone to feel sorry for me. I know what I am. And I know there's a chance I'll go to hell for this.

~50~

Alice's college friend from Petaluma was driving home for the weekend, so Alice hitched a ride to check in on Grace and have a couple of days in the city. And now she was caught behind a streetcar and two tourists on scooters as she tried to maneuver her mom's Volvo down Taraval Street to get to the beach, where something happened to Max.

Grace had been out of breath on the phone, and she said that she needed Alice to get down there right away.

When Alice turned onto 47th Avenue, she saw a man wearing just the bottom half of a wetsuit. The top had been pulled down so that his tanned skin was exposed, while the arms of the suit were dangling around his knees. He was talking to a lady in a tie-dyed maxi dress. She was holding one of those little umbrellas that a geisha might carry. Both she and the surfer were barefoot.

They were in the bike lane looking down at the sidewalk, and when Alice drove up a little closer, she could see that they were talking to three kids sitting on the curb.

Alice double-parked and ran around the car to see if everyone was all right. When she got close, the surfer turned around and said, "Alice?"

He was older than she originally thought. Maybe around forty. In great shape though. "I'm Alice?" she said as a couple of cars drove around hers, the drivers giving her the stink eye.

"Well, you got here quick, darlin'," he said and stepped to the side so that she could see Grace and her two friends.

All three were in various stages of wetness. Max's curls were just starting to take shape again. Jill's pink bikini top was showing through her white blouse. And Grace's St. X t-shirt was plastered to her round belly. "Are you guys okay?" said Alice.

"They are now," said the girl in the tie-dyed dress. Alice had misjudged her age as well. Alice originally thought she was an old hippy, but the woman was really a stunning beauty, probably in her late twenties, long blond hair in a loose braid draped over her shoulder. "Our hero over here," she said and smiled at the surfer. "Pulled this one out of the surf." She pointed at Max, who kept his head down.

All three had wet sand stuck to their feet and legs. Max had some on his face and neck as well. "What happened?" asked Alice.

The surfer said, "The undertow's pretty gnarly out here, Alice." The hair on his chest was blonde and grey, and he was scratching at it while he talked. "Barnys get caught in rips out here and try to fight it."

"There's no reason to fight it," said the beautiful woman. "You can't win. You gotta go horizontal before you can go vertical. Then, when you get around the edge of it, you can swim in."

"Ruthy lost her man out there," said the surfer and looked out toward the breakers.

"And he was a great swimmer," she said. "It's just really dangerous, you know?" She opened her mouth like she would say more, but she stopped. She looked like she wanted to explain something but couldn't find the words.

"It's like trying to swim against the current in a big flood," said the surfer. "A lot of work for nothin'. You just have to take the current and ride it back around."

The woman was twirling her umbrella and smiling, a striking beam of a smile that made Alice want to stand closer to her. "Y'all read the Bible?" she said.

Jill said, "We go to Catholic school, so..."

"Oh goody," she said. "So, the flood in the Bible's about judgment and punishment, right?" Alice watched all three kids nod, but Max was still avoiding eye contact with anyone. "Well," she said. "The ocean is about redemption and salvation."

Alice looked at Ruth, but Alice didn't really know what this woman was talking about or why she wanted to share it today. "Uh-huh," said Alice, waiting to see if there would be more.

From her spot on the curb, Grace looked up at Ruth and said, "Why is the ocean about redemption?"

Ruth grinned. "I'm glad you guys are listening to such a weird lady," she said. "Usually people just walk away." Alice doubted that. People never walk away from beautiful women. "Potter," said Ruth. "Tell these guys why the ocean has redemptive properties."

"Second chances, sports fans," he said, tilting his head to the side and shaking the water out of his ear. "Every time you wipe out, kids, you have the choice to paddle in and sit in the sand." He exaggerated a frowny face. "And sometimes a wipeout can feel like you're trapped in a flood, but it's not. So, guess what? You have the opportunity to paddle back out and try to pull into a barrel. That's redemption. And if you get a good one? Salvation." He said it slow and soft. Not a whisper. More like a prayer or an incantation.

Max finally looked up but didn't say anything.

Potter looked down at him and touched Max's head. "Brother, you got lucky today." Max used his hand to shade the sun and look up at him. "But that's okay," said Potter. "Use it."

"What does that mean?" asked Grace, speaking for Max now apparently. "To use it?"

Ruth was walking and twirling her umbrella. "It means," she said, looking over her shoulder like she was posing for a picture, "don't waste the opportunity." She stepped back toward the soaked teenagers and reached out her hand to Grace, who took it and allowed Ruth to help her stand up. "So many people are blessed with a bit of good luck, but they think it's just a momentary gift. It's not. You're supposed to let it propel you."

Alice liked the sound of that. She wanted to be propelled.

Potter said, "Most people sit around and dwell on their *bad* luck. They won't let go of it. Sometimes they let it ruin their lives. But when the *good* luck comes around, they feel like they're entitled to it. Like they somehow deserve it. And they take it for granted. Then they forget all about it before they can parlay the luck into something epic."

"Preach," said Ruth, laughing and waving a few cars around Alice's mom's car, which was still double-parked. A meter reader came buzzing up, so Ruth said, "You guys better go." She hugged Grace and Jill and said, "Thanks for enduring our platitudes," but she knew they were more than that.

Grace said, "Thanks for everything."

Max was already in the back seat of the car.

Once they were all in, Ruth called to them. "Stay out of the flood."

And Potter said, "Catch a wave, brah." But Alice couldn't tell if Max was listening.

~51~

After they dropped off Jill, Max asked if it was okay to come over to Grace's house for a while.

The sky had turned dark. Huge, black clouds were forming, and Grace didn't know what to make of it. San Francisco didn't really do humidity. Grace only knew rain when it was cold out. This was almost tropical. Confusing.

Grace also thought it was weird that Max wanted to come over. She was still trying to figure out why he ran away at the beach and started swimming like a crazy person. She couldn't even remember what exactly they were talking about when he took off for the water. The general topic was catfishing, but they'd been talking about it for a while before he lost his mind. Something specific had to have set him off.

By the time Potter had gotten him back on the beach, Grace had lost track of the original conversation and didn't want to upset him by asking about it.

When Alice parked the car, Max and Grace went to the back deck. It wasn't raining yet, but she thought she could hear the distant rumbling of thunder, and Sully was trotting around the backyard, sniffing at the air.

"So weird," she said.

"I know," he said. "That's why I wanted to talk to you alone."

"Huh?" she said. "I'm talking about these *clouds.*"

"Oh," he said. "I thought you were referring to my insane Michael Phelps bit earlier."

They were both leaning on the railing the way Grace's mom and dad did when they talked in this spot. "Yeah," said Grace. "That was really weird, too."

Although he tried for a joke, he looked deadly serious, and he'd had this expression since the moment he coughed up all that seawater on the beach. He didn't look angry or upset. He just looked serious.

"Well, I've been wanting to talk to you about something for a very long time," he said, but he wasn't looking at her. His eyes were on the clouds that seemed to be joining forces and forming one super cloud. There was a warm breeze now blowing through the yard.

"Go ahead," said Grace, thinking it was an odd time for him to tell her he liked her when she was standing here damp and seven months pregnant. "No time like the present." Oh my God, she sounded like her grandmother.

"You know how much I like you," he began, and Grace could feel herself smiling. He didn't take long to get to the point. "You know, right?"

"Uh-huh," she said and looked at him. She thought he might want to hold her hand or something while he talked, but he kept a little distance between them.

"Well I did something horrible to you," he said and lost control of the muscles in his face. It was as if his mouth and nose and eyes were all posturing for a fight, but nobody wanted to make the first move. Finally, he got a little bit of control and said, "I committed an unforgiveable sin against you."

***

Running with this huge belly was almost impossible, but it was partly downhill, so Grace was making a go of it. Of course, the challenge was compounded by the fact that it had started to pour, and Sully was off-leash and kept cutting her off as she made her way to Buena Vista Park.

She couldn't be in the same yard as Max.

In fact, she wanted to be in a different city, or maybe even on a different planet, but the only place that made her feel separated from the world was Buena Vista.

It was coming down in buckets, sheets, torrents—all at the same time. Every step produced a splash that shot up all the way to her face. She could hardly see with the water running in front of her eyes, but Sully knew where he was going, so she followed him.

She wasn't crying. She was trying to remember every one of Max's sentences, but they were quickly falling away and then streaming down the gutters and into the storm drains. So she was remembering only the feelings, and they were complicated.

They were coming together like that first black raincloud into a kind of super-emotion that she couldn't separate into parts. It was overwhelming her, and all she could think to do was keep running even though she knew the act of concentrating on her steps on the slick pavement was making it harder for her to think.

Sully didn't slow down when they had to cross the street into the park, and Grace was literally running in his wake. The main road up looked too steep in this rain, so Grace tried to whistle to Sully to come back, but there was too much water running into her mouth. "Sully," she yelled and took the dirt path instead. The slope wasn't nearly as steep, and it was at least partially covered by trees.

Sully followed her and quickly passed by as they zigzagged their way toward the dog run near the Frederick Street entrance.

The rain was still dumping on them, and Grace's shirt, which was being soaked for the second time today was starting to hang off one shoulder. The rainwater was reactivating the seawater in her clothes and hair, and she could smell the salt, but her breathing was getting difficult. She spotted a bench on the paved path ahead where it intersected with her dirt path. Sully was looking back down at her. He was standing and panting by the bench. She knew she better sit down. She needed to catch her breath, slow down her mind, and sort out Max's story. She needed to figure out how she could simultaneously hate him and like him. She was supposed to hate him for what happened. He was supposed to help her. He was supposed to protect her. He did that. But he didn't.

She was just walking now, taking long strides up the trail, but the dirt and gravel path had turned into a muddy rivulet now, and every step was labored. When she finally got to the top, she reached with her left hand for the bench so that she could pull herself up to the pavement.

But just before she could grab it, her front foot began to slide and her whole body began to tilt forward. She extended her hand to make a quick grab for the back of the bench, and she got it. She pulled herself up straight, but she overcompensated and began to lean backward.

Her hand slipped off the wet wood.

Then she separated from herself. She felt as if part of her was still holding the bench, but she was not. She was falling backward. Instead of reaching back with her hands to brace herself, she was still grasping for the bench, which was now fading from her vision.

The first blow wasn't bad. She hit some soft ivy to the side of the dirt path. But the ivy was covering a five-foot stone retaining wall, and after the initial fall, she did a back roll and dropped from the top level onto a lower terrace. Some of the retaining wall, which had been built from old tombstones, had eroded and the old marble was scattered on the dirt below. Grace's head hit the flat side of one of the stones, and then she rolled over one more time. She was still alert enough to have heard the sickening sound of her skull smacking the wet stone. And for a few moments, she felt the rain on her face.

Grace

The lady and I are floating today. We're moving together with the current in a stream of water that is neither cold nor wet. I know that sounds ridiculous, but I really can't feel the water. I can feel the pressure of it pushing us, but that's it. And I don't really have to tread water or swim. I'm just letting it push me. Or is it pulling me?

The lady is right behind me, like we're on a tandem bike. She says, "Things are making more sense now."

"Are they?" I say, as I watch Sister Margaret float past. She's sitting on her desk, reading the Old Testament, and she doesn't even seem to notice us. "I feel even more confused," I say.

"But now you know," she says.

"I know some things," I say. Maybe the most important thing. "But I have more questions about some of the other stuff."

"Ask me," she says.

"How come the people we're closest to hurt us the most?"

"Can you be more specific?" she says.

I just want her to answer the general question, and maybe I already know the answer, but I don't want to be specific, so I don't say anything. Instead, I turn my attention to the shore, where I see Dr. H.P. Cooper riding a bike through about two feet of water. His long legs are pumping hard, and he's moving just slightly faster than the current. There's a bunch of other things floating around him—a fish tank, office chairs, a Styrofoam cooler. I want to yell, "Hey Coop," but I stop myself. I don't want him to have to stop and help.

So I float on and ignore the lady's question. My body doesn't feel anything. It's like I'm moving through a tide of room temperature gelatin. But my head is out of the water, and it's cold. It's a grey day, and the rain is constant. I have a dull headache that I forget about as long as I'm not thinking about it. Finally, I say, "Jill was trying to help me with that online identity she created."

"Wonderful," she says. "Did it help?"

"I think it did," I say and remember how exciting it was for me to feel like I wasn't alone. "It was nice to have someone who understood."

"Yes," says the lady. "That is nice."

Then she's quiet, and it gives me a moment to look around at the water. It's everywhere, and it's carrying away everything in its path. On our side of the flow, things are moving slowly, but everything to our right is coursing at a dangerous pace. I hear the tree before I see it. Just over my right shoulder, the top half of an enormous redwood is coming in fast. And my Aunt Erin and her Harley are tangled up in the branches. I only see her for a couple of seconds before she drifts past, but I can see that, with one hand, she's trying to untangle the handle bars, and with the other hand, she's gripping the waterlogged photo album. She's holding it up high so that it won't get wet even though it's already ruined.

"What about Max?" asks the lady.

"What about *Max?" I say, and I snap my head around to give her a dirty look. But something strange happens. I have to blink the rain out of my eyes because I feel like I'm seeing things. But there's nothing wrong with my eyes. I'm finally seeing the lady for the first time, and she's not a lady at all.*

She's me.

Maybe I knew it all along.

And before I can even wrap my head around it, I hear a baby crying, and out of the corner of my eye, I can see a floating cradle in the same part of the flood that Aunt Erin and Sister Margaret had been carried away only a few minutes before.

The wooden cradle is drifting away, picking up speed, drifting, still drifting.

~52~

When Alice heard Max screaming up at her from the deck, she opened the back door and told him to shut up. Then she saw the panic in his eyes and said, "What's going on?"

It was raining pretty hard, and Max had to yell over the sound of the downpour pounding the deck and running out of the gutters. "Grace ran off with Sully," he said.

"In the rain?" she asked.

"Yes," he said.

"Why?"

"We were having kind of a heavy conversation, and then—"

"What the hell, Max?" she said. "What did you say to her?"

She grabbed her jacket off the hall tree and ran out the back door. "Which direction?" she asked.

Max pointed toward Buena Vista.

"Well, we have to go find her," said Alice. "She's fucking pregnant, Max." She didn't feel good about berating Max, but this seemed serious. Grace should not be out in this typhoon, and Max was standing there with this his thumb up his ass doing nothing.

"I know," he said, frustrated. "Let's go get her."

It was really dark now. Like almost nighttime dark, so they weren't running. It was too hard to see. They were just walking fast, and it gave Alice a chance to ask Max what they were talking about before Grace stormed off.

Max tried to be vague, but by the time they got to the top of the park, she'd asked him enough questions to get to the truth. And she believed him. Parts of the same story probably happened in a hundred dorm rooms on her campus every weekend. She thought he was disgusting, but she did believe his story. And she didn't have time to hate him just yet. She was still processing the whole thing, and at the same time, looking for Grace.

They were at the patch of grass at the crest of Buena Vista's hill. It was the one place that Alice thought she'd be able to find Grace quickly. Otherwise, Grace could be anywhere: the playground, the tennis courts, the dog run, the lookout. It would take forty-five minutes to search all those places in this weather, and that wouldn't even include the haphazard network of dirt trails.

"Max," she yelled through another cloudburst. "Do you know where she likes to go?"

Max had water puddling up around his shoes; his swimsuit was hanging down below his knees, and his socks had turned the color of dirty snow. He looked like he might be crying, but Alice couldn't tell because there was so much water running down his face. She was about to tell him to get his shit together and *think*, but then they both heard the howling. "That's weird," he said.

"That wasn't Sully," said Alice.

"You think someone else is walking a dog out in this?" Max put his hands out as if to simultaneously shrug and catch the rain in his cupped palms.

Alice didn't answer. She just started running toward the howling.

The acoustics on this hill in this storm made it difficult to pinpoint the source of the howling. At first it sounded like it was coming from somewhere on the east side of the park, but as they got closer to Buena Vista East, the sound seemed to weaken. And then when they ran toward the tennis courts, it got louder and louder until they seemed to just pass through the sound, and it was so muffled that it was as if it were coming from inside a coffin.

Alice stopped at that point, looked at Max, and said, "What the fuck?"

Max looked at Alice and shook his head. Then he started to turn in place. When he got to about a hundred and eighty degrees, he stopped. To Alice, the howling still sounded muffled, but Max was pointing now. "There," he said, with his arm extended and his finger trained toward an area beyond the dog run.

When Alice turned and faced the direction toward which Max was pointing, the sound of the howling became clear and loud again. It was as if they were in some kind of sound anomaly in which the rain and the stone walls and the trees were all participating in this game of acoustic catch—throwing all the noises back and forth among themselves. Alice was thinking it was like a house of mirrors, but instead of their eyes being fooled, it was their ears.

As they walked in the direction that Max had pointed, the howling was definitely getting louder. And when they got to a junction between a sloped dirt trail and the path, they saw the coyotes. The mother was facing Alice and Max—looking right at them—and had stopped howling, but the pup was facing the opposite direction and continued to cry out into the storm.

Alice and Max didn't move. The two animals were only about twenty feet away. When the pup realized he was the only one still howling, he scampered over to his mother and sat down in the ivy. The staring contest went on for about ten seconds before the mother let out one more extended moan, as if she were in physical pain.

Then there was a bark. For a moment, Alice thought it was the pup, but her brain caught up to her ears, and she realized it was Sully's bark. She ran past the bench near the intersection, jumped the dirt path, and landed in soft ground cover. She looked back at Max who was following her but keeping his eyes on the coyotes.

Then there was another bark.

Alice took two steps, and her feet reached the edge of a stone retaining wall. When she looked down, she saw Grace lying in the mud, Sully pawing at her bare shoulder the way he would at her knee when they'd be eating dinner, and he thought Grace might feed him some table scraps.

Before Alice jumped down to the lower terrace, her brain was able to capture the scene as if she were looking at a famous painting. The St. X t-shirt was so stretched out that it looked like a knee-length, off the shoulder white dress. Her white legs were in high contrast against the mud that surrounded her. She was missing a shoe.

The other contrast was between her dark, wet hair, and something white beneath her head. In the split second that Alice paused before she jumped, it looked like it might be a pillow. She blinked once and saw that, yes, it was white, but it wasn't absorbing the water. The water was running off it, giving it a kind of sheen. The edges of it—a stone maybe—were rounded, so that it appeared to orbit Grace's beautiful face.

All this was registering at brain-speed as Alice took one more step and jumped down onto the muddy terrace. Max was right behind her. The two of them each had one of Grace's hands now, and they were begging her to wake up.

Alice wanted to put her own hand behind Grace's neck to see if she could help her sit up, but then she remembered that you're not supposed to move someone who has suffered this kind of trauma. Alice was kneeling in the mud, and she bent down to try to talk directly into Grace's ear. That's when Alice saw that blood was leaking onto the stone. It was diluted by the rainwater, but it was definitely blood. She yelled at Max to call 9-1-1, and then spoke directly into her sister's ear. "Gracie, please open your eyes," she said and was surprised at the calmness of her own voice.

Grace didn't move. She didn't open her eyes.

"Gracie," said Alice again as she heard Max making the call.

Still nothing.

"Where are we?" yelled Max, sounding like he was losing his mind.

Alice looked around and saw through the trees a part of a street sign: ICK. "Frederick Street entrance to Buena Vista Park. You can stand out on the street and tell them where we are. Buena Vista West and Frederick."

Alice looked back down at Grace, whose eyes were open now.

"My baby," she said. "My baby."

~53~

Pat was in the old bar at Gleneagles Golf Course at MacLean Park. He wanted to get in a quick nine with his Dean of Discipline, but it started pouring when they were out on the third hole—farthest from the clubhouse.

There were about fifteen other guys in the bar. They'd all gotten hall passes from their wives and weren't going to waste this gift by going home. One younger dad had called it a *Get Out of Jail Free Card.*

Pat had just bought a round when he got a text from Emily telling him to call immediately. She knew he didn't look at his phone when he was on the golf course, but now she'd called three times in the last minute.

Pat walked outside and stood under an awning to take the call. Emily was loud but almost incoherent. Pat could pick up only a few of the words, but that was enough: *Grace. Accident. Emergency Room. Hurry.*

Gleneagles is way out in the Bayview-Hunter's Point District tucked in next to the Sunnydale Housing Projects, but Pat made it across the city in record time. He'd talked to Emily on the phone as he weaved through Saturday afternoon traffic and found out that Grace had slipped and hit her head. But the doctors said she'd be okay—stitches and a pretty bad concussion.

In Pat's panic, he didn't think about the baby until he was parking illegally on Parnassus and then running across the street to get to the emergency room entrance. His brain was doing complicated calisthenics, and he was embarrassed that a moment passed when the flicker of a thought entered his consciousness—that Grace's life would be so much simpler if she were to lose the baby.

It must have been some kind of depraved pragmatist's reflex, and he was immediately furious with himself for not being able to stop the idea from slipping into the cacophony of voices engaged in the heated discussion in his head. If someone had seen him walking through the lobby, that person might have thought Pat was looking to punch someone. But it was himself. He wanted to fight himself.

Just before he got through security, he started to give himself a break. He thought that maybe the idea only came to him to prepare him for the possibility that Grace could lose the baby, and this kind of thinking was the only way for him to emotionally survive such a tragedy. That idea made some sense to him. Preparation for disappointment.

It really didn't matter. He'd had the thought. He didn't feel that way. He wanted his daughter to be safe, and he wanted the baby to be safe.

As he got to the end of the hallway, he walked past that Max kid, who was sitting in a chair outside the room. When Pat stepped inside, before he even registered who was there, he blurted, "Is the baby okay?"

Alice and Emily just looked at him.

Grace said, "The doctor says the baby's going to be fine." Then she smiled and said, "I'm gonna be okay, too, Dad."

"I know," said Pat, a little ashamed that Grace was poking him. "Mom told me on the phone that you were all right." He walked over and tried to hug her, but it was awkward. They weren't a very huggy family, and Pat was trying to avoid her stitches. "I'm so happy everyone's all right. I'm so relieved," he said and let himself drop down into the cushioned chair in the corner by the window.

Emily and Alice still hadn't said anything.

Pat said, "Is there a reason Max is sitting out in the hallway?"

The three most important women in Pat's life just looked at each other.

Pat asked, "Was he out walking with Gracie when the storm hit?"

Still nothing.

"What's going on?" he said and sat forward in the chair.

***

Emily was still processing the story of Grace's baby's conception. A mother never wants to think of her child in the kind of situation in which Grace had been the night of the party.

When Alice recounted the story to her, Emily had some questions, but none of the answers were going to make her feel any better about the scenario.

Initially, she wanted Max's parents to take responsibility for what happened, but then she remembered a drunk driving disaster that had occurred with a couple of St. X kids who had been partying at another St. X kid's house. The parents of the two dead boys went after the homeowners and how awful it was for everyone involved and how Emily had felt so sorry for that nice couple who'd simply wanted to go to Tahoe for the weekend. And, of course, she'd cried and cried for the families who'd lost their sons.

Everybody involved was ruined.

But Gracie was alive. Did Emily really want this other family to have to take responsibility for the things that happened in their house when they were hundreds of miles away? Should they pay for the sins of their sons?

She wasn't sure how Pat would feel about any of it. After Emily and Alice had team-told the story while Grace sat in her hospital bed listening, Pat stood up from the chair and looked out the window for a long time. When he turned back around, he said, "I love you, Grace." Then he sat back down in the chair. "Emily and Alice, I love you guys very much," he said and folded his hands as if he were going to pray, but he didn't.

He sat for a very long time, and then he stood up again and walked over to the door and looked down the hall. He came back in and closed the door behind him. "Here's the game plan," he said. "First, I'm going out into the hallway, where I'm going to dump Max out of that chair and beat him over the head with it."

He was very calm as he explained this, like he was drawing up a play during a timeout. Alice jumped in almost immediately and said, "Oh stop it, Dad."

Pat looked at her, incredulous.

"Max kind of helped her in a way," said Alice.

"I agree," said Pat. "That's why I'm not going to kill him."

"This is ridiculous," said Alice, and Emily almost said the same thing, but Alice was doing a good job, and maybe Pat just needed to say this, to let it all out.

"It's not ridiculous," said Pat. "This is a good plan." He continued to talk in a voice that Emily imagined he used in faculty meetings. "After

I'm through with Max, I'm going down to L.A. That's where Max's brother ran away to, right Grace?"

Grace ignored him.

"When I get down there," he continued. "Santa Monica? That's where you said he was. When I get down to Santa Monica and find him, I'm going to kill him."

"Please stop," said Emily.

"No," said Pat. "Don't worry. I'm not going to get caught. I'll hide the body, and then I'll just come home. And I haven't figured out yet what I'm going to do about the parents."

Pat looked at Emily as if he wanted her approval, so she decided to give it to him, see if that wouldn't derail his demented rant. "Yeah," she said. "I guess that sounds like it could work. Do you need a ride down to L.A.?"

"Mom!" said Alice. "Why are you playing along with this bullshit? This is so stupid."

Grace adjusted her hospital bed so that she was sitting up now. "Dad," she said. "Sometimes I think you do things like this so we can laugh about them later. I assume that's what you're doing now. When my baby gets to be about my age, and we tell him this story about the hospital, we can all laugh about how dad went crazy. That's the real game plan here, right?"

Pat's head was in his hands, and Emily knew he was breaking down. The only other time she'd seen him do it was when she'd miscarried their first child after nine weeks. Otherwise, he'd done an admirable job of pretending that he was the hero and that no misfortune was so horrible that he couldn't fix it.

Maybe after realizing that his current strategy was, indeed, preposterous, he had no other option but to let himself give up the role of fixer for once. Maybe that's what he was doing in that chair in the corner of this room at UC Medical Center with his face in his hands. He was surrendering just this once to the fact that the Ryan family had been aggrieved in a painful and complicated way.

And there were no last second heroics to save the day. No buzzer-beater. No Steph Curry miracle. Grace had been wronged, and there would be lasting effects. There was no way to go back in time to undo what had been done.

But that was okay because the Ryans were fighters. They would handle this situation better than any other family in the history of the world.

Although this was simply Emily's conjecture about what might have been going through Pat's head, she was comfortable with it. They'd be fine. And she kept thinking this over and over and over until she was finally saying it out loud, "We'll be fine ... We'll be fine ... We'll be fine."

Postpartum

"It is preferable to have a virgin mind than a virgin body. Each is good if each be possible; if it be not possible, let me be chaste, not to man but to God."

— St. Ambrose

~54~

Pat was pushing the stroller up West Portal. Grace and Emily were walking side-by-side just in front of him, talking and laughing. They passed the Empire Theater, where there was a line outside forming for Tarantino's *Once Upon a Time in Hollywood.*

Pat had already seen it and liked it. He thought a lot of Tarantino's other movies were stupid and childish, but there was something about this one. So, Pat wasn't completely shocked when he saw a YouTube video of Bishop Barron praising aspects of the film.

Barron thought the Brad Pitt character exemplified "cowboy virtues," and the Bishop later went on to say that Pitt was actually illustrative of the basic Christian virtues: justice, temperance, courage, and prudence.

Pat didn't necessarily believe there were many people, besides the Bishop himself, who came out of that movie thinking of those virtues, but Pat knew there was some kind of intellectual stirring that he'd experienced while watching the movie—something that sneaked into his subconscious and stuck with him in the days after.

Pitt was in some extremely violent scenes, but he sure had a code of ethics. He was a good guy. An almost good guy. The character was complex, and after Pat's last nine months, he was starting to think that everyone might be complex. Just when you start to think that someone is simple, he's going to do something to surprise you.

Perhaps the person in Pat's life who had remained the most consistent over this tumultuous period was Grace. Even after she'd found out the truth, she still believed she was carrying around a gift. In fact, she eventually named him Sean—Irish for *Gift from God.* And Pat liked the name a lot. Every Irishman knew someone named Sean Ryan. That was a name you could trust. A guy who'd cancel his plans to help you move. A guy who'd pick up the tab before anyone had a chance to pay. A guy who'd take care of his mother. That's Sean Ryan.

And now that Sean was this brand spankin' new part of their lives, Pat knew Grace had been right all along. There was something incredibly pure about her outlook, and Pat was humbled to be her dad. He was proud to be her dad.

After they'd moved beyond the theater line, they walked in front of Barbagelata Realtors and Spiazzo Cucina and Eesy Freezy Market. But before they got to Dr. Cooper's office, Grace turned around and said, "Are you coming up?"

"Does he want to talk to me?" asked Pat, suddenly anxious. Dr. Cooper had warned him about his temper after the diatribe in the emergency room. Pat was hoping Grace hadn't tattled on him for something else he might have done more recently.

"No," said Grace. "I just thought you'd be tired from pushing around the stroller. You could take a break in the office while Coop and I walk."

"Yeah," he said, relieved. "I could sit."

"Okay," said Grace. "Give the baby to mom."

Pat took Sean out of the stroller and handed him over. Then he attempted to fold up the stroller so that he could more easily carry it up the stairs, but he struggled with the task for a few moments before he thought *screw it*, and picked up the stroller as is.

"Stop," said Grace. "Put it down." Then she leaned over and pushed some button or lever that she'd shown him several times before and folded up the stroller like this was Origami 101. Then she handed it to him by the handle and took Sean from Emily. "Let's go up," she said. "Coop hasn't met the boy wonder yet."

***

Grace left the baby with her mom and dad, and she and Coop set off on foot toward St. Francis Wood. It wasn't really the woods. It was tree-lined streets with giant houses, but it was a peaceful walk, and after the last few weeks of being up late with the baby, Grace needed some peace.

"So, what's going on?" asked Coop after they'd finished all the small talk about how big the baby was and how much he weighed and was he sleeping well. Grace knew Coop wasn't all that interested in that stuff.

"I'm good," she said. "My mom and dad have been really helpful."

"Your dad?" he said.

"Believe it or not," said Grace. "He did help raise two kids."

"I'm joking," said Coop. "He's a good man. You're lucky to have him."

It was a nice day, and they were walking on the sunny side of the street, so they were both squinting at each other. It was even worse for Grace because she had to look up at Coop. "Dad has actually really helped with a lot of the big decisions," she said.

"Your mom told me you're taking a break from school?"

"Yeah," she said. "Everyone gets so caught up in the standard route. That's just not going to be for me."

"You're preachin' to the choir," he said. "The educational system in this country is just manufactured constrictions."

"Whatever that means," she said. "I'm just saying, what's the rush? I mean, I could've gone back after a few weeks leave, and we could've figured out how to make it work. But what's the point? I would have missed all this time with Sean. Why would I do that?"

"Exactly," he said. "I like that plan. You only have your first months with your baby one time. You should be with him as much as possible, and you're lucky that your folks are helping out."

"Agreed," she said and walked around a chalk hopscotch grid that someone had drawn on the sidewalk. She was tempted to skip through it, but she caught herself.

"So, what's the plan then?"

"I'll just go back and start sophomore year all over again next fall," she said. "By that time, we'll have created a schedule that'll work for everyone." She took a deep breath as she thought about some of the challenges. "I won't be able to be like in many extra-curricular activities or anything, because Sean will kind of be my extra-curricular, but that's what I signed up for."

"In a sense," he said.

"What do you mean?"

"Well," he said. "Technically, you did *not* sign up for this."

"Oh yeah," she said. "Right. But like we did have some choices. We talked about adoption and other stuff, but I chose this instead."

"Yes. You and I discussed it. But you thought ... what? I can't remember your thoughts on adoption."

"Doesn't matter how the baby came into the world," she said. "He's here, and no matter what, I feel like it's my responsibility to raise him."

"That sounds practiced," he said.

"It is," said Grace. "But that doesn't mean it's not true."

Coop nodded but didn't say anything right away. Then he stopped in the shade of a big Eucalyptus and said, "Would you judge someone in a similar circumstance who chose to put the child up for adoption?"

"C'mon, Coop."

"What?" he said, laughing now.

"No one has ever been in the same situation as me."

"You might be right," he conceded.

"I'm unique," she said and smiled up at him. "Not trying sound like I think I'm special or something, but I do still feel like I'm a virgin." Then she had to think for a minute. This wasn't coming out quite as she wanted it to. "Not that I have any judgment toward girls who aren't virgins. I'm not really like that. But in a couple of different ways, I still am, and even though no one will ever see me that way again, me and God know."

Grace and Coop walked for a long time after that one. It was a lot. Had a lot of layers to it. She could tell that he was pondering it or trying to decide what to talk about next. And that was okay with Grace. Sometimes they would just walk and be comfortable with each other.

Eventually he said—and this was actually related to the last stuff—"How is your relationship with Max?"

"Max is a good person," she said.

"That's not what I asked?" he said.

"It's kinda tricky," she said and thought about all the conversations she'd had with her mom and Alice and Jill. "He is Sean's father."

"Yes," he said. Sometimes he did that. He would just confirm something she'd said and leave it at that.

"But I don't really think he can be part of Sean's life."

"Really?" said Coop.

"As I said before, I think he's a good person. But his parents have already pulled him out of St. X, and I just don't see our relationship growing after all this."

"I see."

"C'mon, Coop. You know it's best. We're only sixteen. What are the odds that we were gonna stay together?"

"So, this baby will never know his father?"

"I guess that depends," she said. She really hadn't planned it out that far yet, but she was willing to let things happen naturally. "I'm going to leave that up to Max. If he wants to be some part of Sean's life ... I don't know. The circumstances, y'know?"

"Indeed," he said.

"Maybe when we're both older," she said. "It'll make some sense that Max should meet his son."

"Maybe," said Coop. "Until then—and I wouldn't say this to just anyone—I think you're going to be a hell of a mom."

"Thank you," she said because she believed he meant it.

"You're going to make mistakes," he said. "But that's okay. And Sean's going to make mistakes. And that's okay, too."

It felt to Grace like Coop was ready to head back to the office, but he was looking for some nugget that would propel her into this new stage of her life. "And?" she said.

"Okay, try this," he said. "Make your mistakes into milestones."

"Did you make that up?"

"I think I did."

"It's not bad."

About the Author

Tim Reardon is the author of two previous novels, Shadow Lessons and Part of the Game. He lives with his family in San Francisco, where he is Principal of Archbishop Riordan High School.

ALL THINGS THAT MATTER PRESS

FOR MORE INFORMATION ON TITLES AVAILABLE FROM
ALL THINGS THAT MATTER PRESS, GO TO
http://allthingsthatmatterpress.com
or contact us at
allthingsthatmatterpress@gmail.com

If you enjoyed this book, please post a review on Amazon.com and your favorite social media sites.
Thank you!

Made in the USA
Coppell, TX
19 November 2020